Rebel Rebel

Compiled by

Gene Kemp

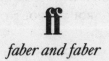

faber and faber

First published in 1997
by Faber and Faber Limited
3 Queen Square London WC1N 3AU

Photoset by Avon Dataset Ltd
Printed and bound in Great Britain by
Mackays of Chatham PLC, Chatham, Kent

A CIP record for this book
is available from the British Library

ISBN 0–571–19520–2

2 4 6 8 10 9 7 5 3 1

Compiled by Gene Kemp

MD

At that moment in the sunshine she was a piece of power, she could do anything and everything, leap in the air, fly to the stars, live for ever.

Gene Kemp, *Jason Bodger and the Priory Ghost*

Got your mother in a whirl.
She's not sure if you're a boy or a girl.

David Bowie, 'Rebel Rebel'

Contents

Here and Now

Then and There

Long Ago and Far Away

Here and Now

Charming!
Jan Mark

Alice and Lydia Pitt were saving up for a padlock. In the meantime they had to rely on the power of fear to keep people out of the garden shed across the lane. Alice had pinned a notice on the door:

CAUTION
DEADLY SPIRITS

The Pitts lived in the garden flat, which was right at the bottom of the house, down the area steps, so the shed was officially theirs, but the lane that ran along the ends of the gardens was a right of way. Anybody could walk down it, and the sheds were on the other side. The rest of the sheds had bolts and chains and keys, but Mrs Pitt said there was nothing in the shed worth stealing, so why waste good money? Alice and Lydia kept quiet. There *had* been nothing in the shed worth stealing, but there was something now. They put threepenny bits in a jam jar – on the rare occasions that they came by a threepenny bit.

'Why don't you ask your daddy to buy you one?' said Maureen, who was poking about uninvited in Alice's bedside cupboard and had discovered the jam jar. Alice and Lydia kept quiet about that, too. If their father was buying anything, it wasn't for them. They could not quite remember when they had last seen him. Lydia thought it was on Bonfire Night, but Lydia was only six. Alice knew that it was not last Bonfire Night, or even the one before that.

Alice's bedside cupboard, and Lydia's, were made out of

orange-boxes, as were the bookcases in the front room and the shelves in the kitchen. Mrs Pitt, who could sew, had made covers and curtains to fit the orange-boxes. One, lying on its side under the window, had a padded top. Alice could sit there to read by the little light that came down the area steps, and Lydia kept her toys inside it.

Mrs Pitt sewed things for other people too, if they asked her, in between cleaning other people's houses and looking after other people's children. While she was out doing all this, Alice looked after Lydia.

Lydia thought that everyone lived this way and didn't mind, but Alice knew differently and often felt badly about it, especially when Maureen came round to play. Maureen liked going down the area steps and knocking at the green door underneath; she liked the darkness at noon down there, below the road; and she admired the dear little orange-box cupboards with frills on. All the same, she would not have liked to be Alice Pitt and live there all the time. Lydia had never lived anywhere else. She was pale and wide-eyed, like something raised under a stone, according to Gregory Beasley's mother. Lydia was thought to be a bit strange. She certainly looked it.

'Let's go and play in the garden,' said Maureen, one summer's day at half past two, when it became too dark in the front room to see even the darns on Alice's cardigan. They went outside and Maureen continued to poke about.

'What's all that green stuff all over the lawn?' she demanded. It was nice of her to call it a lawn. It grew in lumps.

'Spinach,' said Alice.

Maureen began to giggle.

'Why've you got spinach on the lawn?'

'Mum planted it in the flower beds last year,' said Alice, 'but we didn't cut all of it in time and it seeded. Now it's everywhere.'

4

'I'm fed up with spinach,' said Lydia, and daringly wasteful she grubbed up a handful and threw it over the fence.

'You don't eat it, do you?' said Maureen.

'Why not? We can't afford to leave it,' Alice said, sharply.

'But it's wild. Look, it's even growing on the path. It's growing on the rubbish heap. Ugh!'

'It's still spinach.'

Maureen leaned on the fence at the end of the short garden and looked across the muddy lane.

' "Caution deadly spirits." What have you got in that old shed, anyway?'

'It's my laboratory,' said Alice.

Maureen laughed, but not too loudly. Alice Pitt might not have tuppence to bless herself with, but she had plenty between the ears.

'And plenty behind them,' said Gregory Beasley's mother.

'Nonsense. Those two girls are kept spotless,' said Maureen's mother, who liked to be nice about Mrs Pitt.

Gregory Beasley shared his mother's opinion, but the one time Gregory had leaned over the area railings yelling, 'Stinky old Alice, hasn't got a palace. Cess Pitt. Cess Pitt!' Alice herself had come up the steps and given him such a kick that he never dared tell his mates what had lamed him.

'What do you do in a laboratory?' said Maureen.

'I invent things,' said Alice, who spent as much time as she could at the public library, educating herself, since she didn't trust her teacher to do it.

'I want everyone in the class to write an essay about his or her favourite ambition,' said Miss Cornwell. Alice very truthfully wrote about saving up for a padlock. 'I meant your ambition when you leave school, dear,' said Miss Cornwell, and gave her two out of ten. 'Silly old moo-cow,' said Alice, under her breath.

5

'What do you invent?' said Maureen. 'Machines?'

'Potions,' said Alice. 'Herbal remedies.'

'What's a remedy?'

'Medicine and things to put on your skin.' There was a herbalist's shop near the cinema, and Alice enjoyed looking in the window at the jars and white paper packets and cakes of lavender soap, made from real lavender. When she had achieved the padlock, she intended to start saving for some basic ingredients.

'Medicine shouldn't be deadly,' Maureen said, reasonably.

'It isn't,' said Alice, 'but I had to think of something that would keep people out.'

'I should think it would make people want to look inside,' said Maureen.

'I know.' Alice sighed. She had seen Gregory Beasley lurking.

'Can *I* see inside?'

'All right. But you mustn't touch anything and you mustn't tell.'

'What'd you do if I did?' said Maureen. 'Put a spell on me?'

'I'd kick you,' said Alice. Alice's kicks were famous. 'And I won't get you any more library books.' Alice had access to the whole family's library tickets, including her father's, and Maureen was grateful for the loans. Maureen's mother would not let her go to the library in case she met nasty men on the way, in the Memorial Gardens where there were bushes.

'Alice never meets any nasty men,' said Maureen.

'Alice kicks,' said Maureen's mother.

Alice opened the door of the shed. Inside were shelves and cobwebs, grey and thick as floorcloths, and leaning towers of flower pots. The little cracked window was so dirty that everything outside looked brown, like an old photograph. Half a bicycle hung from the rafters, beside a watering can with a pot-mender in the bottom, and along one wall was a bench with the remains of a vice screwed to it. The bench had been thoroughly dusted and scrubbed, and ranged on it were jars, and bottles and little cold-cream pots.

'It stinks,' said Maureen. 'It's all filthy. Mummy would skin me if she knew I was here.'

'Don't tell her, then,' said Lydia. Maureen ignored her. She had no intention of telling her mother that she had been in Alice Pitt's back shed, but she thought it would do Alice no harm to know that she was breaking rules on Alice's behalf.

'It only smells of creosote,' said Alice. 'There's a can of it down there.'

Maureen looked under the bench.

'Where'd you get all this stuff?'

'It was here when we moved in,' said Alice. She closed the door and lit a candle. The shed was dusty-dark, and warm.

'A lot of those things are poisonous,' said Maureen, seeing weedkiller and paraffin and anonymous rusty cans with conical tops. 'They aren't your medicines, are they? You could kill people.'

'No I couldn't,' said Alice. 'My things are all up here.' She put down the candle on the bench and pointed to the row of jars. Maureen peered.

'What's all that in there? Rose petals?'

'Yes.'

'What are you going to do with them?'

'Make scent,' said Alice.

'Aren't they a pretty colour – hey! You pinched them off Dr Hardy's roses, didn't you?' Dr Hardy lived in the next road, and his long garden stretched halfway down it. Rose bushes hung over the fence.

'I didn't pinch them,' said Alice. 'But you know how they get when they open right up, all loose? Well, if you hold out your hands underneath and breathe hard, all the petals drop off and you can catch them. They'd just fall on the ground, otherwise, and people would squash them,' she added, rationally.

'I got little red ones,' said Lydia.

'She threw them all up in the air,' said Alice.

'It was like weddings,' said Lydia.

'It was a terrible waste,' said Alice. 'We put some out on a tray to dry for pot-pourri, but it got windy while we were out shopping, and they'd all blown away, time we got back. They were wasted, too.'

'Well, what are you going to do with those?' said Maureen, pointing to the petals in the jar. 'They don't smell like scent to me. They smell like – vinegar.'

'I did put some vinegar in. Vinegar preserves things. I had to see if it would work,' said Alice. 'But it didn't.'

'I like these.' Maureen fiddled about with the cold-cream jars. 'Where'd you get them from?'

'Rubbish heaps,' said Alice. 'You can nearly always find cold-cream jars on rubbish heaps. And whelk shells. I don't know why. I'm making face-cream.'

'What with? Not real cream?'

'No. Dripping and cucumber mostly, and bluebell seeds; and mignonette.'

'Bluebell seeds and *dripping*?'

'I got the recipe out of an old book. It's supposed to be lard, but we haven't got any. Dripping's near enough,' said Alice. 'I thought the bluebell seeds might make it smoother. They're all gluey when you pop them.'

'I never tried,' said Maureen.

'The mignonette's to make it smell nice. Cucumber's right, though,' said Alice. 'It did say cucumber.'

Maureen unscrewed the lid from one of the little pots and

discovered a mouldy puddle inside, the colour of old kerb-stones.

'I have to experiment,' said Alice, defensively. 'Inventions never come right the first time. It took years to discover penicillin. And it's so hard to get things to put in,' she added sadly. 'No one round here grows herbs.'

'It's not really herbs, is it?' said Maureen, hurriedly replacing the lid. 'I don't think mignonette's a herb. Cucumbers aren't herbs.'

'Mint's a herb. We've got mint all over – where it isn't spinach. I put some in a lotion –'

'Potion?'

'No, lotion. With dock leaves. I thought it might be good for nettle stings.'

Maureen did not bother to ask if the lotion had been a success.

'You can eat nettles,' said Lydia, suddenly.

'Like spinach,' Maureen jeered.

'Mrs Witkowski told me.'

'Mrs Witkowski's *foreign*.'

'I suppose,' Alice said, diffidently, 'I suppose your mum hasn't got any old jars?'

'Jam jars?'

'No, this sort. Little make-up jars. My mum doesn't wear make-up.'

'I'll ask her,' said Maureen. Alice's mum didn't even put her hair in curlers. Poor Alice.

'Jars for Alice?' said Maureen's mother. 'Is she going to sell them? I gave all ours to that Scout who came round collecting.'

'Not jam jars,' said Maureen. 'I meant those little glass white ones with face things in, or Daddy's Brylcreem jars. She plays with them.'

9

'I would have thought Alice was a bit old to be playing with jars,' said Maureen's mother. 'Don't you mean Lydia? She's too young to be playing with glass.'

'She doesn't play like *that*,' said Maureen. 'She invents things and puts them in jars, like make-up. It's only pretend.'

Maureen suspected that if Alice had been able to get hold of the things she needed, there would have been less experiment and no need for pretence. Her mother fetched out some jars and an old cut-glass scent bottle as a treat.

'It's slightly chipped on this side. Tell her to be careful.'

Maureen would have liked the little bottle for herself. With the stopper out it still smelled pretty, but she knew that one ought to be kind to Alice, and handed it over with the jars.

Alice was very pleased and gave Maureen some pink lip-salve made of squashed geranium petals.

'It's not poisonous, but you'll have to use it up quickly, or it goes a funny colour,' said Alice, pounding nasturtium leaves with the handle of a trowel.

'Lots of lipsticks do that,' said Maureen, generously. 'I saw it in *Woman's Own*.'

'Alice put her ocean on my nettle sting and it went away,' said Lydia.

'*Lotion*,' said Alice.

'Maureen could put your ocean on her wart.'

'I haven't got a wart,' said Maureen.

'Yes you have, I saw,' said Lydia.

'Let's have a look,' said Alice, wiping her hands on her apron, very professional.

'I haven't *got* a wart.'

'It's on her thumb.'

'Shut up, Lyddy. You go on with the nasturtiums,' said Alice, prising Maureen's clenched thumb away from her palm. 'It's a big one, isn't it?'

'I keep knocking it. Mummy put caustic on, but it won't go away. Gregory Beasley said you get warts off being dirty,' said Maureen, pink with shame.

'Gregory Beasley thinks everybody's dirty,' said Alice feelingly.

'Gregory Beasley does things behind the shed,' said Lydia, in a faraway voice. 'I saw.'

'Did your nettle lotion really work?' Maureen asked, hopefully. 'The caustic didn't.'

'It only works on nettles,' said Alice. 'I'll have to charm this.'

'Don't be daft.'

'It's not daft. It's not half as daft as some of this lot,' said Alice, shrugging at the laboratory. 'I had three on my finger, and my gran charmed them away. It really works.'

'I bet it doesn't.'

'Won't do any harm to try, will it?' said Alice. 'It won't cost you. That's better than spending good money on caustic pencils that don't work, isn't it?'

'Caustic doesn't cost much.'

'*We* couldn't afford it,' said Alice. 'Charming's got to be done free or you lose the power, but you'll have to steal something.'

'I'm not stealing anything,' said Maureen. 'Mummy wouldn't like it.'

'Mummy wouldn't like it,' chanted Lydia, in her little, little voice.

'What'd I have to steal?'

'A bit of meat.'

'You steal it.'

'We haven't got any meat,' said Alice. 'It's baked beans and bacon today. I don't think bacon would work.'

'Chops on Saturday,' said Lydia, happily.

'You can't take bits off chops,' said Alice. 'Anyway, Mum

11

would notice. Anyway, it's your wart, Maureen, and you have meat every day.'

'There's some beef in the pantry.'

'That'll do. Rolled up?'

'No, all floppy. I could get a bit of that.'

'It needn't be a very big piece, not just for the one wart. Is your mum home, Maureen?'

'Shopping.'

'Go on, then.'

'I think it's silly,' said Maureen, but she went home and returned to the shed ten minutes later, with a little bit of raw beef wrapped up in her handkerchief.

'Ugh. It's all bloody,' she said, unwrapping it. 'I'll have to tell my mother I had a nosebleed.'

'Of course it's all bloody. If it didn't have blood in it, it wouldn't be red, would it?' said Alice. 'Give it here.' She took the meat and rubbed it carefully all round and over the wart.

'Ugh,' said Maureen, again. 'It's still there. Now what are you going to do?'

'Bury it,' said Alice.

'The wart?'

'The meat.'

'Come on, then,' said Maureen. 'Where shall we put it?'

'You mustn't know that, or it won't work.'

'All right. I won't look.'

'Oh no,' said Alice. 'You must go home and don't come back till it's gone.'

'You're just trying to get rid of me,' said Maureen. 'It won't go.'

'Yes it will, but you mustn't come back until it does.'

'I don't believe that.'

'It doesn't matter, as long as I do,' said Alice. Maureen began to be frightened, there in the dark shed beside solemn, raggedy Alice and batty Lydia, mumbling and pumping up and down like a little engine, with her trowel handle.

Three days later, Maureen woke up in the morning and found that the wart had gone. She went over to the bedroom window where the sun shone, and examined her thumb, but there was no sign at all of any wart; not even a scar.

'What are you doing?' said her mother, coming in with clean clothes.

'My wart's gone,' said Maureen.

'So it has. Fancy, after all this time.'

'Alice Pitt charmed it.'

'Don't be silly,' said Maureen's mother. 'It must have been the caustic.'

'Yes,' said Maureen.

'Wart-charming is a silly superstition. I don't want to hear any more nonsense like that.'

'No.'

'It was the caustic.'

'Yes,' said Maureen, but she didn't believe it. Mint-flavoured nettle lotion and grey face-cream were one thing; this was real. It had worked.

When she went down the road later, she saw Alice in the gutter, turning a rope for Lydia to jump over. 'Salt – mustard – vinegar – pepper. Salt – mustard – vinegar – pepper.' The other end of the rope was tied to the area railings.

'It's gone then,' said Alice, as Maureen drew close.

'How'd you know, clever-pot?' said Maureen.

'You wouldn't have come back, otherwise,' said Alice, calmly. 'Let's see.'

'I *would* have.'

'No.' Alice stopped swinging the rope and stood in the gutter, very sure of herself. 'I knew you wouldn't come back till it went.'

'I'm never coming back again, neither,' Maureen shouted. 'You're horrible. I hate you!' And she ran home, crying.

'Funny,' said Alice. 'She didn't mind the geraniums, and they don't work at all, hardly.'

'That's why,' said Lydia.

Alice gazed long and hard at her little sister, but Lydia only stood on one leg, and scratched, and sucked her thumb, like anyone's little sister.

'Well,' Alice said finally, 'we'd better not tell her what *you* can do. Come on, Lyddy. *Salt* – mustard – vinegar – pepper. *Salt* – mustard – vinegar – pepper. *Salt* – mustard – vinegar – pepper . . .'

The Animal House
Sandy Brechin (aged 12)

I have a lion, a furry faced lion.
He dominantly controls the household.
He eats a lot of meat and he snarls if I pester him.
He is out most of the day. I call him dad.

I also have a dove.
She works all day too, but she works at home,
She is soft, gentle, kind and cares for her young,
She is always there if I need her. I call her mum.

I have a peacock.
She has a head with lots of different colours.
She has green eyes and a beautiful coat.
She has a tuft of glittery hair at the front. I call her my
    punk sister.

I have a kitten.
He is so small and smooth.
He has teeny little eyes and a wet nose.
He drinks milk a lot, and cries a lot. I call him baby
    brother.

Then there's me.
I know what I am.
I'm the black sheep.

A Very Positive Moment
Tim Kennemore

'I hate the first day of term,' said Tamsin, stomping across the
tarmac, hands stuffed crossly in coat pockets. She was in a bad
mood, and prepared to hate almost anything. 'Especially this
term. I hate January.'

'Everybody hates January,' said Judith, who didn't see why
Tamsin should have the sole rights to it.

'But *not as much as I do*,' said Tamsin, in tones of dark
triumph. 'Christmas is all finished. Nothing nice happening
for ever. It's all right for *you*. You've got your birthday in a few
weeks. Mine's not till *August*.' This reminded her of another
grievance. 'And I hate being the youngest in the form! I'm
going to be twelve still, while everyone else is thirteen. I'll be
the only one not to be a teenager.'

'I don't think being a teenager is all it's cracked up to be,'
said Judith, whose sixteen-year-old sister was currently
verging on nervous collapse over her impending mock GCEs,
and had boyfriend troubles to boot. Tamsin had been Judith's
best friend since their junior-school days; there were times

15

when she wondered why, but on the whole Tamsin was worth it, even with her moods and moanings. Tamsin was smart, and always right in there at the thick of the action: action which would have left Judith-without-Tamsin hovering wistfully on the sidelines. 'Anyway – who cares if you're the youngest? It doesn't show. It's much worse to be the smallest. Look at Gillian Phelps.'

'I'd rather not,' said Tamsin, and, rummaging in her satchel, she extracted that week's copy of The Magazine. The Magazine was Tamsin's Bible. It was cruelly named *Fifteen*, but it was amongst the second-formers that it was most popular. It provided tantalizing glimpses of the sophisticated lifestyle that lay just around the corner. 'Look at this dress, Jude. I mean, look at it. It's *beautiful*. When I'm a teenager that's what I'm going to look like. And I'm going to have matching leather boots and shoulder bag like these, and Mary Quant eyeshadow and nail varnish . . .'

'Let me know what bank you're going to rob,' said Judith. 'Or are your parents going to start giving you a tenner a week when you turn thirteen, as a reward for having lived so long?'

Tamsin said nothing; there was nothing to say. It was the truth. On the allowance she got, she was often pushed, by Thursday, to find the cash for The Magazine, let alone the glorious things pictured inside it. By the weekend she was invariably stony broke, reduced to fingering the fabulous fashion clothes in Snazzy boutique, drooling with longing, while salesgirls watched suspiciously. It was no good; she would have to find a way to make a lot of money. They'd be having Religious Instruction first lesson in the afternoon: she'd think about it then. Something like the principle of the Loaves and the Fishes; little tenpenny pieces must be persuaded to go forth and multiply into meaty ten-pound notes. What Tamsin could do with a tenner . . .

16

'Hey, you two – come here a minute.' The little squirt herself – Gillian Phelps, red-nosed and yellow-haired, clutching a pad and a pen.

'The bell's going to go,' said Tamsin, frostily.

'Not for another five minutes it isn't. Your watch must be fast.' Gillian Phelps was the kind of person whose watch is always exactly right. 'D'you want to bet ten pence on who'll be elected form captain? Here's the odds, look. Rachel Wilcox is favourite at three to one . . . but if you fancy an outsider, what about Madeline Drury? Fourteen to one – very generous odds. I must be mad. One pound forty you'd get, cash, plus your original ten pence back . . .'

It was no good. They had to look. Every time they vowed *never again*, and every time they fell for it. Which house would win the school sports? Whom would they get for form teacher next year? Who would come top in the science exam? Always they had a bet, and nearly always they lost. The only winner was Gillian, crafty little Gillian, the bookie's daughter. They knew this. The whole form knew it. And yet . . .

'Tamsin Mitchell, six to one,' read Tamsin, running a finger down the list.

'You'd be favourite, except that you did it one term last year.'

'Hmmm. Rachel Wilcox, though? What've you made her the favourite for?'

'Oh, everybody likes her. And she's never even been vice-captain. It seems like her turn. I've got a feeling about Rachel this time.'

'You're barmy. She's such a goody-goody little creep – none of Sarah Pike's lot can stand her. Yeah – what about Sarah Pike? She's much more likely. Go on then – *twenty* pence on Sarah Pike. I'm confident.'

'Twenty pence at seven to one,' muttered Gillian, filling out a slip. 'What about you, Judith?'

'Oh, I'll put twenty pence on Sarah too,' Judith said. It would be more fun if they were rooting for the same person. Judith herself was rated at fifteen to one; this, she thought glumly, pretty well summed her up.

Tamsin was still scanning the list. Right at the bottom, at twenty-five to one, was Caroline Stanmore. 'You're wasting your time even writing her down.' Caroline Stanmore was a nonentity, silent, spotty, sullen and stupid. When the class had to choose partners for gym, games or dancing, Caroline was always the one left out, the one who had to dance with the teacher. She never spoke in class; she had no friends. She didn't always smell very nice. 'She's as much chance of being form captain as I've got of being pope. She should be a million to one – and still nobody would bet on her.'

'I'll give you fifty to one,' said Gillian, hastily scribbling out the twenty-five. 'There, look. Twenty pence gets you ten quid.'

'No chance,' said Tamsin, preparing to move on. It was a mug's game, this betting business. The only way to win a lot of money was to back somebody you knew couldn't win. So there was *no* way to win a lot of money. Still – Sarah Pike might come good. One pound forty was a whole lot better than a kick in the teeth.

The first day of term did have its good points. Assembly was more than usually prolonged and tedious – Tamsin tuned out when Miss Ramsay started ranting about 'the thrills and challenges of the weeks that will unfold' – but after that there wasn't a thing to do until lunchtime, except to sit around gossiping in the classroom while the form teacher – a young, intense type called Miss Flynn – organized things like dinner arrangements, the exchanging of new books for old, and the election of form officials. And so slow, so earnest, so easily distracted was Miss Flynn, so subtly disruptive were Form H2, that it all took a very, very long time. Miss Flynn would make a move towards getting down to business, and Heather Gilmore or Sarah Pike would suddenly ask, what did you get for Christmas, Miss Flynn? Do you really believe in God, Miss Flynn? and Miss Flynn, who believed that her pupils were her equals, and that their every question deserved her serious attention, would answer, often at length.

Three people took no part in any of this. Caroline Stanmore, hunched at her desk, peering short-sightedly at a green exercise book. Gillian Phelps, in her corner, quietly counting money and jotting figures in her rough book. This was not unusual. The silence, however, of Tamsin Mitchell was altogether without precedent. She, too, was scribbling figures in her rough book, an expression of furious concentration on her small round face. Occasionally, she looked up and gazed at the window, on to which small patters of rain had lately begun to dash.

'No,' said Miss Flynn, 'I'm not very well informed about the current pop charts, but I do think the Beatles wrote some very nice tunes.' It was now ten-thirty: fifteen minutes before break. 'Oh dear,' said Miss Flynn. 'We don't seem to have got very much done. I wonder if we've got time to vote for form captain . . .'

'Miss Flynn!'

'Yes, Tamsin?'

Tamsin had dropped her pen, and was now sitting bolt upright, paying full attention. 'Miss Flynn – do you honestly think that form captains are a good thing? I mean, in a comprehensive school where everybody's *equal*, do you think it's right to pick one person out, and say, sort of, OK, you're more important than everyone else?'

Miss Flynn's eyes lit up. It was the sort of question, intelligent and concerning a matter of principle, that touched her soul. She had not been so moved since Madeline Drury had shyly asked her opinion on the topic of vivisection, later spoiling the effect by saying that *she* thought cutting rats up was more fun than almost anything.

'Well, Tamsin! Although there are sound arguments for that point of view, I must admit that I personally...'

She was off. 'What are you doing?' hissed Judith to Tamsin. 'What's all that you've been writing?'

'I've worked out a way to get some money. Just pray that it keeps raining. It's worth ten quid. *Each.*'

'How? What d'you mean?'

And Tamsin leaned across and told her. 'Now,' she said, 'this is what *you've* got to do.'

'. . . therefore not incompatible with the principles of democracy,' said Miss Flynn. The bell rang, abruptly cutting off the flow. 'Oh dear – already? We really *must* get on with things after break, H2.' She glanced at the window. 'It'll be a wet break, obviously, so sit quietly in the classroom. The tuck shop isn't open till tomorrow. If you want to use the lavatories, please return here straight away. If you haven't got anything to do,' she added hopefully, 'you could get on with your reading of *A Midsummer Night's Dream*. We'd reached the beginning of Act Three . . .' The class shrank back as if in pain. Miss Flynn taught English. People like Miss Flynn always did. 'Well, anyway, try not to make too much noise,' she said, and scuttled off to the staffroom, where – they knew, because they'd seen through the door – she would instantly light one of the cigarettes she so eloquently pleaded with them never to touch.

Tamsin looked round surreptitiously. To her relief, most people seemed content to stay where they were, giggling and nattering in their little gangs. A few were making for the door, but they'd probably be back in time. Break lasted twenty-five minutes. 'OK,' she said to Judith. 'Off you go, and for God's sake get it right.'

Judith strolled out of the room, along the corridor, and down the steps towards the cloakrooms, keeping a sharp eye out for a suitable victim. Ah – there was just the thing, huddled against the wall, looking lost and terrified. A first-former – one of those tiny grey undeveloped ones, uniform spanking clean and immaculately pressed, hair strained back in trembling ponytail. Judith advanced. She was one of the tallest in H2, which was the reason Tamsin had delegated this task to her. Height equalled authority.

'Ah!' she said loudly. The first-former looked up in fright. Judith could see her little brain desperately trying to work out what she had done wrong, and wondering what was to be her punishment. 'Would you run along to room 14 – you know where that is?' – squeak of assent – 'and tell Gillian Phelps and Caroline Stanmore that Miss Ramsey wants to see them. They're to wait outside her office until she fetches them in. Got that?'

'Gillian Phelps and Caroline Stanmore,' said the first-former, nodding furiously, and off she went, muttering the names under her breath. Really, Judith thought, it was marvellous being in the second year. It gave you something to feel superior to. Mission accomplished, she went off for a few minutes to loiter in the loo.

Tamsin, back in the classroom, was boiling herself up into a fever of impatience. What was Judith doing? Had she messed it up? Judith was normally reliable enough, but . . . ah. Tap on the door, nervous little head peering round, face like a peeled potato. What a little weed. Where had Judith dug her up from? The weed was looking alarmed; no nice safe teacher to whom she could whisper her message. But 'What d'you want?' called Sarah Pike, and the weed unburdened herself, and fled. Sarah relayed the message. Exit Gillian and Caroline, Gillian shaking her head in bewilderment, no, she hadn't a clue what it was about. She took her money with her, Tamsin noticed, stuffed into her blazer pocket. Caroline just trailed out, eyes obscured by greasy strands of fringe. Caroline's eyes rarely saw daylight. Shortly afterwards, Judith returned, strutting jauntily across the room with the air of one who knows she has done well.

'Right,' said Tamsin. She went over to Miss Flynn's desk and banged the board duster on it. Clouds of chalk flew upwards; H2 looked up in surprise.

'Everybody listen,' said Tamsin, 'and listen carefully, because there's not much time. How would you all fancy making a tenner? A crisp ten-pound note, one for each of you?'

H2 regarded her with deep suspicion. 'Oh yeah?' somebody said. 'You going into the betting business now, are you?'

'Sort of,' said Tamsin. 'I want to rig the election for form captain.' Immediately there was a buzz of interest. 'If we fix it so that we know who's going to win, and put a big last-minute bet on, we could get a whole load of money out of little Miss Millionaire Phelps.' She had their full attention. Nearly everyone had had a bet with Gillian at one time or another; nearly everyone was poorer as a result.

'Who shall we vote for to be captain then?' asked Heather Gilmore, who had quite fancied her own chances, and was hoping it would be her.

'Caroline Stanmore,' said Tamsin. Howls of indignation and scorn. That smelly slob? That revolting creature? She had to be joking. They'd never . . .

'Oh, don't be so stupid!' They really were morons. She's always suspected it. 'What d'you want – to vote for Rachel or somebody? Rachel's three. We'd hardly make anything. It wouldn't be worth the trouble. Caroline Stanmore is *fifty to one*. Fifty. That means we'd win fifty times as much as we bet. I've worked it out.' She picked up her rough book. 'Twenty-seven of us in the class, minus Gillian and Caroline, makes twenty-five. If each of us contributes twenty pence, we could put a five pound bet on. And at fifty to one, that makes' – she paused for effect – 'two hundred and fifty quid. Ten each.'

There was a long, awed silence. A strange, yearning look was discernible in the eyes of form H2. Ten pounds. Mentally they were caressing the crisp brown piece of paper already. Skirts, shoes, visits to the cinema, the skating rink . . . money! Money could do almost anything, and none of them ever had enough of it. Ten pounds.

'It's a brilliant idea,' said Sarah Pike, slowly. 'But there's a couple of things bother me about it. Will she take a five-pound bet? Nobody ever bets that much. She's bound to wonder.'

'I don't think Gillian would wonder about anything once she actually saw the money. She'd be *begging* me to make a bet with it. She's not that bright. It's just a question of doing it really casually. Look, I don't know. I think she'll fall for it. If she doesn't we haven't lost anything, have we?'

'No – but the other thing is, two hundred and fifty pounds is an awful lot of money. Even if she's got it, would she part with it? I mean . . .'

'She'd bloody well have to! A bet's a bet. If she didn't pay, nobody would ever bet with her again, and that would be the end of her little income. And of course she's got it! She's been bleeding all of us for a year – don't you think she's got all that cash salted away somewhere? Course she has. And you think we're the only ones? She does exactly the same with the kids in her street. And what about junior school? Gillian Phelps has probably been taking bets since she learned to *write*. And if she hasn't got it, she can damn well get it off her father. Anyway – ' she glanced nervously at the door, expecting at

23

any minute that Gillian would walk back through it and spoil everything – 'you've got to decide *now*. There's no time to argue. Yes or no?' Most people were nodding yes, and a few were already getting out their purses, but there were still some undecided and hesitant faces.

'Oh, come on,' Sarah Pike said. 'What're you all afraid of? That smarmy little snake has made enough money out of us in the past. It's about time she got taught a lesson. Who're the cowards who won't join in?' She glared balefully around the room. 'Right. That's better. Now, if I start collecting the money . . .'

'Wait a sec,' said Tamsin. Sarah's support had probably clinched it, but she needn't start thinking she could take over, just the same. 'First we've got to organize the election. We can't have everyone voting for Caroline, or nobody'll believe it. I mean, no one ever gets all the votes. This is how we do it. The two rows on the left – ' she waved her arm – 'you vote for Caroline. That's eleven votes. Then we've got to have another candidate with strong support, so that the next row must all vote for the same person – Sarah, say. So you six vote for Sarah, and I will too – that's seven. Everyone else vote for whoever you like, as long as it's not Sarah or Caroline. Just don't all go for the same person, that's all. Everyone got that?' They nodded as if hypnotized. With half of their minds they were in Snazzy boutique, browsing through blouses, trying on dresses. 'Right. Money.' Sarah got up and began collecting. 'You do that side,' Tamsin said to Judith, and she herself took the two rows in the middle.

'Ramsay never sent for those two at all, did she?' Sarah said to Tamsin as they passed in the aisle. 'You fixed that.' There was a mixture of admiration and envy in her voice. 'You really planned it out.'

'You have to plan things,' said Tamsin, rattling silver, 'Or

24

they don't work. That reminds me.' She raised her voice. 'When Gillian comes back and I make the bet with her, *don't watch me*. Don't take any notice at all.' She could just picture it: the whole form craning their necks and giggling, and Gillian cottoning on. They were so thick, H2, you practically had to tell them their own names.

By the time the money had been collected there were only three minutes left before the bell. Tamsin sent Judith to lurk outside the staffroom, waylay Miss Flynn when she emerged, lungs well coated with tar, and engage her in conversation.

'What'll I say?' asked Judith.

'You'll think of something,' Tamsin said unkindly. She was rather worried by the amount of small change. There was one pound note, but all the rest was in silver: five, ten and twenty-pence pieces. 'This won't do,' she said. 'We need a note. Who's got a five-pound note?'

'Well – I've got one,' Joanne Burke said, 'but you can't have it, I need it. I mean, I'm going to Snazzy after school to get this blouse in the sale, and I can't carry all that silver . . .'

'Oh, shut up waffling and give us the fiver,' said Tamsin. 'If this comes off you can get three flippin' blouses.' She tipped the money on to Joanne's desk; Joanne blinked, her eyes following the silver stream. It was like winning on a fruit machine. She hardly noticed as Tamsin extracted the five-pound note from between her fingers. And just in time, for the door burst open and in came Gillian, snarling and raging.

'I'll get that bloody kid! Who was she?' She looked round the room, as if one of H2 might be harbouring the criminal inside her satchel. 'Ramsay hadn't sent for us at all. I'm so mad I could kill someone. *Who was that kid who brought the message*?' There was a great deal of shrugging, and, to Tamsin's horror, some giggling. But then, somebody always was giggling about something: Gillian saw nothing odd in it, and went over to her desk, still cursing under her breath. Caroline Stanhope slipped inside the room like a shadow; the bell rang.

Tamsin sidled over to Gillian's desk. 'Bloody little first-form scum!' said Gillian by way of greeting.

'Throttling's too good for her,' agreed Tamsin, perching nonchalantly on the edge of the desk. 'Ah, well. How's the betting going?'

'Fine,' said Gillian, instantly appeased. She brought out her list and pad. 'Nearly everyone's had a go. There's been quite a bit put on Heather Gilmore. Hope she doesn't win.'

'She won't,' said Tamsin.

'You want another last-minute bet, then? It's your last chance.'

'Maybe.' Tamsin picked the list up again. 'Caroline still at fifty to one, is she? Anybody backed her?'

'Nah. The wet weed. Stood by me outside Ramsay's office for fifteen minutes just now and didn't say a word. Wouldn't even have a bet! I think she's mentally ill.'

'Oh. Not much point in putting money on her, then, I suppose. I'd be wasting my time.'

'Oh, not necessarily!' Instantly, Gillian transformed herself to Salesperson. 'All sorts of weird things happen, you know. I bet lots of people like her really. She never does any harm. And, I mean, even if they don't they might vote for her out of spite. I mean, nobody likes being form captain. It's a real drag.'

You lying toad, thought Tamsin. She slipped her hand into her pocket and brought out the five-pound note. 'I was thinking maybe I'd have another bet. This is all I've got, though. I haven't got any change.'

Gillian's eyes popped. She opened her mouth to say: 'I can give you change,' but thought better of it. 'Sound little investment, a fiver,' she said weakly. Her fingers were twitching. She had already mentally added five pounds to the not

26

inconsiderable sum in her savings account.

'Yeah – but it's a lot of money. Too much to bet, really, isn't it? I found this fiver on the way to school, you know. I was walking along, and I looked down, and I thought, no, it *can't* be – and it was. So I was thinking just now, even if I bet and lose, I won't be any worse off than I was when I got up. And fifty to one is such a lot of money I could win . . . but, there, there wouldn't be much chance with Caroline.'

'I reckon you've got *every* chance,' said Gillian, reaching for a pen and hovering over the betting-slip pad. 'Of course, it'll break me, if Caroline wins . . .'

'Better not do it, then . . .'

' . . . but I'll risk it,' she said generously, tweaking the note out of Tamsin's hand with much-practised fingers. 'Here's your slip.'

'I'm sure I've just thrown five quid down the drain,' said Tamsin sadly, heading back to her own desk, and winking gleefully for the benefit of anyone who could see.

Judith returned, with Miss Flynn two paces behind her, looking anxiously at her watch. 'Really, H2, we have *no time to lose*. I hope you've been thinking deeply about the election for form captain – which of your fellow classmates has the necessary qualities of responsibility and leadership . . .'

'Oh yes, Miss Flynn,' they chorused. Never before had they thought about an election quite so deeply. Judith scrambled to her seat and glanced enquiringly at Tamsin.

'We have lift off,' said Tamsin, pointing to the betting slip which poked out of her front pocket. 'All systems go. You did well, to keep her so long.'

'I asked her to tell me some good books to read. She went sort of delirious. She said it was moments like this that made her certain she's found her vocation. What's a vocation?'

'I thought it was a holiday,' said Tamsin, and shrugged;

they'd always known Miss Flynn was mad, it was nothing new.

'Write down *one* name,' Miss Flynn was saying, 'and then fold up your papers. Think carefully. Don't automatically vote for your best friend. Look at her and *think*. Is she suitable? Is she worthy? If not, think again.' This was too good to resist; in perfect unison the class turned, scanned their dearest chum thoughtfully, and shook their heads with mournful regret. 'Everyone finished *already*?' said Miss Flynn. 'Very well. Pass your papers forward.' She collected the slips, took them to her desk and began to sort them, her mouth curving upwards into a knowing little smile. You could see her thinking: how meaningful this is. What a wonderful rehearsal for adult life. What a splendid introduction to the principles of democracy.

The class watched silently as Miss Flynn's busy fingers unfolded, smoothed, sorted. Little piles were beginning to form on her desk, and one pile was already visibly ahead of the field. Nothing can go wrong now, thought Tamsin, but her fingers, arms and legs were crossed just the same. She'd have crossed her eyes if she hadn't been watching the piles so closely. It was going to work. Ten quid – ten crisp tasty smackeroos. And suddenly it seemed rather unfair that she, the deviser and organizer of the whole scheme, she who had done all the work, should profit by not a penny more than everyone else. What had the rest of those subnormal nerds done except to reach into their purses? Tamsin was their agent, and agents were entitled to ten per cent of their clients' income. She'd have one pound from each of them – they could keep nine, and be grateful. Except for Judith, maybe, and Sarah, because they'd helped. That left twenty-two people – twenty-two pounds, plus her own ten, made thirty-two. Wow and double-wow. Thirty-two quids' worth of goodies. She could hardly imagine it. Never before had she had so much money to spend. And there were sales on everywhere! How could she possibly have hated January? It was a *brilliant* month.

'Well – we have a result,' said Miss Flynn. Nobody breathed. This was the all-important moment. With a teacher less daft than Miss Flynn, the plan could never have worked. Anyone with half a grain of common sense would be aware of Caroline Stanmore's status, or lack of it, and would *know* it must be a fixed result. But Miss Flynn, as yet untempered by age or experience, was so idealistic, so full of belief in the good in everyone, so blind to harsh realities . . . wasn't she?

'In third place, with five votes,' said Miss Flynn, 'is Tamsin Mitchell. Second, with eight votes, and your vice-captain for this term' – how she did love to build up the suspense – 'Sarah Pike.' Eight? It should have been seven. But then, Gillian and Caroline must have voted for somebody. 'And the clear winner with eleven votes – your new form captain – Caroline Stanmore! A round of applause for Caroline, everyone.' Tamsin turned to Judith in jubilation. *They'd done it!* The class erupted into a frenzy of clapping and cheers.

Miss Flynn beamed benevolently around the room. Such nice, good girls! She herself had long been trying to devise some method by which Caroline might be brought out of herself a little. The poor girl was so very lacking in confidence. And now this – this *remarkable* form had, spontaneously, given her the boost she needed. Form captain – it would be the making of Caroline. A very special form, H2. So mature, so unselfish. And so clearly delighted by the result. Except – and Miss Flynn's face fell slightly – except for Gillian Phelps, who was really looking most hostile. *Most* hostile. She looked, in fact, almost murderous. Such a pity, one person showing negative feelings at what was a very positive moment. And now, here was Caroline rising to her feet and making her way to the front of the room. Perhaps a short speech of thanks and acceptance. Miss Flynn could discern a change in the girl already. New spirit – new life in those dull eyes. Caroline came up to her desk, bent over and spoke.

'I'm not being form captain,' she said. 'It's some joke they're playing. I won't do it. I'm not going to do it.'

'Oh – but, Caroline! Of course, you don't have to if you don't want to – but don't you think . . .'

'No,' said Caroline. Miss Flynn stared sadly at the two large red spots on her chin; so close were they that they appeared to be on the verge of joining, blending into one huge megaspot. Could spots do that? 'I don't think,' said Caroline, 'and I'm not doing it.' Miss Flynn considered launching into her 'I shall feel that you're letting me down personally' speech, but it was no use. Caroline was already slinking back to her seat and to obscurity. Sighing deeply, Miss Flynn rose to her feet, trying to think of a way to tell H2 as tactfully as possible, and without hurting any feelings, that their new form captain would be Sarah Pike.

'Two hundred and fifty quid you owe me,' said Tamsin.

'Get lost.'

'I had a bet,' said Tamsin, 'on who would be elected form captain. Caroline Stanmore was elected. She got the most votes. Whether she accepted or not is nothing to do with it. Now, how do you want to pay?'

'Go stick your head in a microwave oven,' said Gillian. 'You cheating vermin. I don't owe you anything. The bet was on who'd be the new form captain. Sarah Pike's the new form captain. Nothing more to say.'

Tamsin knew she'd lost. She knew where she'd gone wrong, too: she'd been too greedy. They should have voted for someone like Judith, at fifteen to one. It would have been so much simpler and safer – and though the rewards would not have

30

been so great, Tamsin would still have been comfortably off with her ten per cent agent's fee. Still – she hadn't given up yet. 'The bet was on who'd be *elected*,' she repeated. 'That's what you said.'

'Prove it. And then prove you didn't cheat.'

'Who's cheating? You shouldn't be so stupid as to take bets from people who decide the result of what they're betting on.'

Gillian swung round in fury. 'Look. Here's your rotten fiver back. Keep your lousy stake money. And that's all you're getting. As far as I'm concerned the bet never happened. I'm not standing here arguing with you all day.'

'I beg your pardon,' said Tamsin. 'If you're not paying out on Caroline, you must be paying out on somebody else. Or have you decided not to have any winners this time?'

'I'm paying out on Sarah, of course,' said Gillian, and then she remembered.

'Good,' said Tamsin, 'because I put twenty pence on her, at seven to one, and so did Judith. Here's the slips. That's two pounds eighty, plus our original forty pence, makes three pounds twenty, please.' Just as well she'd had that bet on Sarah as insurance. At least she'd made *some* profit. It hadn't been a wasted experience. One pound forty clear. And there were those gorgeous little pots of glitter nail varnish in the sale at Snazzy boutique . . .

First Day at Boarding School
Prunella Power

Like a trapped bird
she hid behind her hair.

Confident buxom girls
crowded the corridors

on their bedroom walls
pictures of pop-stars kissing.

What did they comprehend
of Africa's space and silence?

Like a caged animal
she sniffed the stuffy air,

heard the head's platitudes
resolved never to 'settle down',

pledged herself to wildness
to bursting through closed doors

behind which they said
she must learn a new language.

Suddenly There Came a Crack in the Ice
Petronella Breinburg
(*A story set in the Hague*)

'You? You of all people!'

The words came back to Cita as if from the cold wind blowing against her face. She pulled her woolly hat closer over her ears. The hat in itself seemed to be a symbol of defiance. 'Teachers,' she laughed. 'They hate anyone who wears such a hat which displays the colours of the new Surinamese flag.' Cita was right. Girls, and boys too, had more than once been told by their teachers to 'take that ridiculous thing off your head.' That is, the Creoles got told off. They were the ones brave enough to wear them. Cita, like the other Hindustani girls from Surinam, liked the colours, but was afraid to wear one.

'Funny,' Teneke had more than once laughed, 'how people could hate a simple hat.'

Teneke was Cita's best friend in those days. Now it was Teneke who had got her into trouble. If it wasn't for Teneke, none of this would have happened. Cita felt sure that it was Teneke who went and told Mr van Oost, the teacher on break-duty, that Cita was speaking Surinam. The teacher came and caught Cita. Maybe if she had stopped speaking, the teacher would have just given her a warning cough or clearing of his throat.

For an unexplained reason, Cita did not stop. She continued to explain the maths homework to a young third-year, in Hindustani. The girl was new, from the special-class where all foreign pupils went before they were transferred to the general class. She was terribly nervous and unsure of herself. Because of that nervousness, Cita felt sure, the girl could not do the work. The girl was getting very low marks, so the tutor told her off, and this made her more nervous and caused her to make more mistakes.

That day Cita had found the girl in tears in the girls' toilet. She managed to speak to her and bring her back to the home-work room. Cita had begun to explain in Dutch, but the girl didn't seem to understand the problem, and continued to sniff. It was then that Cita broke one of the most important rules of the school, the rule that said none of the Surinam languages were permitted in school. People who broke that rule were severely punished. They had to stay in after school and do their Dutch homework, or if they were behind in French or German, they were allowed to do extra work in those subjects.

33

'Damned unfair.' Cita stamped in the ice. It had been snowing again and the Zuider Park, near the school, was high with soft ice in places.

'It's like sugar, lots and lots of white sugar.' Cita began to run along the ice, kicking sprays of it into the air.

That action brought back to her mind the first day she met Johan. If it wasn't for Johan, she and Teneke would have still been best friends. Teneke would not have told on her. Cita would not have been called to the tutor's office, and she would not have been told off and told to report for staying in after school. And she would not have refused to take punishment for speaking her own language. And she would not have been given a choice.

'Either you take your punishment or you take suspension. You know the rules.' Cita pursed her lips to imitate the tutor.

'Bloody scarecrow she is,' Cita swore under her breath, then automatically looked round to see if anyone had heard her. Because, brave as she was only an hour ago, she still could never swear for anyone to hear.

'Crunch, crunch,' the hardening ice said under her feet.

'It's like walking on broken glass,' she smiled in spite of her sadness.

How Cita liked the crunching of half-hard ice when she first arrived in Holland from Surinam, exactly five years before. She had arrived in 1977 and now it was 1982. She liked Holland then and still would like it now. 'If only the school didn't have those silly rules,' she thought. 'Why can't the Surinam children speak Surinam when the Moroccan children and the English children are all allowed to speak their mother tongue. Not fair, not bloody fair, and I don't care if I am suspended! Don't care one damn!'

Cita's thoughts were braver than she actually felt. What would she tell her father? 'Dad will go berserk. He wants me

34

to do well, and I *am* doing well. I got top marks in English, my German is brilliant – even that scarecrow with her giraffe neck said so. My French is not too bad either. I must work harder on my French, that's all. Anyway, I was the first Surinam girl to move up from the school's low stream to a high stream, so I can't be bad. No Surinam girl ever got out of a low stream before. God, what am I going to tell my dad?

'Maybe I should go back to school, go back and say I'm sorry. Other people have done it, why not me? Why can't I be like all the other girls and say I was sorry for speaking Hindustani? I've done it before, another time when I was caught speaking it?' Next moment Cita asked, 'But why should I? That damn Teneke, damn her, damn Johan, damn the whole school, damn Holland! I'm fed up! Wish I was back in St Maria School in Paramaribo. There you don't have all these stupid rules. And you don't have people like that Teneke.'

Cita had been jogging while thinking but had now got to stop. She had jogged a long way and was tired. She found herself a bench and sat down. 'Oh, God, what am I going to do now? I can't go home and tell them I was suspended, I just can't. They'll kill me, they'll skin me alive . . . they . . .'

'Cita,' a voice called loudly from behind her. That voice startled her. She knew that voice well. She had heard it for the first time, right here in that very park. She had heard it many times since. She had heard it at the local community centre where she and her brothers had gone to a festival of Hindustani art. She was surprised to find him admiring the exhibits because he was no Hindustani, he was Creole.

'What happened? Teneke said you got suspended and that you're blaming her. What *is* going on? You can't get suspended! Not you, you're the best girl in the school. The best girl in the whole of den Haag even, you're, eh, my eh, special girl.' He sat himself, uninvited, beside her.

'Don't talk nonsense, I'm not your girl, special or not special. Anyway, I *can* get suspended if I want to.'

'No you can't! You'll go right back there and stay in school.'

'Who are you to tell me what to do?' Suddenly Cita was angry. He looked so handsome that she had to be angry with him. If she wasn't angry with him she might love him. And if she loved him he might notice it. And if he noticed it he might want to see her more often. Teneke would go berserk, and when Teneke went berserk, the whole school shivered. Cita remembered the incidents when something had upset Teneke, making her scream and shout. Cita recalled her 'beating people up'.

'Look,' he said, not looking at her. 'I know how you feel. It is like the old days back home when our grandparents were beaten if they spoke Sranan.'

'The Hindustanis were beaten too,' she joined in.

'True, but did that stop Hindustani or Sranan? No, it didn't, not one bit it didn't. All the boys at my school speak Sranan or Hindustani. They even have a place in Amsterdam where you can learn to write in Sranan.'

'What's that got to do with me here, that's what I want to know? Amsterdam is Amsterdam, maybe there the teachers are more, eh, civilized. Anyway, you'd better go.' Cita got off the bench and pulled nervously at her woolly hat.

On one hand, his presence made her very uncomfortable. On the other hand, she wished he would stay. He was a nice boy. Why couldn't he stay and talk to her if he wished? 'Teneke'll kill you if he does, that's why,' the ice crunching beneath her feet seemed to say.

'You cold?' he asked.

'Of course I'm not.' Yet she seemed to have goose pimples all over her.

'Look, go back to school. Take the punishment. Anyway, it is no punishment if it doesn't hurt. So don't let it hurt. Just do any homework they set you. You're clever anyway, you'll finish it in no time and go home. When you leave school, you'll go to Amsterdam and learn to write in your own language. Nobody can stop you then. Nobody can stop them speaking Dutch no matter where they live, so nobody can stop us.'

He speaks like a grown man. He sounds so clever, Cita thought, and wondered why he was sent to a technical school instead of a HAVO, which is a higher school. It was to HAVO that all the clever people went. Everybody knows that 'technical school' is a nice name for 'dumb school'. He is no dumby, and he looks so handsome. He could be a president one day if he wanted to. He could be anything, God even, if he wanted to . . .

'I know you're cold. I can tell. You're shivering.'

'Well, I am a bit. I got so mad I came out without my coat.'

'Take mine.' He pulled off his coat and put it over her shoulders.

Side by side they continued to walk through the park. Occasionally she'd kick some soft ice. He too would kick some, and pretended that he could not kick further than she could. She knew he was pretending. He could kick much further than that. He was pretending, to make her happy, and the thought that he wanted to make her happy, made her happy.

'Hi . . .' A long cry came and jerked Cita from her romantic dream. She looked round, but need not have done so. Somehow she knew that voice. It belonged to Teneke, Teneke Groen, who else?

'Oh, bloody hell! Where're they all going?' he said.

'Hi, you! I knew I'd find you here,' said Teneke, and a group of about six girls, led by The Teneke, ran up to where Cita and Johan were.

Teneke puffed, so the other girls puffed as well. None of them would have dared not to puff if Teneke was puffing.

'We've (puff) got it all (puff) organized.' Teneke took a deep breath.

'Yes, and Tien is our leader, aren't you?' a girl said. It was little Liesje. Poor Liesje who agreed with everything Teneke said, or got her face smashed in.

'Now, if *you* get suspended, we all take suspension. All the Surinam girls, don't know about the boys.' Teneke gave Johan a dirty look. 'And some of the Dutch girls too.'

Cita was puzzled. Was Teneke saying that she was actually on her side? Cita wanted to say something more, but just managed a guttural, 'What?'

'See, I told you!' Johan smiled. 'You got supporters, I told you!'

'I am no footballer.' Cita seemed to find her voice at last.

'Where is the paper? Who's got the damn paper?' Teneke said in coarse Sranan.

The two Dutch girls in the group could not, of course, understand, so they looked vaguely at Teneke.

'Who's got the paper with the names?' Teneke repeated.

'Names, what names?' asked Cita.

'Come on ladies, you can't stand here chatting in the ice, that child is going to get in an accident there, the ice is cracking!' Johan pointed to children playing, but the group took no notice.

The group began to walk along while Teneke explained, to Cita's horror, that all the names on the list were of girls who said that they'd stand by Cita.

'You've got a right to speak your own language,' said Marelijn. 'My dad said so. He said, as long as you write in good Dutch you can speak Plat-Haagse if you want to. "Let any teacher punish you for it, and I'll come to that school and break necks," he said,' Marelijn laughed.

'And he will too, I've seen him at his market stall,' said Teneke.

'My dad can't break necks, you see.' Cita felt better. If these girls could be on her side then all was well. She wouldn't even mind being punished.

'No, but if my dad and other parents . . .' Marelijn began, but Teneke stopped her.

'No parents, just us, right?' Teneke stared into Marelijn's blue eyes.

'Just us,' all the girls, except for Cita, said in unison.

'Now, we'll sign a petition. Telma, you're doing typing, you type out the words . . . "We the girls of . . ." Oh, who's best at Dutch? Who should write it.'

'That would be Anne. She's top at Dutch,' said someone.

'Yes, I will,' said Anne.

'What are you grinning for?' Teneke asked Johan.

Cita had, for the moment, forgotten Johan's presence.

'And don't you, Cita, go telling people I got you in trouble, and because of him. I did not for one thing, and for him? You must be joking. She can have him, can't she girls?'

'Oh, yes, she can,' the girls chorused.

'But now we must plan. Tomorrow, you, Cita, you come to school as usual. You say sorry to the old scarecrow. Of course, you wouldn't call her scarecrow to her face. You must be all nice and stupid, and say, well, blame it on . . .' Teneke whispered to Cita. 'Say it's your menstrual, your . . .'

'Sh!' Cita pushed Teneke away and blushed, even though she was sure that from where Johan was standing he could not have overheard.

'Then we'll start the petition rolling.' Teneke continued to give orders. 'We'll need . . . Hi, Helen, your dad's photocopier's working again, is it?'

'Yes, I can make one for each of us six. Eh, five assistant

39

leaders take a copy round to the whole school and you keep a copy,' Helen said.

'What about other schools?' asked Anne.

'Ladies, may a mere boy speak?' Johan mocked.

'Yes, you may.' Teneke gave permission before Cita had a chance to open her mouth.

'The boys at my place, can they sign as well?' asked Johan.

'I'm not going to go round asking boys,' said Cita.

'I can do it,' said Johan.

'But you're not at our school,' reminded Helen.

'His girl is, so he can help,' said Teneke.

'I'm, eh, not his girl, eh,' Cita stammered.

'Of course you are, liar! We'll give him a copy to take to his place. I say so. Now, let's get to our houses, leave these two lovebirds.'

With that Teneke and the girls went as suddenly as they came, waving.

'Strange girl that Teneke. She makes me, well, I can't speak when she's around. And I thought she was, well, your girl.'

'Nah, she's got another boy, thank God. She was beginning to get on my nerves with her bullying. She's turned her attention to Ronald.'

'Poor Ronald. Anyway, I must go home now.'

'And you are my girl, aren't you? I can only take the petition around if you are.'

Cita wanted to speak but it was as if something held on to her tongue, and unless you move your tongue, you cannot speak.

She did not speak for a long time while they walked side by side, until he said, 'The ice is beginning to melt. See over there.'

'Ja, that child had better be careful staying on that pond.'

'Ja, it's beginning to crack,' said Johan.

For Cita, it was as if a very new beginning was following

the end of an era. She pulled her woolly hat back into place to cover her ears. 'I'm going to school tomorrow, and won't let that Teneke do all the talking, either!'

'Good, I'll wait for you in the playground, no matter how long your punishment homework, OK?'

'Yes, wait for me.'

A Knife with Sixteen Blades
Antonia Forest

[from *Autumn Term*]

Train journeys, Nicola decided, were awfully dull. After the first half-hour no one seemed to want to talk any more, so that unless you had something to read you sat and looked at Karen and Lawrie and Rowan opposite or right and left at Ann and Ginty. Actually, Nicola had a book on her lap (Karen had seen to that before they left Victoria) but she wasn't in the mood for reading. She seldom was. Nicola's world had to be very calm and settled before she could sit down quietly with a book, a remedy frequently suggested by her weary relations as an antidote to Nicola's general air of being all agog.

It had been suggested very often in the last week or so; for even the excitement of going into town almost daily with her mother and Lawrie to be measured for their new uniforms and buy the startling number of new underclothes necessary for school, and (crowning glory) eat lunch and tea in a restaurant and order exactly what they liked (which meant that Lawrie stuck to chicken and ice-cream and Nicola dodged all over the menu to make sure she was missing nothing), had not, as

41

Rowan so hopefully prophesied, tired her out. She still came back and stood on one leg near Karen or Rowan or Ann (Ginty was too unreliable) and went on asking questions:

'Will Miss Keith see us when we get there? Where do we go first? Do new girls have to sing on First Night like they do in books? Who will be games captain this term? Mother says I can wear Ginty's old blazer. Can I? Do people? Wouldn't it be better if Lawrie wore her hair a different way so that we don't look so much like twins? Will people be funny about it? Shall we share a sisters' room with the rest of you?'

'I hope not,' said Rowan emphatically. 'The first thing I do when I get back is look at the dormitory lists; and if we are in the same room I'm going straight to Matron to protest.'

'Oh, Rowan. Why?'

'Because I like my nights quiet, peaceful and undisturbed. I can't honestly feel that they'd be that with you around. And do go away, Nick. I'm supposed to have read this wretched book by the time I get back.'

Nicola went away and found Giles, who was the eldest, and was doing nothing at all but lie peacefully on his back in the sun.

'They won't tell me things,' she complained, sitting down cross-legged beside him. 'And I want to know so as to be prepared.'

'Prepared for what?' asked Giles sleepily.

'Just prepared. So that I don't do anything awfully silly and have people laughing at me like they do. And so that I know what it's going to be like.'

'No good worrying about being laughed at. There are sure to be thousands of new brats all making the same mistakes at the same time. And as for telling you what it's like – no one can do that.'

'Why not?'

'Because, my idiot sister, the same thing looks quite different to different people. Karen can't possibly tell you what the kindergarten-'

'IIIA,' said Nicola indignantly.

'Kindergarten,' said Giles firmly, 'looks like from the Sixth. Father tried to tell me what the navy was like before I got there, but it wasn't like that at all. Not to me, anyway.'

'Oh,' said Nicola.

So she had, to the relief of her family, almost stopped asking questions. Not entirely, of course. But they only came out now when she had to ask or burst.

The train journey continued dull. Nicola swung her legs and looked crossly round the carriage, piecing together from her own and her sisters' uniforms the things she knew about Kingscote. The three black felt hats in the rack with the blue and scarlet hatbands meant that Rowan and Ann and Ginty were seniors. The fourth hat, with the plain scarlet band, was Karen's and meant she was a prefect. Head girl actually, thought Nicola accurately, and she had a special badge to pin to her tie. The two scarlet berets with the bright blue crest belonged to Nicola and Lawrie and showed they were juniors. What else was there? There was Rowan's plain blue tie because she was in the netball team, and Ginty's striped girdle for second-eleven hockey. Ann wore a Guide badge on her coat - but that wasn't particularly a school thing. Nicola yawned and kicked Ginty accidentally-on-purpose.

'Couldn't Lawrie and I go and stand in the corridor for a bit?' suggested Nicola hopefully, when the commotion had died down a little.

'For heaven's sake, let them,' said Rowan. 'If Nick's starting to fidget no one'll have any peace.'

'Well – all right,' said Karen. 'But *don't* go and fall out of a window. Miss Keith wouldn't be a bit pleased if the train were

43

late because one of the school was careless about a little thing like that.'

She spoke in her head girl's voice which had returned to her a day or two before term began, making Giles salute and say: 'Yes, *ma'am*,' in a way Karen found particularly aggravating. But Nicola was only concerned with what Karen said, not how she said it. She sprang to her feet, knocking Ann's book from her hand, trod on Rowan's foot and tumbled out into the corridor followed by Lawrie. Rowan closed the carriage door firmly behind them.

'Good,' said Nicola. 'Now we can talk.'

Lawrie nodded. Like Nicola she was thin and blue eyed with straight sun-bleached hair and an expression of alert inquiry. But she talked less than Nicola, and although she was just as interested, she was inclined to leave it to Nicola to find out and tell her all about it when she had done so.

'What time is it?' asked Nicola.

Lawrie looked at her watch, a parting present from her parents. Nicola could have had a watch too, but when she had been told to choose her present she had plumped for the knife with sixteen blades which had dazzled her for months every time she passed the ironmonger's window where it was the centrepiece. Her father had warned her that if she had the knife she would have to do without a watch till she was twenty-one. Nicola thought this no drawback. There were always clocks. And bells. Especially in school. One wouldn't need a watch. Whereas a knife with sixteen blades – she took it out of her pocket and stroked it affectionately.

'It's ten to three,' said Lawrie.

'Another hour,' said Nicola despairingly. 'I do think trains are dull, even in the corridor.'

'I wonder if we'll like it,' said Lawrie nervously. She meant, as Nicola promptly realized, since Lawrie had been saying the

44

same thing every night for weeks, school, not the train.

'I don't see why not. The others do.'

'They're used to it,' said Lawrie.

'So will we be used to it,' said Nicola firmly. 'In two weeks, Giles said.'

'I hope Giles knows,' said Lawrie. She sighed deeply.

A few compartments down, a door slid back and a girl came out. Like Lawrie and Nicola she wore the scarlet beret of the juniors. She looked at them and then pretended not to look, leaning against the partition and staring at the scenery.

Nicola nudged Lawrie. 'Is she new too, d'you think?'

'I don't know,' whispered Lawrie.

'I think she may be or she'd be inside talking to people,' decided Nicola. She edged down the corridor and said, 'Are you new like us?'

The other girl turned and grinned. She had short, rough dark hair, and her face was tanned the colour of a brown egg. Her eyes were a lighter brown, with greenish flecks in them. Nicola, whose favourite looks just then were sleek black hair and grey eyes, could not decide whether she thought her pretty or not. Lawrie, who had already decided, thought she wasn't.

'New as paint,' said the other girl.

'Good,' said Nicola. 'How old are you?'

'Twelve and a half; how old are you?'

'We're twelve. That's Lawrence and I'm Nicola. Nicola Marlow.'

'Well,' said the other girl. 'I'm glad other people have odd names too. It makes me feel better.' She had a dry, amused voice.

'They're not odd at all,' said Nicola, affronted.

'Not odd,' conceded the other girl, 'but not ordinary. Not like Joan and Peggy and Betty.'

'Well – no,' admitted Nicola, 'I suppose not.'

'Now mine is definitely odd,' said the other girl. 'And you may as well know it at once and that will be two less people to tell. It's Thalia. Thalia Keith.'

'*Failure?*' said Lawrie startled. She was farther away than Nicola and the train had blurred the sound of Thalia's voice. 'Why did they call you that? Because you weren't a boy? That's why they called me Lawrence, 'cos they'd got it all saved up.'

'Not Failure.' She said it patiently as though she had said it many times before. '*Thalia*. It's the name of the Comic Muse. Mother would have it, though Father did his best.'

'It's quite all right,' said Nicola politely. Privately, she thought it very odd indeed.

'It's terrible,' said Thalia calmly. 'But people call me Tim. And if you don't mind, I'd rather you began at once.'

'All right. They call us Nick and Lawrie, actually. At least, they do at home.'

'Tim, Nick and Lawrie,' said Thalia thoughtfully. 'Tom, Dick and Harry. No, I think our way's better. Did you say your name was Marlow?'

'Yes.'

'Head girl's family?'

'How did you know?' asked Nicola, surprised. 'Or have you got sisters here too?'

'Not sisters,' said Tim impressively. 'An aunt.'

'An aunt?' said Nicola, horrified. 'What kind of aunt?'

'The ordinary kind,' said Tim. Or perhaps not so ordinary. Actually it's – well, I call her Aunt Edith. You call her the Head.'

'The headmistress?' said Lawrie. 'Good gracious. She can't be.'

'She is, though.'

'How awful for you,' said Nicola, deeply sympathetic. 'It's

46

bad enough being the head girl's sister. At least, I think it may be. But think of being related to Miss Keith.'

'I don't. Not more often than I can help,' said Tim. 'I told Father that it was simply silly and that I'd much better go to another school – if I must go to school –'

'Haven't you been to school before?' Lawrie interrupted.

'Not properly. At least, not for long at a time. We were always shifting because Father wanted something new to paint. I've been to school in America and Spain and France and Italy and Holland – all over the place. So, of course, I don't know a thing except languages. I do know those.'

'Gosh,' said Nicola, uncertain whether she was impressed or merely astonished. 'We haven't been to school either, much. Every time we started we always caught something. But we haven't caught anything now for six months –'

'Touch wood,' said Lawrie hurriedly.

'Touch wood,' agreed Nicola. 'So Father said we'd better get to Kingscote while the going was good.'

'It was Aunt Edith got at Father about me,' said Tim gloomily. 'He decided to come home for a bit and paint here, and of course Aunt Edith was asked to stay. And then she began finding out, in a nasty sort of way, all the things I didn't know – What were the Wars of the Roses, Thalia dear? – Don't know, Aunt Edith, and care less – you know the kind of thing – and then she sat down and had a long talk with Father and said the dear child simply must start her education, which hiking round Europe and America was *not*. And I said (when they mentioned it to me, which was pretty late in the day), "If I must go to school I must, but not to Aunt Edith's seminary." And Aunt Edith said, "Why?" And I said, "Because it's bound to be awkward." And Aunt Edith said, "Nonsense, Thalia dear, of course you will be treated exactly like the others." And I said, "That's just the point. If I go to an ordinary school – all right. But if I go to my aunt's school, I don't see why I *can't* be treated like the headmistress's niece. *Why* can't I have special privileges and sit in your garden and that kind of thing?" She didn't see it, though,' said Tim bitterly, 'but I still don't see why not.'

Nicola and Lawrence listened, fascinated. It had been impressed on them also, by both Karen and Rowan, that they were on no account to give themselves airs simply because they happened to be the head girl's sisters. They had accepted this dictum meekly, protesting: 'Of course not, Kay. We wouldn't dream of it.' But there did seem to be something in what Tim said, although Nicola, at least, was aware that if she tried anything like that, Karen would certainly snub her, hard.

'Aunt Edith – I suppose I shall have to remember to call her Miss Keith,' continued Tim, 'she was full of helpful hints about lying low and showing the other girls that there was no difference between us. But lying low sounds so *dull*. I don't see why I should have to pretend to be a nonentity just because I'm her niece, and she doesn't want to be accused of – of nepotism – '

'What's that?' asked Lawrie, horrified. 'It sounds dreadful.'

'It only means favouring your nephews. Or nieces, too, I suppose. But I don't see why I should be expected to come to Kingscote and be quiet and dreary and – and *crushed*, when I could go somewhere else and be perfectly ordinary. I told Aunt Edith all that, and she laughed in that idiotic way grown-ups have, and said, "Never mind, Thalia. You'll soon settle down in the Third Remove and find your own level – "'

'Third Remove?' cried Lawrie. 'Oh. What a pity!'

'Why?' asked Tim.

'Well, because we'll be in IIIA and I don't suppose we'll see much of you once we're there – '

'Do you know your form?' asked Tim, surprised. 'I thought no one did until they'd taken the form exam. Aunt Edith said I'd be in the Third Remove because of only knowing languages. But I didn't know anyone else was told.'

Nicola had gone rather red. She frowned at Lawrie.

'We don't know, really,' she said awkwardly. 'But all our family always have started in an A form and – well – you know – we've got to, too.'

'None of the others have ever been in a B form,' supplemented Lawrie. 'Not even Ginty and no one thinks she's a bit clever. And IIIA is the one for our age.'

'Aunt Edith talked quite a lot about your family,' said Tim digging her hands into the pockets of her coat. 'Karen, of course – she's the head girl, isn't she? – she thinks an awful lot of her. And what's the next one – Rowena?'

'No. Rowan.'

'Yes, of course. Sorry. Rowan. She's the one who's good at games, isn't she? She said – what was it? – something about her being an excellent person to have in a team because she always played best on a losing side.'

Nicola and Lawrie blushed with pleasure. 'Except for Giles, Rowan is the nicest,' said Nicola. 'Kay's all right, but she can be pretty snooty when she likes.'

'And then there's – Ann, is it? – the Guide one, anyway. Aunt Edith said she was kind and competent – very good with juniors – and the other one – Virginia, I think she called her – '

'She is Virginia, really,' said Lawrie, 'but she's always called Ginty.'

'Oh. Well, she said she was rather wild but that she had a lot of good stuff in her.'

'She didn't say that on her report,' commented Nicola. 'She put, "Virginia's conduct leaves much to be desired and she must make a real effort to improve".'

49

'There you are,' said Tim impishly. 'It just shows what hypo-crites headmistresses really are.'

'It does, doesn't it?' agreed Lawrie, deeply moved.

There was silence for a moment. Then Nicola sighed. 'It's an awful lot to live up to,' she said sadly.

'How do you mean?' asked Tim.

'Well, you can see for yourself the kind of reputations they've got. Kay's awfully clever, and Rowan can play any-thing, and Ann's a Patrol Leader and she's got her First Class, and Ginty – well, even Ginty's pretty good at games and people like her a lot – '

'And have you got to do all that too?'

'We must,' said Lawrie earnestly. 'We've simply got to be credits to the family. Specially as we're starting so late. All the others came to Kingscote when they were *nine*. We decided in the holidays,' said Lawrie confidentially, ignoring Nicola's warning frown, 'that first we've got to get into the junior netball team, so that next year Nick can be captain and me vice. And then – we've been Brownies at home, you know – so we're going to pass our Tenderfoot and fly up and get our Second Class badges all in one term.'

'Do shut up, Lawrie,' said Nicola gruffly, interrupting her at last. 'It sounds so mad when you say it like that. It probably doesn't matter with Tim, but you can't go round *saying* things like that to people.'

'"Vaulting ambition,"' said Tim solemnly, shaking her head at Lawrie, '"which o'er leaps itself, and falls on the other."'

'Gosh,' said Lawrie, abashed. 'Whatever's that?'

'That's Macbeth,' said Tim, 'and look what happened to him.' Nicola and Lawrie were vague on this point, but they looked as intelligent as possible.

'But you won't say anything to people about what Lawrie said,' urged Nicola. 'They might – well – you know – they might think we were conceited – and we're not. We just – it's only because – ' she floundered unhappily.

'I won't tell,' said Tim. '"Crorse me 'eart an' 'ope to die."' It sounded trustworthy.

'Thank you,' said Nicola. 'Lawrie does talk an awful lot.'

'I don't,' said Lawrie indignantly. 'Nothing *like* as much as you. You know perfectly well, Nicola, that only last week Father said – '

'All right,' said Nicola hurriedly. 'I don't suppose Tim's a bit interested.'

'Where are your family?' asked Tim tactfully. 'I'd like to look at them from a discreet distance.'

'Second compartment up. Kay and Ann are by the windows and Rowan and Gin this end. Kay and Rowan have their backs to the engine 'cos they don't get sick in trains.'

'I don't expect head girls do,' said Tim, amused. She strolled off to look.

It was obviously the same family. They all had the same fair hair and blue eyes, although the others, except Karen, had curly hair, which Ann wore in plaits and Rowan and Ginty in short crops. Tim strolled nonchalantly past the compartment and back again.

'And very nice too,' she remarked. 'I'm glad to have seen the famous Marlows at last.'

They looked at her doubtfully.

'You're teasing,' said Lawrie at last.

'A little,' agreed Tim candidly. 'I think it's just a scrap funny to be so frightfully much esteemed. You don't mind, do you? Are there any more at home?'

'Not at home,' said Nicola a little stiffly. 'There's Giles and Peter. But they're away now.'

'Where do they come in? And what do they do?'

'Giles is the eldest. He's in the navy. And Peter comes

between us and Ginty. He's at Dartmouth,' said Nicola briefly. She still felt rather sore.

'I like the navy,' said Tim. She grinned at Nicola with her friendliest expression. 'I like the navy better than anything.'

Thawing, Nicola grinned back. 'So do I. Do you know – '

'No,' interrupted Lawrie. '*Please* don't talk navy now. *Please*, Tim. If you lived in our family you'd want a rest from it too, sometimes. When Giles comes home, Nick always wants to know what he's done every single minute he's been away. And then she wants to tell me all about it. It isn't that I don't quite like the navy; but I do get tired of having it all the time.'

'All right,' said Tim sadly. 'Only it's rather hard on me if I'm going to be in the Third Remove and probably never speak to you again because you're in IIIA. Never mind. Have some chocolate.'

She tugged a large bag out of her coat pocket and offered it. 'We may as well finish all we can,' she added with her mouth full, 'because I don't suppose we're allowed to keep sweets. Unless I can persuade anyone that as I'm Aunt Edith's niece I ought to be allowed to keep them. I shall try, anyway.' She looked into the bag and added: 'But I expect it would be *safer* to eat them now.'

They munched steadily, occasionally flattening themselves against the partition as other and unknown members of King-scote passed up and down the train, looking for their friends. One tall dark girl smiled and gave them a lordly: 'Hullo, twins,' before disappearing into the Marlow compartment.

Lawrie choked and blushed.

'Who's that?' asked Tim.

'That's Margaret Jessop. She's the games captain. She stayed with Kay one holiday,' said Lawrie, blushing more deeply still.

'Lawrie's awfully keen on her,' explained Nicola unnecessarily. 'She's all right, you know. Quite matey.'

52

'She won't be matey at school,' protested Lawrie hurriedly, 'and you can't expect it, Nicola.'

'I don't,' said Nicola calmly. 'Is that the last piece, Tim? Because if so, you'd better have it as it's your bag.'

'All right,' said Tim. She put the square of chocolate into her mouth, squashed the bag into a ball and lowered the window to throw it out.

'Let's leave it down,' said Nicola. 'It's awfully stuffy.'

'Mother said –' began Lawrie.

'We're not leaning out,' Nicola forestalled her. 'Mother didn't mean we were to suffocate. What time is it now?'

'Twenty to four,' said Lawrie. 'Look, Tim. This was my parting present.'

'Super,' said Tim. 'Haven't you got one, Nick?'

'No,' said Nicola proudly. 'I've got a knife. Look. Sixteen blades *and* a corkscrew *and* a file *and* a thing for taking things out of horses' hooves –'

She handed the knife to Lawrie to pass to Tim. As she did so, the train rounded a curve, swinging them all against the farther side of the corridor.

'Ow!' cried Lawrie in anguish, as she knocked her knee. 'That hurt.'

'My knife!' cried Nicola in sudden horror. 'You dropped it! I saw you!' She pushed Lawrie out of the way and leaned out of the carriage window, her hair blowing wildly in the wind. 'It's on the step,' she gasped. 'Look!'

Leaning over her shoulders, the other two looked down. There was the knife, jigging a little with the motion of the train, and quite out of reach.

Tim said hopefully, 'Perhaps it'll stay there till the train stops and we can get it . . .'

They watched in silence. The knife jigged a little this way and that; sometimes nearly over the edge, then back against the train. It seemed as though Tim might be right.

'Look out,' cried Lawrie suddenly. 'There's a tunnel! Nick!'

They pulled in their heads sharply.

'Oh, quick,' groaned Nicola to the express. 'Do hurry, you beast. Quick, quick, quick.'

There had never been so long a tunnel. The choking smoky darkness came into the corridor. Tim wrinkled her nose, but did not care to suggest that they should close the window. Nicola stamped angrily. 'Oh, do *hurry*, you – you *goods* train!'

The drift of smoke lightened a little. In another moment they were out of the tunnel and rushing through the last of the smoke. Nicola's head went through the window.

'It's gone,' she said after a moment in a too-calm voice. 'It's fallen off.'

'In an emergency,' Commander Marlow was given to telling his family, 'act at once.' On occasion he amplified this, saying that it was also necessary to think clearly and sensibly and not act upon impulse. Nicola, however, had absorbed only the dictum that she was to act immediately. Before Tim or Lawrie realized what she was about she had ducked back into the corridor and pulled the communication cord.

How Does Your Garden Grow?
Vivien Alcock

Old Mr Hewitt was ill. Again. An ambulance had carried him off to hospital. Again. In his garden, weeds began to grow among the flowers. Brambles sneaked under the fence and rioted behind the lavender. Roses dropped their petals untidily on the neat concrete paths. Everywhere plants spread out in the sunlight, like heedless children unaware of danger.

Mrs Hewitt came out through the french windows of her sitting room, and put a pair of gardening gloves on her fat red hands. She was a short, square woman, with a face like a painted brick.

Two pairs of eyes looked down at her from the apple tree on the other side of the fence; one pair frowning and intent, the other with a slitted yellow stare. The dark eyes belonged to Gina Hobb, a skinny girl with long black hair and a thin, pointed face. The yellow ones belonged to her grandmother's cat, Rumar, who was old and fat and lazy, his once black fur grown rusty from too much lying in the sun.

Mrs Hewitt was their enemy. They hated her.

The fat woman seemed unaware of the watchers in the apple tree. Or perhaps she guessed they were there, knowing it to be their favourite perch, and was glad to have a helpless audience for what she was about to do. She put her hands on her hips and surveyed the unprotected garden with a nasty little smile. Then she walked towards the garden shed.

'Trip! Trip! Fall flat on your face!' Gina muttered, trying to will the woman's feet to stumble on the path. Mrs Hewitt disappeared into the shed.

The watchers glared at the closed door. Rumar, the cat, hated Mrs Hewitt because she threw stones at him whenever she saw him, and though she was a poor shot, she hit him occasionally, forcing him to scramble back over the fence in an undignified fashion, to the amusement of all the birds. He was too lazy, however, to be good at hating. Soon his eyes wandered away to watch the petals blowing over the paths, as if he was remembering the days when he'd been young enough to enjoy chasing such inedible toys.

But Gina was good at hating. She stared at the shed with her fierce black eyes, trying to will it to fall down on Mrs Hewitt's head.

'Crash, crush, crump,' she muttered.

Gina hated Mrs Hewitt for what she had done to the old man's garden. Every time Mr Hewitt had had to go into hospital, his wife had destroyed something he loved. First the trees went. Mrs Hewitt disliked trees because they were untidy and dropped their leaves where they chose, not respecting other people's property. Even the apple tree, on which Gina and Rumar sat, was lopsided. Over their garden, the branches grew to their full length, bowing down over a ragged lawn full of buttercups and dandelions. On the other side, the branches were chopped off short at the boundary fence. Not so much as a twig was allowed to grow over the garden next door.

'You're an old man now,' Mrs Hewitt had told her husband when he came home and saw what she had done. 'You don't want to spend your time sweeping up leaves.'

His grass had gone next, replaced by a square of concrete that would never need mowing.

'I have to look after you,' Mrs Hewitt had said, with her false smile. 'It's not good for you to be pushing that heavy mower at your age.'

And she had bustled back into her house, duster in hand, ready to pounce on any speck of dust that dared settle on her shining furniture, leaving Mr Hewitt standing in his treeless garden, looking sadly down at the square of concrete that had once been his treasured lawn.

'I'm sorry,' Gina had said from her perch in the apple tree. 'I couldn't stop her.'

He had smiled up at her. They were fond of each other, the gentle old man and the fierce young girl. They both liked living things; trees that shed leaves, flowers that dropped petals and harboured greenfly and welcomed bees, and cats that left their hair on furniture and sharpened their claws on table legs.

'She meant it kindly,' Mr Hewitt said, for he never complained. 'It's true I can't do as much as I used to. Oh well, perhaps it's all for the best.'

It made Gina angry that he was so meek. 'You should biff her one,' she advised. 'Stamp on her plastic flowers. Scratch her precious furniture. You can borrow Rumar for that, if you like. He's very good at it. Only wait till she's out or she'll throw things at him and he's too fat to run fast.'

Mr Hewitt had stopped her, shocked at these suggestions. 'I'm fond of my wife,' he'd said stiffly. 'Please don't say such things to me again, Gina.'

So now Gina said them to herself and her grandmother's cat and the leaves of the apple tree. She watched Mrs Hewitt come out of the garden shed, chopper in one hand, spade in the other, and muttered under her breath, 'What's she up to now, the horrible fat pig?'

The trees had gone. The grass had gone. Only the flowers were left. Surely she couldn't . . . Even *she* wouldn't . . .?

Mrs Hewitt pulled up the flowers and left them with their roots drying out in the hot sun.

'What are you doing?' Gina shouted. 'They'll die if you

leave them like that. What are you doing to his garden?'

Mrs Hewitt straightened up and looked with grim satisfaction at the furious face in the apple tree.

'Suppose you mind your own business and leave me to mine,' she said. 'My husband's ill in hospital. Someone has to see to things while he's away.'

'I'll do it! I'll look after his garden for him,' Gina promised anxiously. 'I'll do whatever you want me to – weed it, tie back the plants, sweep the paths. I promise. Please, Mrs Hewitt, please let me do it.'

In her agitation, she was bouncing up and down on her branch. A small leaf fell down into the garden next door. Mrs Hewitt picked it up between gloved finger and thumb, as if it were dirt, and tossed it back over the fence.

'If you've so much energy to spare, I suggest you do something about your own garden,' she said. 'It's a disgrace to the neighbourhood.'

Mrs Hewitt disliked Gina quite as much as the girl disliked her. She knew who posted dead leaves and old bus tickets through her letterbox. She knew who dropped sticky toffee papers on to her newly scrubbed front steps. She knew the hard green apple that had hit her on the head had not fallen from the tree next door, but had been thrown all too accurately by a small grubby hand. And so she had told the girl's grandmother who, to do her justice, had apologized handsomely and said that she would see that it did not happen again. Old Mrs Hobb was a lady and knew how to behave. How she'd ever come to have such a wild and wicked granddaughter was a puzzle.

With great pleasure, Mrs Hewitt told Gina what she was planning to do, knowing the girl was powerless to stop her.

'I'm going to have the whole garden covered with concrete,' she said, 'and them coloured paving stones laid on top. Orange

58

and green I fancy – or maybe pink. There'll be plastic chairs that don't need taking in and out every time it rains, and a table with one of them striped umbrellas – like at the seaside. Everything nice and bright and neat, and no trouble to anyone. Now what have you to say to that, miss?'

'He'll hate it!' the girl cried, looking quite demented, with her black hair all tumbled and her black eyes blazing.

Mrs Hewitt turned her back on her and dug up a rose bush, chopping at its roots with her axe.

'You'll be sorry!' Gina screamed at her. 'I'll make you sorry for it!'

She jumped down from the apple tree and ran into the house to find her grandmother.

Mrs Hobb was in the kitchen, shelling peas. She was a thin, tall old lady, who must have been beautiful once, though her cheeks were now sunken and lined, leaving her nose too prominent on her narrow face. Her hair, though grey, was still thick, coiled at the back of her head and fastened with a silver pin. She was vain of her appearance. There were rings on her knobbly fingers, fine pearls hiding her scraggy neck, and her clothes were both expensive and fashionable.

She looked up when her granddaughter came banging in, and surveyed her with mild displeasure.

'What was all that vulgar screeching about?' she asked. 'Have you been quarrelling with Mrs Hewitt again? I thought I told you to leave her alone.'

'Gran, she's going to bury his garden in concrete! You've got to stop her! You've got to!'

Mrs Hobb held up her hand. 'There's no need to shout. I'm not deaf. Did you comb your hair this morning? It certainly doesn't look like it.'

Gina hastily smoothed her hair with her hands. 'He loves his garden, Gran. Don't let her destroy it. Please, Gran.'

Mrs Hobb's face softened, but she shook her head.

'I'm not going to interfere. I'm sorry, Gina, but after all, it's her garden. She can do what she likes with it, I suppose.'

'It's not hers! It's his! Can't you warn him –'

'No,' Mrs Hobb said firmly. 'It would be unkind – and quite useless. He's far too weak, in more ways than one. What she says goes in that house, like it or not.'

'I hate her! I hate her!' Gina raged, stamping on the floor in her fury.

'That's enough of that,' her grandmother said sharply. 'You're too fond of hating people, Gina. There's a wildness in you. I can't think where you get it from. I'm tired of apologizing for your spiteful tricks. There's to be no more of them, do you understand?'

'Yes,' Gina muttered sulkily.

'No spiders in a chocolate box left on her doorstep. No molten wax poured down her outside lavatory. No slugs or snails tossed in through her open windows. You're to leave her alone, Gina, or you'll be in trouble.'

Three days later, workmen came with their machines into the garden next door and covered it with concrete, right up to the boundary fences on all sides. No longer would old Mr Hewitt smile with pleasure to see the first shoots poke up from the rich earth in spring. No longer would he talk to his flowers in summer. He would sit in a garden as neat and grim as a tomb, and wither away like his murdered flowers.

Gina could not sleep that night. She kept tossing and turning, seeing in her mind the concrete garden, as hard and grey as Mrs Hewitt's eyes.

I hate her, she thought, getting up and going over to the window. I hate her. I wish she were dead. Dead and buried in earth.

She stared down. The concrete garden was bleached by

moonlight, a pale immaculate oblong, as cold as a tombstone.

I'd plant flowers on her grave, that would serve her right, Gina thought. No rest in peace for you when you're dead, Mrs Hewitt. Roots will nudge you in the dark, weeds wrap round your bones and squeeze and crack –

Crack! Like an echo of her thoughts the sound came, hard and sharp in the night air. Leaning out of her window, she saw the concrete was now marred by a jagged black line. She'd done it!

'Crack! Crack! Crack!' she commanded, and saw with delight dark lines spreading over the whole garden like a black spider's web.

She beat her fists on the windowsill with excitement and began to chant:

> 'Earth! Earth! Give up your dead.
> Every flower that died and bled,
> Ivy green and roses red,
> Bramble, thorn and poppy head,
> Rise! Rise! Rise!'

The cracks gaped wide, and out of each one came a writhing mass of tendrils, like thin grey snakes, bending their narrow heads to heave the broken concrete aside and make room for others to follow.

Gina leaned out of the window, her black hair blowing in the night wind, her eyes blazing. Then she turned and ran out of her room, down the stairs and out into the garden. The grass moved restlessly beneath her bare feet, and the air was filled with a strange scent, both sweet and rotten. She climbed the apple tree and looked down over the fence. The plants were thick and strong now, with pale leaves groping like hands and thorns as sharp as daggers.

'Revenge!' she shrieked. "Kill! Kill! Kill!'

*

Mrs Hewitt had gone to sleep in front of her television set. She sat wedged upright in a small armchair, her hands folded in her lap, her ankles neatly crossed, and her mouth only slightly open.

A tidy sleeper in a tidy room. Everything was in its place. On the mantelpiece, the china shepherd and shepherdess were kept a proper distance apart, separated by a forbidding marble clock. Mr Hewitt's empty chair was immaculate, the cushions plump and undented, no messy newspapers scattered on the carpet beside it. The highly polished furniture shone beneath the pink-shaded lights. The plastic flowers, newly washed that morning, made bright splashes of colour in their sparkling crystal vases.

Something tapped on the window.

Mrs Hewitt awoke with a start, smoothed her hair, pulled her skirt down over her fat knees, and looked round. The sight of her orderly room reassured her. Really, she thought, it's much easier to keep things nice without a man tramping in and out all the time. Not that she wouldn't be glad when Mr Hewitt came home, of course –

The tapping came again.

Who's that? she wondered, looking at the french windows.

She was a hard, selfish, mean-minded woman, but she did have a certain stubborn courage. Picking up a poker, she went over to the windows and peered out.

At first, she could only see her own face reflected, looking oddly pale and distorted. Then she noticed dim shapes moving behind the glass, long, thin and sinuous. Suddenly something flopped on to the window, and she stepped back, her heart thudding uncomfortably. It looked like a human hand, horribly misshapen. Then she realized it was a large leaf.

She went closer and pressed her nose against the glass,

62

shading her eyes with her fingers. The window was covered with leaves. Twigs tapped insistently against the panes, like tiny drums calling an army to attack.

That girl! Mrs Hewitt thought furiously. This is one of her tricks. Piled up rubbish against my windows, has she? We'll see what her grandmother has to say about that.

Grunting, she undid the bolts and opened the doors wide. A swaying curtain of leaves and flowers hung before her, grey in the moonlight. Slashing her way through them with the poker, she strode out on to the terrace – stopped dead and stared.

Her whole garden was alive and crawling with plants. Giant brambles humped their way over the broken concrete like monstrous serpents. Ivy slithered and wriggled towards her feet. Huge roses turned their blind faces from side to side, as if trying to sniff out their prey.

They were coming for her, all of them! Something touched her ankle. Leaves gagged her mouth so that she could not scream. She tried to run back into the house, but they were behind her now: ivy and rose, bramble and poppy, lavender smelling of old ladies, lilies smelling of death. They pressed their soft, scented faces against hers, their thorns scratched her arms and tore at her hair. Brambles wound around her legs. Ivy crept up her arms. They were pulling her down, down, suffocating her, crushing her, wrapping her up in a shroud of flowers ready for her funeral . . .

'No! No!' Gina cried in horror, appalled by what she had done. 'Gran! I didn't mean it! Gran!' she wailed, like a small child who had broken something precious.

Her grandmother was beside her, in a temper, black eyes burning hot enough to scorch. She climbed up the apple tree with surprising agility for one so old and frail-looking.

'Out of my way!' she cried, pushing so ferociously that the girl fell off her branch into the garden next door.

Her grandmother leapt down beside her and strode out over the mass of twisting, wriggling stems. She stopped some way from the house and held her arms up above her head; an odd-looking figure, tall and gaunt, her grey hair sticking out in two short plaits, and the sleeves of her cotton nightie falling back to show her skinny arms.

'Back! Back! Away with you!' she shrieked in a high, cracked voice. 'Back into your holes this minute, or I'll bring winter down on you! Frost that bites and kills! Snow that buries and breaks!'

With a sullen whisper of leaves and a crepitation of twigs, the plants slithered past her, baring their thorns like teeth, but not daring to touch her. Only the ivy defied her, coiling round her feet and hissing.

'Back, you impertinent weed!' she screamed in high fury, stamping on the ground so hard that it shook. 'Root-rot and leaf-blight infect you! Frog-fly and mealy-bug infest you! Lightning burn you! Secateurs snip you!'

The ivy fled after the others, back down through the cracks into the earth below. Now the garden was leafless again under the quiet moon.

Gina, crouching trembling on the ground, looked up nervously at her grandmother.

'That was clever of you, Gran,' she said, attempting an ingratiating smile.

But Mrs Hobb was not so easily appeased. She grabbed hold of her granddaughter's arm and dragged her towards the terrace.

'Come and see what you've done, you bad girl,' she said.

Mrs Hewitt lay flat on her back, her eyes shut, her mouth open. Her face and arms were patterned with scratches, her

64

hair ripped out of its tight curls, threads plucked from her dress, and her tights torn and laddered. Her breath whimpered painfully in her throat.

Mrs Hobb looked down at her. 'Well, at least she's still alive and not much hurt. That's a blessing. And more than you deserve – '

'I didn't mean it, Gran! I didn't, honestly. I didn't think it would work – it never has before. I – I sort of got carried away. But I didn't mean them to hurt her. Not really. Not like this.'

'Hmmm,' her grandmother said. 'Help me carry her in. Lord, what a weight . . . Here, on the sofa. Put a cushion behind her head.' She stretched herself wearily, clutching her back, and scowled. 'Now I suppose I'll have to put things right again. It's too bad. I'm old and my bones ache, and I should be allowed to enjoy my retirement in peace. I'm fed up with you and your pranks, Gina,' she said, turning on her granddaughter, who shrank away nervously. 'I've a good mind . . .' Her eyes narrowed, and she began to trace patterns in the air with her thin, beringed fingers; slow, undulating patterns.

'No! No, Gran! Not a slug again!' Gina backed away, crying. 'Please! I'll be good! I'll never do it again. Please, Gran, not a slug. A toad, a wasp, anything – '

Her grandmother lowered her hands slowly. 'I'll give you one last chance, Gina. One more, that's all. Another trick like that, and I'll turn you into a slug – and forget the spell to bring you back. Your father wanted you brought up to a respectable profession. A doctor or a civil servant. He was right. You're far too wild to be a good witch. Now go and make some tea in her kitchen, and take your time about it.'

'What are you going to do, Gran?'

'Mind your own business, and do as I tell you.'

Gina went meekly into the kitchen, relieved at having been let off so lightly. When she came back with the tea, she found her grandmother and Mrs Hewitt sitting side by side on the sofa like old friends. The scratches had vanished from Mrs Hewitt's face and her hair was back in its curls. Only her dress showed here and there a plucked thread that Mrs Hobb, growing shortsighted, had missed.

'I'd never have had that concrete laid if I'd known there was an underground stream beneath our gardens,' Mrs Hewitt was saying. 'It's hardly surprising it's cracked. I'll have to get it cleared away.'

'You want to put grass down,' Mrs Hobb said firmly. 'The roots hold the earth together. Grass and flowers and trees, that's what you need.'

Mrs Hewitt's face went pale, and she looked uneasily towards the window.

'Flowers,' she muttered. 'I suppose I do need flowers. I suppose, in the end, we all have to have them.'

The Trouble with My Sister
Brian Patten

My little sister was truly awful,
She was really shocking,
She put the budgie in the fridge
And slugs in Mummy's stocking.

She was really awful
But it was a load of fun
When she stole Uncle Wilbur's
Double-barrelled gun.

She aimed it at a pork pie
And blew it into bits,

She aimed it at a hamster
That was having fits.

She leapt up on the telly,
She pirouetted on the cat,
She gargled with some jelly
And spat in Grandad's hat.

She ran down the hallway,
She ran across the road,
She dug up lots of earthworms
And caught a squirming toad.

She put them in a large pot
And she began to stir.
She added a pint of bat's blood
And some rabbit fur.

She leapt up on the Hoover,
Around the room she went.
Once she had a turned-up nose
But now her nose is bent.

I like my little sister,
There is really just one hitch,
I think my little sister
Has become a little witch.

from The Boy
Jane Gardam

I opened the envelope and pulled out a thick, shiny, white card.

> Mrs Archibald Fanshawe-Smithe
> requests the pleasure of the company
> of
> Miss Jessica Vye
> at a Children's House Party
> at The Rectory, High Thwaite,
> from Friday, December 20th
> until Saturday, December 21st
> RSVP

Underneath it said

> Bus leaves Cleveland Sands bus-station 1.20 p.m. Friday, returns
> Thwaite Lane End Saturday, 2.30 p.m.
> Bring additional clothes for snowballing, Saturday a.m.

'Snowballing,' I said out loud. 'How'd she know it's going to snow? It sounds like a children's book. Who is she anyway? She's very good at working things out if she knows it's going to snow. What's she mean, House Party?' I stood on the fender and put the card up on the high mantelpiece behind the three brass monkeys and a broken clock used for teaching Rowley to tell the time and a couple of diseased old palm crosses. I caught sight of myself in the mirror with the scarf tied on the top of my head and I examined myself. 'I am sunken-eyed,' I thought, and I drew down my mouth and rolled my lower lip outwards so that the shiny part showed and blew air into my

68

cheeks at the same time. This is something I have a habit of doing when I am alone. 'Spare a copper for a pore ol' woman,' I said. 'Me gel's goin' away tilt Big 'ouse, a-snowballing with the gentry.' Then I fell off the fender and the cat went streaking under the cupboard. 'Eeeeh, I's got t'fever!' and I tottered out of the kitchen feeling for the walls. I can never do anything like this when we have to stand up and do *Midsummer Night's Dream* at the front of the class for old Dobbs.

'Actually,' I heard myself saying in my ordinary voice in the passage, 'I do feel a bit funny.' I gathered up the eiderdown, rolled upstairs and back to bed where I slept till dinner.

It was a week later – oh quite a week – and I was sitting in a clear patch in the so-called sitting room writing to Florence Bone when there was a terrible shriek from the kitchen. I took my left hand out of my hair and thought, 'Now what?'

'For goodness' sake!' came Father's voice from the study. We both came into the passage and saw Mother, her face brick red and covered with knobs, holding the piece of cardboard in her hands.

'When did this come? What on earth is it? Why didn't you tell me?'

'I don't know,' said Father. 'Let's have a look-see.'

'Oh that,' I said, and started back to my letter.

'Mrs Archibald Fanshawe-Smithe – that's old Fan's wife up at Thwaite. Well I never, what's she up to? Poor old Fan!' He began to laugh like mad. 'House party, by Gad! Whatever next!'

'Well, I can see it's from Mrs Fanshawe-Smithe, but . . .'

Father rocked and roared. 'Well I never! My stars. God is working his purpose OUT as year succeedeth YEAR!'

'But I don't see . . .'

'Don't suppose you do. You didn't know the Fanshawe-Fiddles at Cambridge for which my lamb and my love may you be truly thankful,' and he went back into his room and shut the door. He began to sing Jesus bids us shine with a pure, clear light and after a bit there was another great bellow of laughter.

Mother came into the sitting room with a very determined step. 'Now then,' (she sat down) 'you will please tell me when this invitation came, why I was not told about it, and why you hid it behind the clock.'

'I didn't. I like that!'

'It was absolutely out of sight in a whole lot of clutter. If I hadn't decided to give the kitchen a really good do . . .'

'I wish you hadn't.'

'What did you say?'

'Nothing much.'

'You said "I wish you hadn't", didn't you? I suppose that means you don't want to go.'

'I don't know. I haven't thought about it.'

'Oh yes it does. I know you, Jessica. We're going to start a tremendous to-do now for the next week, sulks and slams and grumbles just because someone's been kind enough . . .'

Well you know the sort of thing so I won't go on.

'. . . meet some nice new people,' she ended up.

'I didn't say I didn't want to go.'

'And what excuse am I going to make? I can't say we'll be away. Parsons can't say they're going to be away at Christmas.'

'Perhaps she won't know.'

'Won't know what?'

'That parsons don't go away . . .'

'Well since she *is* one herself.'

'She's a parson! Crikey.'

'No, no, no. Do listen. Her husband's one is what I mean.' (This conversation is absolutely typical of my mother. You can hear this sort of thing in our house every day of the week.)

'. . . If you'd only listen. Oh dear . . .'

'I don't know what a children's house party is anyway,' I said after a minute. We glared at each other.

'Neither do I.'

She began to laugh and as a matter of fact I joined in and Father shouted 'For the love of *God*!' through the wall, and then more politely, 'For the love of Mike must you make such a row?'

'Let's think about this then, Jessica,' she said a bit quieter. 'Now I do think you ought to go, dear. They're quite different from the usual run round here and they live in a lovely house. He's the Rural Dean you know – much older than she is I believe, but, oh, much nicer. They've got dozens of children but they're all at boarding schools so you've not met them. They're quite a different kettle of fish from the high school. Now I want you to go, Jess.'

'What's wrong with the high school?'

'Oh nothing's wrong with it. It's just that, well, it's nice for you to meet a different *type*.'

(She does this. Just when we start to talk she says something really awful like this. It makes me absolutely wild.)

'What on earth,' I said, 'are you talking about? You must be mad. There are thousands of different types at the high school, and a lot better types than . . .'

'Yes but . . . Well dear, no. It's wrong to say it but there *is* a difference. Boarding-school children do have a sort of *something*.'

'What do they have?'

'Well it's hard to say. But I think you'll see. It's a sort of *poise*.'

'You ought to see Iris Ingledew. Or even Helen Bell come to that, when she's sitting down at a piano. She's got so much poise she's nearly falling over backwards.'

'No, Jessica. These people do have *something*.'

'Sounds like money. If they've got thousands of children all at boarding schools.'

'No, no, they haven't got money. You'll be surprised. They wear terrible clothes and hardly have anything to eat. You'd think they were nobody if you met them on a walk – until you look again and you see they have this – something. Oh, they must make real sacrifices to send their children away to good schools.'

'Well I'm glad you don't.'

'We couldn't. We haven't anything to sacrifice. And anyhow your father wouldn't hear of it – it's quite against his principles. He would have a fit if he knew about even the shilling dinners. It is different for us.' She got up and went quickly to the kitchen and immediately turned round and came back again. Her hair had frizzed up and she was all knobs again. 'As a matter of fact they *have* got money. You'll see, Jess – you'll see. They'll go talking on and on about having no money. Never discuss money, it says in all the books of rules but they never talk about any blessed thing else. "Penniless", they'll say and "pass the salt" and it'll be in a Georgian silver salt cellar. Just you see if I'm not right. Just you see when you go.'

She was crying or something pretty like it. 'Crikey,' I said, 'whatever's wrong?'

'Nothing.' She sniffed and vanished into the kitchen.

'Well you needn't worry,' I shouted through, 'I'm not going.'

'Yes you are,' she shouted back.

'No I'm not.'

'FOR THE LOVE OF HEAVEN!' came out of the study.

'Ma,' I said, standing at the kitchen door, 'I'm not going. They sound frightful people. You're a fool even to think of letting me.'

'If I'd called my mother a fool . . .'

'Yes, and I bet the Fanshawe-Fiddleshaws never call their mother a fool either. They're all sweetness and light and lies and slop. I can't bear people like that. I'm not going.'

'And I can't bear insolence and rude girls hardly thirteen.'
'Too bad. I'm not going to stay with people you hate.'
'I love you, I love you,' she said with a hop (she's mad).
'You are going to the Fanshawe-Fiddleshaws and that is that.
Anyway, I want to hear all about them.'

Adventures of Isabel
Ogden Nash

Isabel met an enormous bear,
Isabel, Isabel, didn't care;
The bear was hungry, the bear was ravenous,
The bear's big mouth was cruel and cavernous.
The bear said, Isabel, glad to meet you,
How do, Isabel, now I'll eat you!
Isabel, Isabel, didn't worry,
Isabel didn't scream or scurry.
She washed her hands and she straightened her
    hair up,
Then Isabel quietly ate the bear up.

Once in a night as black as pitch
Isabel met a wicked old witch.
The witch's face was cross and wrinkled,
The witch's gums with teeth were sprinkled.
Ho ho, Isabel! the old witch crowed,
I'll turn you into an ugly toad!
Isabel, Isabel, didn't worry,
Isabel didn't scream or scurry.
She showed no rage and she showed no rancour,
But she turned the witch into milk and drank her.

Isabel met a hideous giant,
Isabel continued self reliant.
The giant was hairy, the giant was horrid,
He had one eye in the middle of his forehead.
Good morning, Isabel, the giant said,
I'll grind your bones to make my bread.
Isabel, Isabel, didn't worry,
Isabel didn't scream or scurry.
She nibbled the zwieback that she always fed off,
And when it was gone, she cut the giant's head off.

Isabel met a troublesome doctor,
He punched and he poked till he really shocked her.
The doctor's talk was of coughs and chills
And the doctor's satchel bulged with pills.
The doctor said unto Isabel,
Swallow this, it will make you well.
Isabel, Isabel, didn't worry,
Isabel didn't scream or scurry.
She took those pills from the pill concocter,
And Isabel calmly cured the doctor.

Private Marmalade
Andrew Davies

It was a peaceful scene in the Atkins house. Mr and Mrs Atkins
were drinking tea and gobbling rum truffles in the living room,
while Marmalade was playing with her new toys. It all seemed
too good to be true. And it was.

'Marmalade,' said Mrs Atkins. 'Those rum truffles are for
ladies to nibble at, not for little girls to throw about.'

'What rum truffles, cock?' asked Marmalade.

Mrs Atkins took a closer look at the rum truffle in Marmalade's grimy hand, and then at the toy gun on Marmalade's shoulder, which suddenly didn't look like a toy gun any more. Then she dived for the telephone.

'Hello, Harrods!' she shrieked. 'You've made the most terrible mistake! I ordered lemonade and trifle, not grenades and a rifle!'

Marmalade pulled the pin out of the grenade, tossed it over the back of the sofa and stuck her fingers in her ears. 'Bet it doesn't work, anyway,' she said. But it did.

The following afternoon, Wendy Wooley came to tea with the Atkinses. The rum truffle grenade had caused surprisingly little damage. There was quite a draught from the hole in the wall, of course, and the sofa had disappeared, but Mr and Mrs Atkins looked years younger without any eyebrows, and it was great fun sitting on packing cases and tea chests instead of chairs.

'One thing you learn in social work,' said Wendy Wooley, 'is that things aren't always what they seem. And every problem's an opportunity in disguise.'

'Come again, Wend?' said Mr Atkins.

'Well, gosh, what I think is . . . she's just trying to show affection in her own special way! She wasn't trying to blow you up, honestly! She was making a plea for love and attention!'

'See your point, Wend,' said Mr Atkins doubtfully. 'Very deep, that. But couldn't she just have sent us a Valentine card, sort of thing?'

'Look, gosh, I know you're feeling just a little bit miffed, but all this has given me an ace new idea for Marmalade's work experience! Something where she can really put herself about!'

'Now you're talking, cock,' said Marmalade. 'Have a rum truffle?'

'Gosh, super, thanks,' said Wendy Wooley. 'I really shouldn't . . .' The rum truffles looked rather large and metallic, and Wendy couldn't see very well through her shaggy fringe.

'No, you really shouldn't!' yelled Mr and Mrs Atkins, diving for cover.

'Super great big ones,' said Wendy Wooley, taking one.

'You just pull that little stalk thing out,' said Marmalade helpfully.

'No! No!' screamed Mr and Mrs Atkins.

Wendy Wooley pulled the little stalk thing out.

When the smoke had cleared, Wendy Wooley was still sitting on the edge of the tea chest. Most of her clothes had gone, and her face was black with soot, but she still had that eager trusting smile on her face.

'What I had in mind, Mr and Mrs Atkins,' she said, 'was the army.' Then she closed her eyes and toppled slowly off the tea chest on to what was left of the carpet.

First thing next morning, Mr Atkins took his little girl down to the Army Recruiting Office, and there, below a poster telling you how you could put yourself about in the modern army, sat Sergeant-Major Spratt. He had a face like a giant tomato, bright blue glaring eyes, and a moustache so huge and stiff you could hang out the washing on it (which is what he sometimes did on active service).

'And what have we here?' he bellowed delightedly. 'I will tell you what we have here! We have two lovely recruits what wants to serve their Queen and Country!'

'One lovely recruit,' said Mr Atkins hastily. 'I've done my bit, squire! Now it's the turn of the younger generation.'

'And what's your name, my lovely?' said Spratt, turning a horrible smile on Marmalade.

'Marmalade Atkins, cock. What's yours?' The sergeant-major's eyes bulged a little wider. 'I am Sergeant-Major Spratt, and that is what you will call me, my lovely boy, because when little squaddies call me cock, d'you know what I do with them?'

'Pat 'em on the head and give 'em a biscuit, cock?'

'No, my lovely, I bites their little heads off and spits out the pips!'

'Do it! Do it!' shouted Mr Atkins excitedly.

'I'm off to join the navy,' said Marmalade, making for the door.

'No, no, no, just my little joke!' boomed Spratt, hauling her back by the collar. 'Haven't signed the forms yet, have you? No, all good pals in today's army, my lovely boy. It's all ping-pong and sing-song and jolly japes in tents!'

'You sound like a great big softy, cock,' said Marmalade.

'Oh, I am, my lovely boy,' said Spratt craftily.

'Now look here, squire,' said Mr Atkins, who didn't much like the sound of all this. 'What I want to know is, is the training tough? I mean, do you make 'em march till their toes come through their boots, do you make 'em polish buttons till they're cross-eyed, do you tear their arms and legs off if they're cheeky?'

'Oh, no, nothing like that,' said Spratt, winking craftily at Mr Atkins. 'It's all teddy bears and bedtime stories now. Mind you, he is a bit short. You sure he's over sixteen?'

'You must be joking, cock,' said Marmalade. 'And I'm not a boy either!'

Mr Atkins put a bundle of pound notes on the desk.

'Right, sign here,' said Sergeant-Major Spratt. 'Twenty years.'

'Twenty years?' said Marmalade. 'What if I don't like it?'

'Too late now, my lovely boy,' said Spratt. 'You're in the

army now!' And before Marmalade knew where she was, she found herself in a huge cold drill-hall with a lot of other new soldiers who all looked much bigger and tougher than she was. Sergeant-Major Spratt issued Marmalade with one uniform, baggy; one pair of boots, clodhopping; one rifle, heavy; one pack, very heavy; and one hat, silly.

'Now, my lovely boys!' roared Spratt. 'I will tell you what you are going to do. You are going to march till your toes come through your boots, you are going to polish buttons till you are cross-eyed, and if you are cheeky I am going to tear your arms and legs off. Any questions?'

'Yes, cock,' said Marmalade. 'Has anyone ever told you you look like a beetroot with a moustache?'

Sergeant-Major Spratt's face went so red with rage that he looked like a beetroot with a moustache.

'Ooh, my lovely boy, we're going to have some fun with you,' he roared. 'Squad! At the double on the spot ten miles running go!'

Marmalade found herself pounding up and down between two enormous soldiers, while Sergeant-Major Spratt went off for a nice cup of tea.

'Here, cock,' said Marmalade. 'This is terrible. Don't you ever get tired?'

'Not us, shorty,' said the soldier on her left.

''Cos we are tough!'

'Yer, and hard,' said the soldier on her right. 'He's Private Tuff and I'm Private Hardman!'

'Yer,' said Private Tuff. 'And we're not only tough and hard, we are thick as well. Sergeant Spratt said so,' he added proudly.

Marmalade had an idea.

'Here,' she said. 'I bet you're not thick enough, I mean I bet you're not tough enough, to carry your packs and rifles and me as well.'

'Yer, we could, we could do that easy!' boasted Private Tuff and Private Hardman.

'Don't believe you,' said Marmalade. When Sergeant-Major Spratt came back from his nice cup of tea to see how his brave lads were getting on, he found Private Tuff gasping for breath ('I'm clobbered, Sergeant!') and Private Hardman buckling at the knees ('I'm kippered, Sergeant!') but, strange to tell, Private Marmalade didn't seem tired at all.

'Right my jolly boys!' said Sergeant-Major Spratt. 'Polishing the shiny buttons go! One two, one two, one two, one two . . .'

Marmalade lay on her bunk reading the *Beano* while Private Tuff and Private Hardman polished buttons so hard that they went cross-eyed. After a while they were so cross-eyed that they didn't realize they were polishing Marmalade's buttons instead of their own. When Spratt came round to inspect them he was most impressed.

'Private Tuff and Private Hardman,' he said. 'Look at the shine on Private Marmalade's buttons! You can stay up all night, my jolly boys, and polish till your buttons is as bright as what hers is!'

In the morning, it was Unarmed Combat, but poor Private Hardman and Private Tuff were so clobbered, kippered and cross-eyed that they could scarcely stand up, let alone fight.

'Right, my lovely lads!' roared Sergeant-Major Spratt. 'Unarmed Combat, into the centre rush, last man on his feet is the winner, putting yourself about, GO!'

Private Tuff and Private Hardman stumbled, clobbered and kippered to the centre of the gym, banged their heads together and collapsed in a heap. Private Marmalade sat on top of the heap and fanned her face with the *Beano*.

'Unarmed Combat, cock? Easy!' she said.

'Private Marmalade,' said Sergeant Spratt. 'You have vandalized two of my best men. There is only one thing to do with you!'

'Whassat then, cock?'

'I am promoting you to patrol leader in the SAS!'

'What do they do, cock?'

'The SAS, my jolly boy, are the hardest and the fittest and the toughest men in the whole army. They storm embassies, they run in and out of people's houses shouting FREEZE, they swim thousands of miles with knives between their teeth – all because the lady wants a box of chocolates . . . it's a great honour I'm offering you!'

'Good old Private Marmalade!' gasped Tuff and Hardman.

'*Corporal* Marmalade, now,' said Sergeant Spratt.

Mr and Mrs Atkins were delighted when they heard how well Marmalade was getting on in the army. Mrs Atkins ordered three new fur coats from Harrods, and put them all on at once to celebrate, and Mr Atkins bought himself a new Rolls-Royce and drove it down to the Suparich Gulf State Embassy in Mayfair, where he was hoping to sell Nelson's Column to the Sheikhs for three hundred camels.

His business deal went very well, and he was just working out the final delivery details with the Chief Sheikh (it is not an easy matter to transport three hundred camels on the tube to Trafalgar Square) when two enormous men brandishing giant leeks leapt in through the window.

'Afternoon, gents,' said Mr Atkins. 'These your camel wallahs, then, Sheikh el Shifteh?'

'No! No!' quavered the Sheikh, cowering under the ottoman. 'I have never seen them before! They are bandits!'

'Throw down your weapons, boy bach!' said the first enormous bandit.

'Unless you want a leek across your chops, look you!' said the second enormous bandit.

'Look, squire,' said Mr Atkins, falling on his knees. 'No need to be hasty. I'm sure we can work out a deal on this one!'

'No deals,' said the bandits. 'We are seizing this embassy in the name of the Welsh Liberation Front!' And waving their leeks above their heads, they sang two rousing choruses of 'We'll Keep a Welcome in the Hillsides'.

'Er, look, squire,' said Mr Atkins politely, when they had finished. 'I don't want to cause any aggravation, but I think you might have made a blunder. This is not the Welsh Embassy you've seized here. How about trying next door?'

'We know it's not the Welsh Embassy! We know all that, boyo! That is the whole point of what we are doing, look you! We haven't got an embassy of our own to seize, so we're seizing this one. Well, it was the first one we come to, see. So it's the Welsh Embassy now! All right?'

'All is now clear,' said Mr Atkins, who was no fool when it came to business. 'How would you like to buy Nelson's Column? I'm letting it go cheap today. How about four hundred sheep?'

Meanwhile, back at SAS headquarters, the jolly boys were waiting for their first mission. They were all ready, kitted out in balaclavas, wetsuits, goggles and flippers. They had parachutes, ropes, guns, knives and chocolate boxes. But it was a quiet day for emergencies. No one had invaded the Isle of Wight, no one had seized London Airport, and there didn't even seem to be any ladies in castles wanting chocolates.

'Keep on your toes, my lovely boys,' said Sergeant-Major Spratt. 'The SAS are always on their toes!'

'Blinking difficult in these flippers, cock,' said Corporal Marmalade.

'But if that red alert goes, my jolly boys, we shall shoot into action like corks out of ginger-beer bottles!' And even as Spratt spoke, the red telephone rang!

'Suparich Gulf State Embassy, lads!' said Sergeant Spratt. 'And don't forget the chocolates!'

Mr Atkins was just working out the final details of his deal with the Welshmen.

'Right, squire, four hundred sheep to travel first class on the Cardiff express, arriving Paddington three o'clock tomorrow afternoon,' he was saying, when there was a huge crash, followed by the sound of splintering glass, and the gallant SAS squad swung through the embassy window on ropes.

Unfortunately, in the excitement, Private Tuff and Private Hardman had put their balaclavas on back to front. It is also very difficult to storm an embassy in frogmen's flippers.

'Freeze!' they yelled and stumbled blindly across the room and straight out of the opposite window. Sergeant-Major Spratt found himself standing between two giant Welshmen, evil smiles on their faces, giant leeks poised to strike.

'Steady on, boys,' said Spratt apprehensively. 'No violence. I'm a bit on the Welsh side myself.'

Two giant leeks swung simultaneously, and Spratt sank lifeless to the carpet.

'Now for the dwarf in the flippers!' said the Welshmen, turning to Marmalade.

'Let's have you then, Taffy,' said Marmalade.

Now Welsh bandits are a bit impulsive and excitable, and these two really should have stopped and thought that Marmalade was two feet shorter than Sergeant Spratt. But they didn't. Two giant leeks swung simultaneously into two Welsh heads. And two Welsh bandits fell in a heap on Sergeant-Major Spratt's unconscious body.

'Mission accomplished!' said Marmalade, taking off her balaclava.

'Marmalade!' said Mr Atkins.

'Hello, Dad. Fancy a chocolate?'

'Well, I'll . . . I don't know what to say,' gasped Mr Atkins.

'Say nothing, Dad. And now I must leave you. I have other worlds to conquer. The army is too soft for me. Goodbye!'

And clinging to the rope with her flippers, she jumped out of the window and was gone.

'Well, I never,' said Mr Atkins to the astonished Sheikh who was crawling out from under the ottoman. 'My little girl!' he said proudly. 'Fancy a choc, Sheikh?'

They both took one.

'Funny,' said Mr Atkins. 'These remind me a bit of those rum truffles we . . .'

I expect you remember the pictures of the explosion at the embassy on the TV news, and how they said it was something to do with a top secret mission, and the story could never be told. Well, now you know what really happened.

Lizzie Dripping Runs Away
Helen Cresswell

It all started with Lizzie Dripping losing the baby. The fuss they had made about it, you would have thought he had been lost *for ever* instead of hardly even an hour. And considering that when they found him Toby had only just begun to feel hungry, and considering that he always *was* hungry, anyway,

Lizzie couldn't for the life of her see that any real harm had been done.

But during the days that followed nobody let her forget about it for a single minute. Everybody in Little Hemlock knew about it – Aunt Blodwen had seen to that. Lizzie had been without bubble-gum for five days now, rather than go up to the village shop again and risk having people make rude remarks about it.

But it was worst at home. Patty kept bringing it into everything. That very morning, Lizzie could not find her box of chalks.

'Seen my box of chalks, Mum?' she asked Patty, who was rolling out pastry as if she were rolling her worst enemy flat. 'I want to play hopscotch.'

'Don't you go chalking on our yard,' said Patty, without looking up. 'You want to play hopscotch, you play it on the road where it belongs. Chalk on the pavement, out of my way.'

'Can't chalk anywhere,' Lizzie said. 'That's the whole point. I keep telling you. I can't find my chalks.'

'*That* don't surprise me,' retorted Patty. 'If you can go losing your own brother, you can lose anything. Wonder to me is you've got your own head left on your shoulders.'

Here we go again, thought Lizzie. On about that dratted baby again. Might have *known* she'd drag that into it.

'Nice thing if I can't rely on a great girl like you, Lizzie, to keep an eye on your brother for half an hour,' Patty went on.

Lizzie, wisely, said nothing. She simply stared glumly at her mother, waiting for the rest of it.

'Can't think where you *get* it from,' said Patty, sure enough. 'Head in the clouds, dreaming along from morning till night. Not *my* side of the family, that *is* certain.'

Nag nag nag, thought Lizzie wearily. She don't really love me at all, you can see that. Toby's all *she* cares about. Wouldn't care two pins if it'd been me that was lost.

'Pity you can't find something useful to do, instead of sitting about gawping,' said Patty, who was cutting the pastry now, making *mincemeat* of her enemies.

Lizzie stood up, feeling that by doing so she was at least showing willing.

It'd be all right if I knew what she *expected* me to do, she thought. After all, 'tis Saturday. Holidays, I thought Saturdays was meant to be.

'Is there any jobs you want doing?' she asked, because she really had no clues herself what she was supposed to be doing.

'Well, I daresay there would be,' said Patty, 'if I could think. And if you was to be *relied* on, Lizzie. Look at that half-pound of butter you left lying in the graveyard on'y last week. I *ask* you – butter in the graveyard! I should think it's on'y time there's been butter in graveyard since world began.'

'I ran straight back up for it,' protested Lizzie. 'Didn't come to no harm.'

'That ain't the point, Lizzie. It's the very *idea* of it. It nearly made me that I couldn't *fancy* it, knowing where it'd been.'

'Well is there anything *else*?' asked Lizzie desperately. '*Besides* errands.'

'Oh, do give over *pestering* me, Lizzie!' cried Patty, rummaging in the cupboard.

First I annoy her doing nowt, thought Lizzie. Now she don't want me to do owt. Can't do anything right.

She took advantage of Patty's turned back to slip out the back door. She stood casting about for inspiration. Her eye fell on the riot of flowers round the little yard – dahlias and Michaelmas daisies and a few roses.

That's what, she thought. I'll pick her a bunch of flowers and arrange 'em in that jug of hers shaped like a cat, and put 'em in front room. She'll like that.

She knew it was unlikely that Patty, engrossed in her baking, would look out through the tiny scullery window. All the same, she picked the flowers hastily, a few here, a few there, until she had a fair-sized bunch.

Now wait for her to go into't larder, or upstairs, she thought. She peered cautiously through the crack in the open door. The kitchen was empty.

Upstairs! she thought jubilantly. She ran through the kitchen into the best room, and took the white cat jug (with tail curled up for handle) from its place on the mantelshelf. Hastily she ran back and filled it at the sink and put it on the draining board while she stuck the flowers in, curling rakishly over the cat's face.

She was halfway through when she heard Patty on the stairs. She grabbed the rest of the flowers, picked up the jug and made across the kitchen. Her foot caught – in a crack in the lino – against the chair leg – she never knew which, and she pitched forward. The jug flew from her hand and fell with a smash smack at the feet of Patty herself, just come in.

Lizzie raised her head. Around her lay the strewn flowers, broken white pot, water. Above her was Patty's face, furious and disbelieving.

'That's my jug!' she cried. 'My best jug!'

'I was – I was putting flowers in it, for a surprise!' cried Lizzie, nearly sobbing now. 'And if you hadn't come down so quick I wouldn't have tripped and now – oh, I'm sorry, Mum, I'm sorry!'

Without answering, Patty went to the broom cupboard.

'Stand out way, Lizzie,' she said. 'Next thing, you'll have glass run in your feet.'

Lizzie watched her mother sweep the fragments into a dustpan, then she herself went and picked up the strewn

86

flowers while Patty fetched the floor cloth and mopped up the water.

'That's that, then,' she said. 'And now what?'

'I've said I'm sorry, Mum,' said Lizzie. 'I *am* sorry. I tripped.'

'And you had to pick my best jug to do it with,' said Patty. 'That's what beats me. Couldn't have broke a jam jar, or that old brown pot of your grandmother's. You drive me to absolute *distraction*, Lizzie, I swear you do. You can't be turned back on five minutes together. That *baby's* more to be trusted to be left than you.'

She wouldn't carry on at me like this if she knew I'd got a *witch* for friend, Lizzie thought. She'd look out what she said to me, if she knew that.

For a moment, she was tempted to tell.

Fat lot of good that would do, she thought. Don't suppose she even believes in witches!

But remembering about the witch made her feel better, and gave her an idea.

I know what, she thought. I'll go and see if she's there. And if she is, I might get her to do a spell. What if she could do a spell so's Mum'd never find fault with me again, *ever*?

The idea was irresistible, beautiful. She got up.

'Just going out for a bit,' she said, and went out. Toby's pram was standing just under the window and she gave it a shove as she went by, and was rewarded by hearing his yells following her as she turned into the street.

'*Now* who's a little pettie pie?' she muttered under her breath. '*Now* who's Mummy's little fat lamb?'

As she passed through the rusted iron gate into the church-yard she willed the witch to be there.

Not all of them, she thought. Just mine.

She turned by the corner of the church, scanning cautiously about. It seemed important that she should see the witch before the witch saw her. At the moment, however, it did not seem as if either one thing or the other was likely to happen. She listened, and heard only the wind in the trees and dry grasses, and the far-off drone of a tractor.

'Witch!' she said softly. Then, a little louder, 'Witch! Witch, where are you?'

No reply. Lizzie's eyes raked the churchyard looking for a wisp of black, the tip of a pointed hat behind a tombstone, that might betray the witch's presence.

Could be playing hide and seek, she thought. She had seemed that kind of a witch.

'I see you!' came a shrill voice.

Lizzie jumped.

'I see you!' came the voice again.

'Well, I don't see you,' said Lizzie.

There was a cackle.

'Couldn't if you tried!' came the witch's triumphant voice. 'Invisible!'

'Couldn't you be visible, please?' said Lizzie. 'Just for a minute?'

No reply.

'Please?' said Lizzie.

Then she screamed. The witch *was* visible, and only a yard away, right under her nose and perched on the stone of *Betsy Mabel Glossop aged 79 years Life's Work Well Done*.

'That made you jump,' said the witch with satisfaction. Then, 'What do you want now?'

'Well – er . . .' Lizzie was taken aback. She hardly liked to say it straight out, just like that.

'Well – er – for one thing, I wondered what your name was,' she said – perfectly truthfully, as it happened.

'Name?' snapped the witch. 'Not telling.'

'Oh!' said Lizzie.

'Don't want folk yelling my name all over from morning till night,' said the witch. She was beginning to sound like Patty herself. 'Might be invisible, but I ain't *deaf*, and if there's one thing I detest it's having folk yelling my name all over.'

'I'm sorry,' said Lizzie. 'All right, witch, don't tell me, if you don't want. But I did just wonder – well, I wondered if you'd do a little spell for me. Just a little one.'

'There ain't such things as little spells,' said the witch. 'Spells is big. *All* spells is big.'

'Well, then, a big one please, witch,' said poor Lizzie, beginning to feel more and more out of her depth. 'But it ain't a bad spell, witch. Not a wicked one – that's what I meant.'

'What, then?' demanded the witch.

'It's to do with my mum, see,' said Lizzie. 'Gone off me lately, she has. Telling me off the whole time – you know . . .'

'Why?' the witch inquired.

Lizzie shrugged.

'Dunno. Not my fault. Mostly because I left that dratted baby up at mill. *Anyone* could've made a mistake like that. Lucky thing is, Aunt Blodwen didn't see you, or there would've been trouble.'

'What spell d'ye want, then?' asked the witch. 'Turn baby into a toad, shall I?'

'Oh no!' Lizzie squealed with alarm. 'Don't do that! Please!'

She pictured Patty bending over the pram and seeing the transformed Toby under the string of plastic animals, and shuddered.

'Mum, then?' suggested the witch. 'Turn her toad, shall I?'

'No!' Lizzie fairly screamed. 'You've got it all wrong! I don't want *anyone* turning into toads! All I want is for you to make Mum like me a bit more, and –'

She broke off. The witch had vanished. Gone into thin air. Taken dudgeon.

'Witch? Are you still there?'

Silence.

'I bet you are!' cried Lizzie. 'So listen, please do! I just wanted you to put a spell on Mum so's to make her – well – you know – *like* me a bit more. Take more *notice*, instead of being always on about Toby. Witch? Witch . . . ?'

Silence. Then a swift glimpse of black rags, a blink of an eye in which she saw again the sharp face of the witch, and a snapped command: 'Do it yourself!' Then nothing.

Lizzie was too astonished to reply, even if there had been time.

'Witch!' she cried. 'Witch!'

This time, not only was there no reply, but Lizzie Dripping knew, deep in her heart, that there would be none.

Not even if I was to wait all day, she thought. All day and all night.

Slowly she turned away and began to walk back towards the gate. Even the witch had turned against her. She blinked hard.

Nobody cares, she thought. Nobody in the whole world.

She heard the witch's voice again: 'Do it yourself!'

She whipped round. No one was in sight. Then suddenly she found herself thinking.

'All right. I *will* do it myself!'

And the way to do it was so perfectly simple that she laughed out loud and took several skipping steps down the path and back on to Kirk Street.

I'll get lost, she thought. I'll run away. And then they'll realize how much they love me, and be sorry. And they'll make a fuss over me like they did over Toby, and Mum'll never tell me off again for the rest of my life, not for *anything*.

And so Lizzie Dripping began to lay her plans. What she really planned was not to run away to the other side of the world for ever and ever, but just far enough and for long enough to make people – and Patty in particular – realize just how much they loved and missed her.

She saw no reason why she should starve while she was waiting to be found, so she took ten pence from her money box, gritted her teeth and marched up to the village shop. There she bought a chocolate biscuit, a bag of crisps and a stock of bubble-gum. Back home, she mixed some orange squash and put it in a bottle. Up in her room she put everything into a carrier-bag, along with a book to pass the time, and a torch in case it grew dark before she was found. Then she wrote her farewell note.

Mum'll be taking Toby for a push round the village in a bit, she thought. That's when I'll go. Nip out before Dad gets back from Mapleburn. Now, where's that letter?

She read it softly out, imagining the reactions of Patty and Albert when they found it lying there, and herself gone.

'Dear Mum and Dad. I have run away from home, and shall not come back not for evermore. I know I am a big trouble to you and that is why I am going. You will still have Toby so you will be all right and not left orphaned. I will often think of you and goodbye for ever. Lizzie.'

It affected her so much that she had to brush away a tear from her own eye.

Then Patty called up: 'Going now, Lizzie!' and 'All right!' she called back, and then the house was quiet. Lizzie ran through into the front bedroom and watched Patty's back view disappearing. Then she took the bag and went downstairs.

And she went down as if it really were for the last time, stepping quite deliberately and aware of each familiar step, in the watery green and swaying light from the little window above the front door with its view of moving boughs.

She went tiptoe into the kitchen though there was no one

91

there to see (unless the heavily ticking grandfather clock knew, minute by minute, the comings and goings of the Arbuckles, whose time it counted for them). She propped the note on the table, against the butter dish, unhooked her anorak from the back of the door, and went out.

Lizzie knew exactly where she was going. Just outside the village was a derelict barn. It was supposed to be haunted, but Lizzie, having met a witch, felt perfectly equal to a ghost. She marched steadily on and met only ancient Mrs Cobb, to whom she nodded and said, 'Hello.' As she reached the outskirts of Little Hemlock she could see the men at work in the ten-acre field beyond the beeches, but was certain that they could not see her.

She went through the mossed and broken five-barred gate into the weed-covered yard, took a last quick scan about to make sure no one was watching, and ran for the barn itself.

She crossed the threshold and there was sudden cool and shadowiness. There were quick stirs and patterings and she thought, Mice rats bats ghosts – help!

The barn seemed bigger and darker and quieter than any barn she had ever known before, and she wondered whether she had picked the right place for a hideout. Somewhere smaller would have felt safer, more homelike. But it was too late now.

She sat down and leaned against the doorpost. She took out the bottle and had a swig of the orange and felt a little better. Then she stared out at the empty yard and already felt as if she were the only person left alive in the world. Worse – she began to feel a little silly. So she opened a packet of gum and worked it up to a fine soft ball and began to blow bubbles, slowly and expertly, to keep herself company.

She looked at her watch and saw that it was only half past four and wondered however she would pass the next couple of hours till it began to grow dark. She took out her book and immediately wished she had brought a different one. Giants seemed all too possible in that high, vacant barn. All the time she was reading she was aware of exactly where she was and what she was doing. She heard every single sound – the bleating of sheep, the muffled roar of cars passing, the odd scratchings and rustlings in the shadows behind her. She reached the end of chapter two, realized that she had not the least idea what the story was about and closed the book. Then she ate the crisps. Then the chocolate biscuit.

Wonder if they found the note yet? she thought.

And in the instant, a picture of the scene at home began to take shape in her mind . . .

Albert came in and hung his cap on the door as usual.

'Where's our Lizzie, then?' he asked.

'Lizzie? Come to think, don't know, Albert,' Patty replied frowning a little. 'Ain't seen her since dinner, come to think. Hiding out of my way, likely. Broke my best cat jug this morning, if you please.'

'Eeh, that's a right shame, Patty,' said Albert. 'Have to see if I can't get you another. Though jugs made like cats don't grow on trees, that's a fact. Liked that jug myself, I did – way his tail curled up to make handle. But the lass wouldn't do it o' purpose, not our Lizzie. Ain't seen her since dinner?'

'No.' Patty was a little alarmed now. 'No, I ain't.'

'Funny,' said Albert. 'Her off all this time and saying nowt.'

'I reckon I was too hard on the lass, looking back on it,' said Patty. 'She's a good lass, our Lizzie, when all's said and done. You don't – you don't reckon she's gone and done summat – summat silly, Albert?'

'What?' Now it was Albert's turn to be alarmed. 'Run off, you mean, or – wuss?'

'Oh!' cried Patty, wringing her hands. The baby outside began to yell but she hardly seemed to hear him. 'Oh, Albert, don't say such things. If owt should happen to our little lass, it'd break my heart. Fair break my heart!'

She lifted her head, saw the note, and in the instant snatched it up. Next minute she gave a despairing cry.

'Oh, Albert, Albert! I can't bear it! I can't!'

'What?' cried Albert. 'What is it?'

'She's gone!' Patty was sobbing now. 'Gone for ever! Run off! It's all here, Albert! Oh, what've I done, what've I done?'

Silently Albert took the note and read it while his usually imperturbable face grew grim.

'I shall have to go after her,' he said. 'We'll ring police – get out search parties. We got to find that lass, Patty, we got to!'

'Oh, Albert!' – Patty was weeping unrestrainedly now – 'Don't leave me, don't! The dearest, sweetest child that ever a mother had, and I've drove her away! 'Twas me that drove her to it!'

Albert put an arm about her shoulders.

'There, lass, there. We'll find her.'

'If on'y she'll come back, if on'y we find her, I'll never say another wrong word to her again!' cried Patty, raising her tearstained face. 'Never, as long as I live! Oh, Lizzie, Lizzie!'

The scene faded. Lizzie brushed a tear from her own eyes and a great hot wave of shame rushed over her from head to foot.

'Oh, Lizzie!' she whispered aloud. 'Oh, Lizzie Dripping, you *shouldn't* have!'

She had made a mistake. She knew it. In the very moment of knowing it, she got to her feet. And then she was running, running as fast as her legs would carry her, back towards home. And she was not running because she was lonely or scared or afraid of the approaching dusk (though she was all of these things), but because the thought of the hurt she had done to Patty and Albert was too much for her. And because she knew, quite certainly, that they did love her, and all the scoldings in the world would never change that.

She turned into Main Street and slowed down, out of breath.

Oh, Lizzie, what a fool you'll look! she thought, but she no longer cared.

She turned in at the gate and saw her father's van there and Toby's pram and everything just as it always was and yet somehow entirely different, as if she had been away for a thousand years. She went in through the open back door, saw Albert and Patty turn towards her, and she burst into tears.

'Here, then, here,' she heard her father say, and felt his arm about her shoulders. 'What's all this about?'

'Come along, petty,' she heard her mother say. 'You come and tell Mum what's the matter, then.'

Lizzie raised her wet face. 'Oh, Mum!' she cried. 'Dad! I'm sorry! I'm sorry!'

They stared.

'What is it?' asked Patty, and her voice was unusually gentle. 'What is it, then?'

It was then that Lizzie, looking beyond them, saw the note. There it stood, exactly where she had left it, propped against the butter dish. She leapt forward, snatched it up, and screwed it in her hand.

They need never know! she thought. They'll never know!

And what with the relief and one thing and another she began to laugh, so that she was laughing and crying at the same time, and she heard herself say: 'It don't matter, really it don't! There's nothing wrong, Mum, not now, really there ain't. And oh, Mum and Dad, I *do* love you!'

They still stood and still stared and in the silence Toby began to yell from his pram outside. Patty shook her head.

'Oh, Lizzie,' she sighed, 'Lizzie Dripping. Shall I ever understand you?'

And then Albert dug in his pocket and took out a little package and said, 'See what I brought you back from Mapleburn, Lizzie,' and Patty went out to fetch the baby, and the world was the right way up again.

Girls!
Stevie Smith

Girls! although I am a woman
I always try to appear human

Unlike Miss So-and-So whose greatest pride
Is to remain always in the VI Form and not let down the
    side

Do not sell the pass dear, don't let down the side,
That is what this woman said and a lot of balsy stuff
    beside
(Oh the awful balsy nonsense that this woman cried.)

Girls! I will let down the side if I get a chance
And I will sell the pass for a couple of pence.

Sick
Shel Silverstein

'I cannot go to school today',
Said little Peggy Ann McKay

'I have the measles and the mumps,
A gash, a rash and purple bumps.
My mouth is wet, my throat is dry,
I'm going blind in my right eye.
My tonsils are as big as rocks,
I've counted sixteen chicken pox
And there's one more – that's seventeen,
And don't you think my face looks green?
My leg is cut, my eyes are blue –
It might be instamatic flu.
I cough and sneeze and gasp and choke,
I'm sure that my left leg is broke –
My hip hurts when I move my chin,
My belly button's caving in,
My back is wrenched, my ankle's sprained,
My 'pendix pains each time it rains.
My nose is cold, my toes are numb,
I have a sliver in my thumb.
My neck is stiff, my spine is weak,
I hardly whisper when I speak.
My tongue is filling up my mouth,
I think my hair is falling out.
My elbow's bent, my spine ain't straight,
My temperature is one-o-eight.
My brain is shrunk, I cannot hear,
There is a hole inside my ear.
I have a hangnail, and my heart is – what?
What's that? What's that you say?
You say today is . . . Saturday?
G'bye, I'm going out to play!'

from It
William Mayne

Getting home changed nothing for Alice. She was still going to be the wrong way out for everybody else. She could see it in everything around her, and she could see it in what she did herself and in what she had ever done.

'I don't know what you are thinking about these days,' said Mum, when Alice had stood and watched something interesting but fatal happen to the gravy in the baking dish. 'You've burnt both.' Alice had, of course. She had stopped stirring and let the gas flame scorch a ring, first of innocent bubbles and then of real cinder, while she had thought about nothing she could remember in words.

'You'll clean that drip-tin,' said Dad, and there was another little argument about that, with Dad using one name for the thing, Mum the other and Alice not being allowed to be on either side.

'Out of my kitchen, both of you,' said Mum, when it was quite clear that no one agreed.

'Now then,' said Dad to Alice as they went out of the door, 'have a care.'

'I have several,' said Alice.

'Happen you have,' said Dad. Then they went to bring their visitors to the table. Grandpa was a visitor in a natural sense; someone who came occasionally. Matthew was a visitor too, and quite like a stranger. Today he was even an important visitor, and a popular one: everyone made a fuss of him, because everyone was pleased that he was going into the Minster choir. Alice was pleased too, but she could tell that

98

her reasons were different. She was pleased because she loved him, which meant that if he was doing what he wanted to do then she was glad and proud.

But perhaps it might be better not to love him. Alice looked at him now, where he was sitting on the arm of Dad's chair rubbing his face and saying it hurt from smiling, and she knew she wanted him to stay at home now for a long time so that she could play Monopoly all the evening and have a fight with him as well. She thought about the rules for a fight and then left them, because there wasn't going to be one. Matthew was going to have lunch, go up to the Minster for a practice with the rest of the choir, go to Evensong with its ceremony, and then go back to the school in the school minibus, somehow cleaned out of her life except for occasional appearances.

'Ready to serve,' said Mum coming through from the kitchen.

'Dishing up,' said Dad to Grandpa.

'I heard the text in the original Greek,' said Grandpa, getting up. He put one hand behind Matthew and the other on Alice's back, to usher them to the table. Alice instantly turned into a tortoise with a hard shell and arms and legs drawn in so that it could not move. She knew at once she was being unfriendly and that Grandpa had come round to forgiving her. She changed her ungrateful attitude by going round Grandpa and helping to propel Matthew forward, which she did by twisting his arm up behind his back.

'Simmer down,' said Mum.

'Side up,' said Dad.

'Sit down and shut up,' said Matthew, and everybody was pleased with that.

The meal began. The gravy was scorched, after being rescued by Mum. The others seemed to think it was the flavour it should be, but Alice scraped hers away and left it and took no notice of a slight shaking of Mum's head about the way she was doing it.

'You're acting disagreeably,' said Mum.

'I'm not acting,' said Alice. 'I'm realling.'

'I doubt you are,' said Mum, and Dad said 'I doubt you aren't,' but they both meant exactly the same thing, only Dad used his town language and Mum used vicarage language that she had been brought up with.

Alice stopped doing anything with the gravy and poured herself a glass of water, slow and careful, right to the top and beyond the top but without spilling, with the water raised in a blister. The spilling came when she lifted the glass to drink from it, and a plunge of water ran down her chin and her thumb and the glass and splashed on her plate.

So for her the meal ended in the next minute, when she got up to take the plate to the kitchen and pour away the water, without thinking of the gravy, and Mum told her to come back at once, and Dad said Right Now, and Alice thought she would go her own way, and put the plate down on the carpet and went out of the room and sat on her bed, while her stomach made a grinding noise and sank empty away.

Much later Matthew came carefully along the passage with some apple pie for her.

'I don't know what it is,' he said. 'Mum said pudding, Dad says afters, and Grandpa says dessert and at school we say sweet.'

'Apple pie,' said Alice. 'Go and get yours, Matt.'

'We've had ours,' said Matthew. 'Are you going to come this afternoon?'

'I've seen them do it before,' said Alice.

'Would you come to our school if they took girls?' said Matthew. 'Then you could be in the choir too.'

'They wouldn't have me,' said Alice.

'No,' said Matthew, thoughtfully and not in the least un-kindly, 'you didn't even get into that other school, did you?'

'No brains,' said Alice. 'I wish you'd brought a spoon, Matthew, because my hair's getting in the plate.'

'You've nearly finished,' said Matthew. 'I think you didn't want to go to that school. You should have gone to St Hilda's, because it's our sister school.'

'I'm your sister anyway,' said Alice, but she had to repeat it because she had her face in the pie now, chasing a slippery crumb. Matthew was not sure whether St Hilda's was sister to the Minster School because of the sisters and brothers in each or whether it was from some other reason he had not worked out yet. Alice gave him the plate, licked quite clean.

'I have to go,' he said. 'I expect it's that rhyme.' He was still talking about St Hilda's, and Alice knew perfectly well what he meant, but it seemed to her that there were things a younger brother ought not to know about.

'What rhyme?' she said. 'I don't know any rhyme, and if I did I wouldn't care, except it's true.'

Then Grandpa was calling for Matthew, because both of them had to leave long before the service, one to practise, the other to see to something in the Minster library.

Alice went with them. She and Grandpa conducted Matthew between them along the quiet dull streets of the city, where all the shops were shut and no one else walked and hardly a car came. Matthew thought it was creepy. Grandpa thought, historically, that the city would have been silent like this after a great plague. Alice thought about St Hilda's. She could remember being near one of the Minster doors a long time ago, with her friend Raddy, and shouting the rhyme at the St Hilda girls as they went in to Evensong. The girls had taken no notice at all, and the Minster door had closed behind them. Raddy and Alice had shouted half the rhyme again after them, the first two lines about green underwear which was true and not very remarkable in a school uniform; but they had each decided not to speak the last two lines, which were only disgusting. Then they had walked off in different directions and not spoken to each other for about two months, and not mentioned St Hilda's since.

Matthew had gone to the Minster School round that time, after passing a difficult exam, and being one of six chosen from seventeen boys wanting to go. Everybody was pleased with him. The next thing was that no one asked Alice her opinion, but suddenly this summer she had gone on a Saturday to St Hilda's and been given a lot of sums and reading and writing to do.

The sums were all easy, the other questions were simple. The only difficult thing was how to tell Mum and Dad or anybody that she did not want to go there, didn't want to live in a dormitory, didn't want to walk about the town only on Saturday afternoons in pairs with another St Hilda girl. She had not wanted to belong to St Hilda's, but she had not liked to disappoint Mum and Dad with a wrong decision. So she had answered all the sums with nine hundred and ninety-nine, used very childish handwriting, and put her own name as the answer to everything else. She had not been able to tell anyone, not even Raddy, and no one had said anything. A great deal of sad disappointment had been about, however, at home, and up in Sarrow vicarage.

Alice had to keep saying to herself that she was right in what she had done, and it was true: she did not want to go to St Hilda's and the simplest way out of it was to fail the exam. But something had been spoilt, and she knew it was her fault and that she should have relied not on being clever enough to fail but on being brave enough to speak out. Each day at home should have been better than it now was. Today, especially, should have been a particularly happy one, with her and Matthew back and everybody glad to see them, and the service in the afternoon belonging to them all. It was not like that in the slightest, because Alice was the odd one out. But she knew she was right. Matthew had wanted to go to his school and he had gone; Alice had not wanted to go to hers and she had not gone. What she had done was what Matthew had done, chosen for herself; but Matthew was praised and she was not.

Bell Tower and Consequences
Jenny Overton

[from *Creed Country*]

Monica was enraptured by the bell tower.

'I wish we could go higher,' she said, standing dissatisfied on the gallery, and gazing up at the long curl of worn steps which twisted round the circling walls, far above them. 'Why can't we?'

'It isn't safe,' Sarah said, wishing David had come. Monica was in a tiresome mood. There was still no news from the Bishop, and it looked as though her great plan which had promised so well – *visits from the Bishop, telephone calls from solicitors*, Monica thought, hugging herself – was dissolving away like a shawl of snow in a thaw.

'Why isn't it safe?'

'Because it isn't,' Sarah said crossly. Monica had no fear of heights whatever, and had frightened her elder sisters nearly to death when taken up Big Ben one time; and Mrs Wentworth insisted that it was wrong to put fears into her head which weren't already there.

But at least, Sarah thought, Veronica was a bit more cheerful. Simon and she were sprawling on their stomachs peering down through the bellrope hole, arguing amiably about Galileo.

'I tell you he dropped a feather.'

'And I tell *you* a feather wouldn't have dropped, it would've floated.'

Sarah thought of the secret courtyard with its high, lichened walls, and silent gutter, and decided to go and find Stephen.

'Why can't we go higher?'

'Oh, have a bit of sense, Nica, do. Can't you *see* it's dangerous? Why d'you suppose it's barricaded off?'

'But it *isn't* dangerous,' Monica argued, with some reason on her side, for the steps, though worn, were broad and had survived a couple of hundred years in the open. 'It's just that there's no handrail.'

'Shut up, for goodness' sake.'

'Why can't we?'

'Because you can't,' Sarah snapped. 'And if you go on bothering me, I'll tell Dad when we get back, I warn you.'

'D'you dare me?'

'I dare you all right. You *are* a clot, Nica.'

Sarah went towards the stairs. She knew quite well what Monica was going to do, and she went quickly so that she could not see her do it. But even so she did not quite believe it – so she told herself; because of course if she did believe it she would have to stay, argue, be authoritative. She went slowly down the spiral stair, pausing on almost every step; but all she could hear from above was the murmur of Veronica and Simon talking.

'I'll bet two and six on it,' Simon said firmly.

'Well, have you *got* a feather? We'll try.'

Veronica scrambled to her feet, and looked around. At first

she didn't see Monica at all; and when she did, she didn't immediately believe it. Monica was feet above her, flat against the sunlit golden stone. For a minute Veronica thought she was standing on nothing at all, but then she saw the stone stair jutting out from the wall; and as she stood there, Monica moved, going cautiously and steadily up another step. Veronica stared, panicked, and did the stupidest possible thing; she shouted, '*Nica –* '; and Monica's head moved, the blur of dark hair swinging to the left, and she looked down; and stuck.

From the bottom of the tower Sarah heard the shout and knew instantly what had happened. She turned and ran, round and round the spiral, higher and higher, until she came out on the gallery, and saw Monica, way up on the wall, and Veronica clinging to the handrail round the bellrope drop, and Simon looking mildly surprised at the commotion.

'She's stuck,' Veronica wailed. 'Oh, Sarah, she's stuck.'

Sarah swore, and shouted, 'Nica, don't worry, stay still.'

She ran towards the steps. As she climbed up and over the barricade, she remembered with startling clarity her father declaring that if Nica was drowning in Linholt bath, he hoped Anne would cut the heroics and run for help. She hesitated. *But Anne's scared of water and I'm not scared of heights.* Besides she, like Veronica, had always wondered what she would be like in an emergency, and if, after all, she would be brave; and with Veronica patently terrified, it was tempting to do something bold and to-the-rescue . . . And then she remembered that Anthony had climbed up this tower after Quentin. (Though Nica, thank God, had picked the inner wall, with steps . . .) *Anthony*, she thought. And because Anthony had the care-for-nothing courage she most longed for, she started up the steps, pressing flat against the wall.

But she got frightened very quickly, six heartbeats, no more.

She wasn't Anthony; she wasn't even David hauling Vero out of the pothole. She called, 'Simon, get Stephen, quick – ' But it would look awful to go back now.

Sarah told herself that what Nico did, she could do.

Simon thought they were making a great fuss about nothing.

He said to Stephen, 'Sarah says, come on.'

'Why?'

'I'll tell you when we get there.'

Thinking how tiresome Simon could be, Stephen followed him, out of the museum, across to the bell tower, up the first stairs.

Sarah looked up, to see how much further it was to Monica; and saw in disbelief that Monica had begun to climb again. She was going on up. Sarah opened her mouth to yell, but checked herself in time. Moving with extreme caution, her face flat against the rough grain of the stone, Sarah went on. She had to pause on every step and turn her head, the stone grazing her cheek, to check that the next step was there, and whole. She became so absorbed in this, and in fighting back the knowledge that the climb was silly and useless, that when she turned her head, feeling the scrape of the stone across her cheek, the swing of her hair, the way her eyelashes caught on the grain, and saw something on the next step, a foot in blue sock and scuffed sandal, she was amazed, and heard the gasp of her own breath, loud in the gap between mouth and stone, fading in the great unseen space behind her.

Monica said casually, 'The next two steps have gone, I don't think we can get to the top after all.'

'Thank God.' Sarah began to shiver. 'Now we've got to get down.'

'What did you come up here for, anyway? I was perfectly

106

all right, no one asked you to come poking your nose in.'

'You *knew* you shouldn't – '

'Oh, nuts, 'tisn't dangerous. Anyway, you shouldn't have said you'd tell tales. You shouldn't have dared me.'

'You're a stupid crazy tiresome little girl,' Sarah said furiously. '*Nica*, what're you doing?'

'What d'you mean, what'm I doing?' Monica said truculently. 'What I like. Try and stop me.'

'I saw you move. I *felt* you move.'

'Okay, I moved, so what? I'm looking *round*, that's all.'

'Nica, you are *not* to.'

But Monica turned her head, her shoulders; shifted her feet as delicately as though she were moving on a sixpence; and looked out into a great shaft of sunlit space, bounded by a sweep of golden stone. Across it plunged an arrow of shadow, so decisive against the strong clear light that Monica drew in her breath. But far below, something moved; she could just catch the movement. She looked down at the gallery.

'Here comes Stephen,' she remarked.

Stephen looked and turned round, heading for the stairs down to the grass.

'Where're you going?' Simon demanded, grabbing his arm; Veronica was just sitting on the floor and refusing to look.

'To get help, of course.'

'But you can't, there'll be the most almighty row. You've got to keep it a secret. Look, there. They're all right. Sarah's coming down – '

'Monica isn't,' Stephen said, glancing briefly up at Monica, who had stuck again. 'Don't be stupid, Simon. Can't you get it into your head that it's dangerous?'

Simon hesitated, caught between Stephen's intransigence

and the passionate belief, underlying all spats and quarrels, that grown-ups should never be told.

But Stephen had no sense of half shades in such a situation. He saw a clear-cut issue.

'Tell Sarah to stay still – yes, I know she's trying to climb down, but it's not worth the risk – ' Then he had gone, racing down the spiral.

Simon looked up: at Sarah, face to the wall; at Monica staring into the sun. It didn't look dangerous to him. As long as they kept their heads and stuck close to the wall, they'd never fall off. But Stephen had rushed straight off to tell. He'd never thought much of Stephen and now was filled with positive dislike.

Veronica said shakily, 'Simon, what's happening?'

'Look, and you'll see,' he said crossly, not having much patience with Veronica's panics. 'Stephen's gone pelting off to get help, that's what, *which* is going to mean an almighty row, and all for nothing.'

'I'm scared,' Veronica wailed. She had always panicked at the promise of danger or trouble, and none of Simon's contemptuous assurances calmed her down. 'There's no rail,' she kept on insisting. 'And they'll be so mad with us – '

Sarah told herself that if she kept her head, she'd be all right. Just stay still and wait, face pressed to the stone. But she could not forget all that space behind her, warm and humming; all that space, all that drop.

Monica wasn't panicking. After the first stunned amazement, she stared confidently out at the sunlight and the cut of shadow across the gold. She rather liked an edge of fear. She moved a little and dislodged a feather, which had clung to the rough grain of the stone. She watched it float down the air.

Stephen came back, breathless from the spiral, and men came behind him, three, four of them, crowding on to the gallery. Monica watched; wondered why they'd come; and thought, resignedly, that it was a pity, because now there'd probably be a row about her being up their old tower.

There was, as Simon had crossly predicted, an almighty row – or rather a whole series of rows, beginning with the Curator and going on through the families. On the way home, shaken by the Curator's telling-off which, though brief, had been extremely pointed, Veronica said, 'D'you think . . . d'you think we ought to tell them?'

'No,' Monica said.

'Stephen will, if we don't,' Simon said, giving Stephen a look of furious dislike.

'Shut up, Simon.'

Simon muttered about tell-tales. Sarah said, 'We'd better – 'cause if we don't, they'll hear from someone else, and then it'll be worse than otherwise.'

They walked slowly back along the road from the Verney Piece bus stop.

'He's not coming in, is he?' Simon demanded, glaring at Stephen.

'Shut *up*, Simon,' Sarah said, wishing he didn't sound so truculent and childish. But if there was going to be a row – and she knew there was, though she tried to push the knowledge aside – she didn't want Stephen there, watching. Especially with Veronica bound to cry. And maybe herself.

'You go home, Stephen.'

'Are you sure? That's what you want?'

'Yes, really.'

It was extraordinarily difficult to tell. At first no one really listened, being full of a letter from Nick in Paris, a card from Theo in Ireland; then, when people realized they were struggling to tell something and listened, they couldn't find the proper words; and once they did start, they kept being interrupted by furious outbursts from their father, and appalled questions from their mother and Anne.

The others weren't much help, Sarah thought, as she struggled to obey her father's demand: 'Slow down, I want a proper account from one of you, not all this hysteria – you, Sarah. Start at the beginning.'

She kept on being interrupted. Monica said several times over, '*I* don't see what all the fuss is about . . .', and could not, Sarah thought, have found anything to say which would have exasperated her father more.

And Simon backed Monica. 'But it wasn't *dangerous*,' he kept on stubbornly, infuriatingly. David said, 'For heaven's sake, Simon, shut up.'

'But it wasn't – ' Simon began.

'Simon,' their father said angrily, 'what d'you suppose would have happened if Monica'd slipped? If a step had given way?'

'Stone – ' Simon began; but his father ignored him.

'They're worn away – no shelter from the weather – hundreds of years old. Stone can crumble just like *that*.' He slammed his hand down on the table, and eyed Simon as though next time it would be on him. 'Now shut up. Careless you may be, but there's no need to be an irresponsible fool.'

Simon shut up.

Veronica, already tearful, made no attempt to argue; she was keeping quiet in the hope no one would notice her.

'*Now*,' their father said, withdrawing his attention from Simon. 'You were at the bottom of the tower, Sarah? Then why didn't Simon or Vero stop her?'

Veronica looked at Simon, and he glared back, his mouth tightly shut. She felt the ready onrush of tears. 'We didn't *see* – I mean, when I looked she was already *up* there – you couldn't blame me – us – '

'So what did you do?'

110

'I – I – '

'She yelled,' Monica said contemptuously, though giving her father a wary look. She was a long way from capitulation, but it was being borne in on her that, stupid or not, they were taking it seriously.

Her father concentrated on Veronica. 'You yelled?'

'But that's the worst thing to do, surely you know that, Vero? Once someone looks down . . .'

'Must you *always* lose your head?' her father asked scathingly.

Veronica began to cry in earnest. Anne said, 'Oh, Vero . . .', giving her a handkerchief.

'So you came back, Sarah? What then?'

'I – well, she'd stuck. Or at least, I thought she had.'

'I had *not*,' Monica said. 'I was just looking. It was terrific.'

Their mother shivered. 'Nica, *please*.'

'So,' Sarah said, to get it over with, 'I thought I'd better . . . well, go up after her.'

'But, Sally – ' David began.

'Be quiet, David,' their father said, cutting in to demolish Sarah. 'If there's one thing that's sillier than any other, it's false heroics in a situation like that. What good did you suppose you could do? Did you at least send Simon or Vero for help?'

He waited for an answer, but he wasn't getting one. Sarah just shook her head. Her father's voice went scathingly on about dramatics, silly risks, irresponsibility.

'Yes, I *know*,' she said desperately.

'Then why on earth did you do such a silly thing?'

Anthony, Sarah thought, but still kept her mouth shut; and Anne, in a mistaken attempt to divert her father's attention, said, 'But someone called help – was it you, Vero?'

'Well, was it? What were you doing, all this while?'

Appalled to find her father once more swinging round

on her, Veronica reached for the handkerchief and muttered, 'Nothing. I – I – I couldn't look.'

'One day,' her mother said in annoyance, 'you're going to *have* to look.'

The dual attack was too much for Veronica, who promptly dissolved. Anne said, 'Well, then, who *did* get help? Or did it just come?'

'Stephen did,' Simon muttered.

'Well, thank God someone had a bit of sense,' their father said.

'But I thought Stephen wasn't there.'

'He wasn't. Sarah told me to get him before she – well, went up – and,' Simon said, rancour bursting out again, 'he just looked and went, just telling tales, he didn't even –'

'I told you to be quiet,' his father said, 'Stephen did what you, or Sarah, or Veronica, should have done immediately.'

'But I was all *right*,' Monica protested.

'We aren't interested in your opinions. If you were so incredibly silly as to go climbing up a railed-off and dangerous staircase, which you knew quite well was forbidden, do you expect us to put faith in your intelligence? You behaved throughout in the stupidest possible fashion. *And*,' he said, struck by a new question, 'why did you go up there anyway?'

Monica flinched; but her disregard for other people's opinions made her always truthful, so she said, 'Because Sarah told me not to.'

'*What?*'

And so, Sarah thought despairingly, they started all over again. Trespassing, wilful disobedience. Stupidity, irresponsibility. Veronica was still sniffing into the handkerchief, Simon looked white and worried, Monica was beginning to look uneasily defiant. Sarah decided she knew exactly how Anthony had felt when he cut loose from his family.

At last their mother and David and Anne began to calm Mr Wentworth down. They had just about managed it when Monica, obstinate to the last, said, 'But it *wasn't* really dangerous . . .', and he was off again.

'I'll make some tea,' Anne said, getting up from the stairs.

'Yes – Sarah, go and help,' their mother said, glancing at their father. 'Vero, either stop crying or go to bed. And Simon . . .'

'Simon can stay right here,' their father said. Simon sat miserably down on the stairs. 'I'll make him see sense if it takes all night.'

As the kitchen door swung behind herself and Anne, Sarah heard him starting up again, 'Now listen to me . . .'; and as first David, then Veronica, came in, she caught snatches of his angry voice.

Anne said, 'Do stop crying, Vero. Bathe your eyes.'

Veronica suddenly blew up in tears and fury, lashing at Anne because she wanted to hurt someone and Anne seemed so perversely invulnerable.

'I *hate* you, and it's all your fault, making everything go wrong, re-reminding them to look at me – and what did *you* do when I fell in the river – '

'Not fell, *walked*,' David said crisply.

'Nothing you didn't do, *nothing*, just *lapped* up all that sympathy, scared of water, *nuts*, it's just put on – and I'll be *glad* when you bury yourself in your convent, so I will – if you want to go off and leave us, *do*, who cares, I *hate* you.'

Anne stood still. Veronica saw her face and knew she had hit Anne hard, and was pleased because it couldn't be harder than Anne had hit her that day she had said suddenly at lunch, 'I may be a nun, Maman . . .'

Then David said, 'Shut *up*, Vero,' so forcefully that even Veronica obeyed; and Anne went on setting out cups in silence.

Then and There

What Has Happened to Lulu?
Charles Causley

What has happened to Lulu, Mother?
  What has happened to Lu?
There's nothing in her bed but an old rag-doll
  And by its side a shoe.

Why is her window wide, Mother,
  The curtain flapping free,
And only a circle on the dusty shelf
  Where her money-box used to be?

Why do you turn your head, Mother,
  And why do the teardrops fall?
And why do you crumple that note on the fire
  And say it is nothing at all?

I woke to voices late last night,
  I heard an engine roar.
Why do you tell me the things I heard
  Were a dream and nothing more?

I heard somebody cry, Mother,
  In anger or in pain,
But now I ask you why, Mother,
  You say it was a gust of rain.

Why do you wander about as though
  You don't know what to do?
What has happened to Lulu, Mother?
  What has happened to Lu?

Paper Matches
Paulette Jiles

My aunts washed dishes while the uncles
squirted each other on the lawn with
    garden hoses. Why are we in here,
I said, and they are out there.
    That's the way it is,
    said Aunt Hetty, the shrivelled-up one.

I have the rages that small animals have,
being small, being animal.
    Written on me was a message,
'At Your Service' like a book of
paper matches. One by one we were
taken out and struck.
    We come bearing supper,
our heads on fire.

Maggie Cuts Her Hair
George Eliot

[from *The Mill on the Floss*]

Mrs Tulliver had really made great efforts to induce Maggie to
wear a leghorn bonnet and a dyed silk frock made out of her
aunt Glegg's, but the results had been such that Mrs Tulliver
was obliged to bury them in her maternal bosom; for Maggie,
declaring that the frock smelt of nasty dye, had taken an
opportunity of basting it together with the roast beef the first
Sunday she wore it, and, finding this scheme answer, she had
subsequently pumped on the bonnet with its green ribbons,

so as to give it a general resemblance to a sage cheese garnished with withered lettuces. I must urge in excuse for Maggie, that Tom had laughed at her in the bonnet, and said she looked like an old Judy. Aunt Pullet, too, made presents of clothes, but these were always pretty enough to please Maggie as well as her mother. Of all her sisters, Mrs Tulliver certainly preferred her sister Pullet, not without a return of preference; but Mrs Pullet was sorry Bessy had those naughty awkward children; she would do the best she could by them, but it was a pity they weren't as good and as pretty as sister Deane's child. Maggie and Tom, on their part, thought their aunt Pullet tolerable, chiefly because she was not their aunt Glegg. Tom always declined to go more than once, during his holidays, to see either of them: both his uncles tipped him that once, of course; but at his aunt Pullet's there was a great many toads to pelt in the cellar-area, so that he preferred the visit to her. Maggie shuddered at the toads, and dreamed of them horribly, but she liked her uncle Pullet's musical snuff-box. Still, it was agreed by the sisters, in Mrs Tulliver's absence, that the Tulliver blood did not mix well with the Dodson blood; that, in fact, poor Bessy's children were Tullivers, and that Tom, notwithstanding he had the Dodson complexion, was likely to be as 'contrairy' as his father. As for Maggie, she was the picture of her aunt Moss, Mr Tulliver's sister, – a large-boned woman, who had married as poorly as could be; had no china, and had a husband who had much ado to pay his rent. But when Mrs Pullet was alone with Mrs Tulliver upstairs, the remarks were naturally to the disadvantage of Mrs Glegg, and they agreed, in confidence, that there was no knowing what sort of fright sister Jane would come out next. But their *tête-à-tête* was curtailed by the appearance of Mrs Deane with little Lucy; and Mrs Tulliver had to look on with a silent pang while Lucy's blonde curls were adjusted. It was quite unaccountable that Mrs Deane, the thinnest and sallowest of all the Miss Dodsons, should have had this child, who might have been taken for Mrs Tulliver's any day. And Maggie always looked twice as dark as usual when she was by the side of Lucy.

She did today, when she and Tom came in from the garden with their father and their uncle Glegg. Maggie had thrown her bonnet off very carelessly, and, coming in with her hair rough as well as out of curl, rushed at once to Lucy, who was standing by her mother's knee. Certainly the contrast between the cousins was conspicuous, and, to superficial eyes, was very much to the disadvantage of Maggie, though a connoisseur might have seen 'points' in her which had a higher promise for maturity than Lucy's natty completeness. It was like the contrast between a rough, dark, overgrown puppy and a white kitten. Lucy put up the neatest little rosebud mouth to be kissed: everything about her was neat – her little round neck, with the row of coral beads; her little straight nose, not at all snubby; her little clear eyebrows, rather darker than her curls, to match her hazel eyes, which looked up with shy pleasure at Maggie, taller by the head, though scarcely a year older. Maggie always looked at Lucy with delight. She was fond of fancying a world where the people never got any larger than children of their own age, and she made the queen of it just like Lucy, with a little crown on her head, and a little sceptre in her hand . . . only the queen was Maggie herself in Lucy's form.

'Oh Lucy,' she burst out, after kissing her, 'you'll stay with Tom and me, won't you? Oh kiss her, Tom.'

Tom, too, had come up to Lucy, but he was not going to kiss her – no; he came up to her with Maggie, because it seemed easier, on the whole, than saying, 'How do you do?' to all those aunts and uncles: he stood looking at nothing in particular, with the blushing, awkward air and semi-smile which are common to shy boys when in company – very much as if they had come into the world by mistake, and found it in a degree of undress that was quite embarrassing.

'Heyday!' said Aunt Glegg, with loud emphasis. 'Do little boys and gells come into a room without taking notice o' their uncles and aunts? That wasn't the way when *I* was a little gell.'

'Go and speak to your aunts and uncles, my dears,' said Mrs Tulliver, looking anxious and melancholy. She wanted to whisper to Maggie a command to go and have her hair brushed.

'Well, and how do you do? And I hope you're good children, are you?' said Aunt Glegg, in the same loud emphatic way, as she took their hands, hurting them with her large rings, and kissing their cheeks much against their desire. 'Look up, Tom, look up. Boys as go to boarding schools should hold their heads up. Look at me now.' Tom declined that pleasure apparently, for he tried to draw his hand away. 'Put your hair behind your ears, Maggie, and keep your frock on your shoulder.'

Aunt Glegg always spoke to them in this loud emphatic way, as if she considered them deaf, or perhaps rather idiotic: it was a means, she thought, of making them feel that they were accountable creatures, and might be a salutary check on naughty tendencies. Bessy's children were so spoiled – they'd need have somebody to make them feel their duty.

'Well, my dears,' said Aunt Pullet, in a compassionate voice, 'you grow wonderful fast. I doubt they'll outgrow their strength,' she added, looking over their heads with a melancholy expression, at their mother. 'I think the gell has too much hair. I'd have it thinned and cut shorter, Sister, if I was you: it isn't good for her health. It's that as makes her skin so brown. I shouldn't wonder. Don't you think so, Sister Deane?'

'I can't say, I'm sure, Sister,' said Mrs Deane, shutting her lips close again, and looking at Maggie with a critical eye.

'No, no,' said Mr Tulliver, 'the child's healthy enough – there's nothing ails her. There's red wheat as well as white, for that matter, and some like the dark grain best. But it 'ud be as well if Bessy 'ud have the child's hair cut, so as it 'ud lie smooth.'

A dreadful resolve was gathering in Maggie's breast, but it was arrested by the desire to know from her aunt Deane whether she would leave Lucy behind: Aunt Deane would hardly ever let Lucy come to see them. After various reasons for refusal, Mrs Deane appealed to Lucy herself.

'You wouldn't like to stay behind without Mother, should you, Lucy?'

'Yes, please, Mother,' said Lucy, timidly, blushing very pink all over her little neck.

'Well done, Lucy! Let her stay, Mrs Deane, let her stay,' said Mr Deane, a large but alert-looking man, with a type of physique to be seen in all ranks of English society – bald crown, red whiskers, full forehead, and general solidity without heaviness. You may see noblemen like Mr Deane, and you may see grocers or day-labourers like him; but the keenness of his brown eyes was less common than his contour. He held a silver snuff-box very tightly in his hand, and now and then exchanged a pinch with Mr Tulliver, whose box was only silver-mounted, so that it was naturally a joke between them that Mr Tulliver wanted to exchange snuff-boxes also. Mr Deane's box had been given him by the superior partners in the firm to which he belonged, at the same time that they gave him a share in the business, in acknowledgement of his valuable services as manager. No man was thought more highly of in St Ogg's than Mr Deane, and some persons were even of the opinion that Miss Susan Dodson, who was once held to have made the worst match of all the Dodson sisters, might one day ride in a better carriage, and live in a better house, even than her Sister Pullet. There was no knowing where a man would stop, who had got his foot into a great mill-owning, ship-owning business like that of Guest & Co., with a banking concern attached. And Mrs Deane, as her intimate female friends observed, was proud and 'having' enough: *she* wouldn't let her husband stand still in the world for want of spurring.

'Maggie,' said Mrs Tulliver, beckoning Maggie to her, and whispering in her ear, as soon as this point of Lucy's staying was settled, 'go and get your hair brushed – do, for shame. I told you not to come in without going to Martha first; you know I did.'

'Tom, come out with me,' whispered Maggie, pulling his sleeve as she passed him; and Tom followed willingly enough.

'Come upstairs with me, Tom,' she whispered, when they were outside the door. 'There's something I want to do before dinner.'

'There's no time to play at anything before dinner,' said Tom, whose imagination was impatient of any intermediate prospect.

'Oh, yes, there is time for this – *do* come, Tom.'

Tom followed Maggie upstairs into her mother's room, and saw her go at once to a drawer, from which she took out a large pair of scissors.

'What are they for, Maggie?' said Tom, feeling his curiosity awakened.

Maggie answered by seizing her front locks and cutting them straight across the middle of her forehead.

'Oh, my buttons, Maggie, you'll catch it!' exclaimed Tom; 'you'd better not cut any more off.'

Snip! went the great scissors again while Tom was speaking;

and he couldn't help feeling it was rather good fun: Maggie would look so queer.

'Here, Tom, cut it behind for me,' said Maggie, excited by her own daring, and anxious to finish the deed.

'You'll catch it, you know,' said Tom, nodding his head in an admonitory manner, and hesitating a little as he took the scissors.

'Never mind – make haste!' said Maggie, giving a little stamp with her foot. Her cheeks were quite flushed.

The black locks were so thick – nothing could be more tempting to a lad who had already tasted the forbidden pleasure of cutting the pony's mane. I speak to those who know the satisfaction of making a pair of shears meet through a duly resisting mass of hair. One delicious grinding snip, and then another and another, and the hinder-locks fell heavily on the floor, and Maggie stood cropped in a jagged, uneven manner, but with a sense of clearness and freedom, as if she had emerged from a wood into the open plain.

'Oh, Maggie,' said Tom, jumping round her, and slapping his knees as he laughed. 'Oh, my buttons, what a queer thing you look! Look at yourself in the glass – you look like the idiot we throw our nut-shells to at school.'

Maggie felt an unexpected pang. She had thought beforehand chiefly of her own deliverance from her teasing hair and teasing remarks about it, and something also of the triumph she should have over her mother and her aunts by this very decided course of action: she didn't want her hair to look pretty – that was out of the question – she only wanted people to think her a clever little girl, and not to find fault with her. But now, when Tom began to laugh at her, and say she was like the idiot, the affair had quite a new aspect. She looked in the glass, and still Tom laughed and clapped his hands, and Maggie's flushed cheeks began to pale, and her lips to tremble a little.

'Oh, Maggie, you'll have to go down to dinner directly,' said Tom. 'Oh my!'

'Don't laugh at me, Tom,' said Maggie, in a passionate tone, with an outburst of angry tears, stamping, and giving him a push.

'Now, then, spitfire!' said Tom. 'What did you cut it off for, then? I shall go down: I can smell the dinner going in.'

He hurried downstairs and left poor Maggie to that bitter sense of the irrevocable which was almost an everyday experience of her small soul. She could see clearly enough, now the thing was done, that it was very foolish, and that she should have to hear and think more about her hair than ever; for Maggie rushed to her deeds with passionate impulse, and then saw not only their consequences, but what would have happened if they had not been done, with all the detail and exaggerated circumstance of an active imagination. Tom never did the same sort of foolish things as Maggie, having a wonderful instinctive discernment of what would turn to his advantage or disadvantage; and so it happened, that though he was much more wilful and inflexible than Maggie, his mother hardly ever called him naughty. But if Tom did make a mistake of that sort, he espoused it, and stood by it: he 'didn't mind'. If he broke the lash of his father's gig-whip by lashing the gate, he couldn't help it – the whip shouldn't have got caught in the hinge. If Tom Tulliver whipped a gate, he was convinced, not that the whipping of gates by all boys was a justifiable act, but that he, Tom Tulliver, was justifiable in whipping that particular gate, and he wasn't going to be sorry. But Maggie, as she stood crying before the glass, felt it impossible that she should go down to dinner and endure the severe eyes and severe words of her aunts, while Tom, and Lucy, and Martha, who waited at table, and perhaps her father and her uncles, would laugh at her; for if Tom had laughed at her, of course everyone else would; and if she had only let her hair alone, she could have sat with Tom and Lucy, and had the apricot pudding and the custard! What could she do but sob? She sat as helpless and despairing among her black locks as Ajax among the slaughtered sheep. Very trivial, perhaps, this anguish seems to weather-worn mortals who have to think of Christmas bills, dead loves, and broken friendships; but it was not less bitter to Maggie – perhaps it was even more bitter – than what we are fond of calling antithetically the real troubles of mature life. 'Ah, my child, you will have real troubles to fret about by-and-by,' is the consolation we have almost all of us had administered to us in our childhood, and have repeated to other children since we have been grown up. We have all of us sobbed so piteously, standing with tiny bare legs above our little socks, when we lost sight of our mother or nurse in some strange place; but we can no longer recall the poignancy of that moment and weep over it, as we do over the remembered sufferings of five or ten years ago. Every one of those keen moments has left its trace, and lives in us still, but such traces have blent themselves irrecoverably with the firmer texture of our youth and manhood; and so it comes that we can look on at the troubles of our children with a smiling disbelief in the reality of their pain. Is there any one who can recover the experience of his childhood, not merely with a memory of what he did and what happened to him, of what he liked and disliked when he was in frock and trousers, but with an intimate penetration, a revived consciousness of what he felt then – when it was so long from one midsummer to another? what he felt when his schoolfellows shut him out of their game because he would pitch the ball wrong out of mere wilfulness; or on a rainy day in the holidays, when he didn't know how to amuse himself, and fell from idleness into mischief, from mischief into defiance, and from defiance into sulkiness; or when his mother absolutely refused to let him have a tailed coat that 'half', although every other boy of his age had gone into tails already? Surely if we could recall that early bitterness, and the dim guesses, the strangely perspectiveless conception of life that gave the bitterness its intensity, we should not pooh-pooh the griefs of our children.

'Miss Maggie, you're to come down this minute,' said Kezia, entering the room hurriedly. 'Lawks! what have you been a-doing? I niver *see* such a fright.'

'Don't Kezia,' said Maggie, angrily. 'Go away!'

'But I tell you, you're to come down, miss, this minute: your mother says so,' said Kezia, going up to Maggie and taking her by the hand to raise her from the floor.

'Get away, Kezia; I don't want any dinner,' said Maggie, resisting Kezia's arm. 'I shan't come.'

'Oh, well, I can't stay. I've got to wait at dinner,' said Kezia, going out again.

'Maggie, you little silly,' said Tom, peeping into the room ten minutes after, 'why don't you come and have your dinner? There's lots o' goodies, and mother says you're to come. What are you crying for, you little spooney?'

Oh, it was dreadful! Tom was so hard and unconcerned; if *he* had been crying on the floor, Maggie would have cried too. And there was the dinner, so nice; and she was *so* hungry. It was very bitter.

But Tom was not altogether hard. He was not inclined to cry, and did not feel that Maggie's grief spoiled his prospect of the sweets; but he went and put his head near her, and said in a lower, comforting tone, 'Won't you come, then, Magsie? Shall I bring you a bit o' pudding when I've had mine? . . . And a custard and things?'

'Ye-e-es,' said Maggie, beginning to feel life a little more tolerable.

'Very well,' said Tom, going away. But he turned again at the door and said, 'But you'd better come, you know. There's the dessert – nuts, you know – and cowslip wine.'

Maggie's tears had ceased, and she looked reflective as Tom left her. His good nature had taken off the keenest edge of her suffering, and nuts with cowslip wine began to assert their legitimate influence.

Slowly she rose from amongst her scattered locks, and slowly she made her way downstairs. Then she stood leaning with one shoulder against the frame of the dining-parlour door, peeping in when it was ajar. She saw Tom and Lucy with an empty chair between them, and there were the custards on a side-table – it was too much. She slipped in and went towards the empty chair. But she had no sooner sat down than she repented, and wished herself back again.

Mrs Tulliver gave a little scream as she saw her, and felt such a 'turn' that she dropt the large gravy-spoon into the dish with the most serious results to the tablecloth. For Kezia had not betrayed the reason of Maggie's refusal to come down, not liking to give her mistress a shock in the moment of carving, and Mrs Tulliver thought there was nothing worse in question than a fit of perverseness, which was inflicting its own punishment by depriving Maggie of half her dinner.

Mrs Tulliver's scream made all eyes turn towards the same point as her own, and Maggie's cheeks and ears began to burn, while Uncle Glegg, a kind-looking, white-haired old gentleman, said, 'Heyday! What little gell's this – why, I don't know her. Is it some little gell you've picked up in the road, Kezia?'

'Why, she's gone and cut her hair herself,' said Mr Tulliver in an undertone to Mr Deane, laughing with much enjoyment. 'Did you ever know such a little hussy as it is?'

'Why, little miss, you've made yourself look very funny,' said Uncle Pullet, and perhaps he never in his life made an observation which was felt to be so lacerating.

'Fie, for shame!' said Aunt Glegg, in her loudest, severest tone of reproof. 'Little gells as cut their own hair should be whipped and fed on bread and water – not come and sit down with their aunts and uncles.'

'Ay ay,' said Uncle Glegg, meaning to give a playful turn to this denunciation, 'she must be sent to jail, I think, and they'll cut the rest of her hair off there, and make it all even.'

'She's more like a gypsy nor ever,' said Aunt Pullet, in a pitying tone; 'It's very bad luck, sister, as the gell should be so brown – the boy's fair enough. I doubt it'll stand in her way i' life to be so brown.'

'She's a naughty child, as'll break her mother's heart,' said Mrs Tulliver, with the tears in her eyes.

Maggie seemed to be listening to a chorus of reproach and derision. Her first flush came from anger, which gave her a transient power of defiance, and Tom thought she was braving it out, supported by the recent appearance of the pudding and custard. Under this impression, he whispered, 'Oh my! Maggie, I told you you'd catch it.' He meant to be friendly, but Maggie felt convinced that Tom was rejoicing in her ignominy. Her feeble power of defiance left her in an instant, her heart swelled, and, getting up from her chair, she ran to her father, hid her face on his shoulder, and burst out into loud sobbing.

'Come, come, my wench,' said her father soothingly, putting his arm round her, 'never mind; you was i' the right to cut it off if it plagued you; give over crying: Father'll take your part.'

Delicious words of tenderness! Maggie never forgot any of these moments when her father 'took her part'; she kept them in her heart, and thought of them long years after, when everyone else said that her father had done very ill by his children.

'How your husband does spoil that child, Bessy!' said Mrs Glegg, in a loud 'aside' to Mrs Tulliver. 'It'll be the ruin of her, if you don't take care. *My* father niver brought his children up so, else we should ha' been a different sort o' family to what we are.'

Mrs Tulliver's domestic sorrows seemed at this moment to have reached the point at which insensibility begins. She took no notice of her sister's remark, but threw back her cap-strings and dispensed the pudding, in mute resignation.

Plaits

Tabitha Tuckett (age 14)

When I was small my mother did my hair
While I stood in the study, obedient,
Rehearsing foreign words encoded on the spines of books,
Taking a view of the landscaped room.
Its ornamental light dulled by real morning on
Firm hills of history and letters round me;
The favoured lake of recent books, piled and reflected by black
    marble;

Creeping art and green poetry growing with me up the walls.
I chanted titles off; she plaited down my hair;
Neatly tied up I'm launched upon the world.

*Dore	*Stoneware and Porcelain
Modigliani, Sacred	Imitations, Life Studies
Circles,	Wallace Stevens
Dore, Modigliani	Stoneware, Porcelain
Scared Circles	Imitations, Life Studies
Monet at	Turner Sketches
Giverny	A Writer's Journal
Duckworth	Richard

Ortega y Gasset	Jefferies
Missing	Animals in Art
Persons	Arms and Armour
Dodds, Phaidon	Playing
Frozen Tombs	Cards
Tibetan Carpets	Unease and Angels
The Word as Image	The Word as Image

Now I plait my own hair
And it's a darker tone;
Daily scales fast; no shelved music;
I read my own books, silent and private;
Gravely I watch my self's reflected flicker past my face;
Late, every morning, I upbraid myself.

*These two plaits are meant to be read simultaneously by two voices.

Jo Meets Apollyon
Louisa M. Alcott

(from Little Women)

'Girls, where are you going?' asked Amy, coming into their room one Saturday afternoon, and finding them getting ready to go out, with an air of secrecy which excited her curiosity.

'Never mind; little girls shouldn't ask questions,' returned Jo sharply.

Now if there *is* anything mortifying to our feelings, when we are young, it is to be told that; and to be bidden to 'run away, dear', is still more trying to us. Amy bridled up at this insult, and determined to find out the secret, if she teased for an hour. Turning to Meg, who never refused her anything very long, she said coaxingly, 'Do tell me! I should think you might let me go, too; for Beth is fussing over her dolls, and I haven't got anything to do, and am *so* lonely.'

'I can't, dear, because you aren't invited,' began Meg; but Jo broke in impatiently, 'Now, Meg, be quiet, or you will spoil it all. You can't go, Amy; so don't be a baby, and whine about it.'

'You are going somewhere with Laurie, I know you are; you were whispering and laughing together, on the sofa, last night, and you stopped when I came in. Aren't you going with him?'

'Yes, we are; now be still, and stop bothering.' Amy held her tongue, but used her eyes, and saw Meg slip a fan into her pocket.

'I know! I know! You're going to the theatre to see *The Seven Castles!*' she cried, 'and I *shall* go, for Mother said I might see it; and I've got my rag-money, and it was mean not to tell me in time.'

'Just listen to me a minute, and be a good child,' said Meg soothingly. 'Mother doesn't wish you to go this week, because your eyes are not well enough yet to bear the light of this fairy piece. Next week you can go with Beth and Hannah, and have a nice time.'

'I don't like that half so well as going with you and Laurie. Please let me; I've been sick with this cold so long, and shut up, I'm dying for some fun. Do, Meg! I'll be ever so good,' pleaded Amy.

'Suppose we take her? I don't believe Mother would mind, if we bundled her up well,' began Meg.

'If *she* goes, *I* shan't; and if I don't Laurie won't like it; and it will be very rude, after he invited only us, to go and drag in Amy. I should think she'd hate to poke herself where she isn't wanted,' said Jo crossly, for she disliked the trouble of over-seeing a fidgety child, when she wanted to enjoy herself.

Her tone and manner angered Amy, who began to put her

boots on, saying, in her most aggravating way, 'I *shall* go; Meg says I may; and if I pay for myself, Laurie hasn't anything to do with it.'

'You can't sit with us, for our seats are reserved, and you mustn't sit alone; so Laurie will give you his place, and that will spoil our pleasure; or he'll get another seat for you, and that isn't proper, when you weren't asked. You shan't stir a step; so you may just stay where you are,' scolded Jo, crosser than ever, having just pricked her finger in her hurry.

Sitting on the floor, with one boot on, Amy began to cry, and Meg to reason with her, when Laurie called from below, and the two girls hurried down, leaving their sister wailing; for now and then she forgot her grown-up ways, and acted like a spoilt child. Just as the party was setting out, Amy called over the banisters, in a threatening tone, 'You'll be sorry for this, Jo March! see if you ain't.'

'Fiddlesticks!' returned Jo, slamming the door.

They had a charming time, for *The Seven Castles of the Diamond Lake* was as brilliant and wonderful as heart could wish. But, in spite of the comical red imps, sparkling elves, and gorgeous princes and princesses, Jo's pleasure had a drop of bitterness in it; the fairy queen's yellow curls reminded her of Amy; and between the acts she amused herself with wondering what her sister would do to make her 'sorry for it'. She and Amy had had many lively skirmishes in the course of their lives, for both had quick tempers, and were apt to be violent when fairly roused. Amy teased Jo, and Jo irritated Amy, and semi-occasional explosions occurred, of which both were much ashamed afterwards. Although the oldest, Jo had the least self-control, and had hard times trying to curb the fiery spirit which was continually getting her into trouble; her anger never lasted long, and, having humbly confessed her fault, she sincerely repented, and tried to do better. Her sisters used to say that they rather liked to get Jo into a fury, because she was such an angel afterwards. Poor Jo tried desperately to be good, but her bosom enemy was always ready to flame up and defeat her; and it took years of patient effort to subdue it.

When they got home, they found Amy reading in the parlour. She assumed an injured air as they came in; never lifted her eyes from her book, or asked a single question. Perhaps curiosity might have conquered resentment if Beth had not been there to inquire, and receive a glowing description of the play. On going up to put away her best hat, Jo's first look was towards the bureau; for, in their last quarrel, Amy had soothed her feelings by turning Jo's top drawer upside down, on the floor. Everything was in its place, however; and after a hasty glance into her various closets, bags, and boxes, Jo decided that Amy had forgiven and forgotten her wrongs.

There Jo was mistaken; for next day she made a discovery which produced a tempest. Meg, Beth, and Amy were sitting together, late in the afternoon, when Jo burst into the room, looking excited, and demanding breathlessly, 'Has anyone taken my story?'

Meg and Beth said 'No,' at once, and looked surprised; Amy poked the fire. Jo saw her colour rise, and was down upon her in a minute.

'Amy, you've got it!'

'No, I haven't!'

'You know where it is, then!'

'No, I don't.'

'That's a fib!' cried Jo, taking her by the shoulders, and looking fierce enough to frighten a much braver child than Amy.

'It isn't. I haven't got it, don't know where it is now, and don't care.'

'You know something about it, and you'd better tell at once,

134

or I'll make you,' and Jo gave her a slight shake.

'Scold as much as you like, you'll never get your silly old story again,' cried Amy, getting excited in her turn.

'Why not?'

'I burnt it up.'

'What! My little book I was so fond of, and worked over, and meant to finish before Father got home? Have you really burnt it?' said Jo, turning very pale, while her eyes kindled and her hands clutched Amy.

'Yes, I did! I told you I'd make you pay for being so cross yesterday, and I have, so – '

Amy got no further, for Jo's hot temper mastered her, and she shook Amy till her teeth chattered in her head; crying, in a passion of anger, 'You wicked, wicked girl! I never can write it again, and I'll never forgive you as long as I live.'

Meg flew to rescue Amy, and Beth to pacify Jo, but Jo was quite beside herself; and, with a parting box on her sister's ear, she rushed out of the room up to the old sofa in the garret, and finished her fight alone.

The storm cleared up below, for Mrs March came home, and, having heard the story, soon brought Amy to a sense of the wrong she had done her sister. Jo's book was the pride of her heart, and was regarded by her family as a literary sprout of great promise. It was only half a dozen little fairy tales, but Jo had worked over them patiently, putting her whole heart into her work, hoping to make something good enough to print. She had just copied them with great care, and had destroyed the old manuscript, so that Amy's bonfire had consumed the loving work of several years. It seemed a small loss to others, but to Jo it was a dreadful calamity, and she felt that it never could be made up to her. Beth mourned as for a departed kitten, and Meg refused to defend her pet; Mrs March looked grave and grieved, and Amy felt that no one would love her till she had asked pardon for the act which she now regretted more than any of them.

When the tea-bell rang, Jo appeared, looking so grim and unapproachable that it took all Amy's courage to say meekly, 'Please forgive me, Jo; I'm very sorry.'

'I never shall forgive you,' was Jo's stern answer; and, from that moment, she ignored Amy entirely.

No one spoke of the great trouble – not even Mrs March – for all had learned by experience that when Jo was in that mood words were wasted; and the wisest course was to wait till some little accident, or her own generous nature, softened Jo's resentment, and healed the breach. It was not a happy evening; for, though they sewed as usual, while their mother read aloud from Bremer, Scott, or Edgeworth, something was wanting, and the sweet home-peace was disturbed. They felt this most when singing-time came, and Amy broke down. So Meg and mother sang alone. But, in spite of their efforts to be as cheery as larks, the flute-like voices did not seem to chord as well as usual, and all felt out of tune.

As Jo received her good-night kiss, Mrs March whispered gently, 'My dear, don't let the sun go down upon your anger; forgive each other, help each other, and begin again tomorrow.'

Jo wanted to lay her head down on that motherly bosom and cry her grief and anger all away; but tears were an unmanly weakness, and she felt so deeply injured that she really *couldn't* quite forgive yet. So she winked hard, shook her head and said, gruffly, because Amy was listening, 'It was an abominable thing, and she don't deserve to be forgiven.'

With that she marched off to bed, and there was no merry or confidential gossip that night.

Amy was much offended that her overtures of peace had been repulsed, and began to wish she had not humbled herself, to feel more injured than ever, and to plume herself on her superior virtue in a way which was particularly exasperating. Jo still looked like a thunder-cloud, and nothing went well all day. It was bitter cold in the morning; she dropped her precious turnover in the gutter, Aunt March had an attack of fidgets, Meg was pensive, Beth *would* look grieved and wistful when she got home, and Amy kept making remarks about people who were always talking about being good, and yet wouldn't try, when other people set them a virtuous example.

'Everybody is so hateful, I'll ask Laurie to go skating. He is always kind and jolly, and will put me to rights, I know,' said Jo to herself, and off she went.

Amy heard the clash of skates, and looked out with an impatient exclamation. 'There! She promised I should go next time, for this is the last ice we shall have. But it is no use to ask such a cross-patch to take me.'

'Don't say that; you *were* very naughty, and it *is* hard to forgive the loss of her precious little book; but I think she might do it now, and I guess she will, if you try her at the right minute,' said Meg. 'Go after them; don't say anything till Jo has got good-natured with Laurie, then take a quiet minute, and just kiss her, or do some kind thing, and I'm sure she'll be friends again, with all her heart.'

'I'll try,' said Amy, for the advice suited her; and, after a flurry to get ready, she ran after the friends, who were just disappearing over the hill.

It was not far to the river, but both were ready before Amy reached them. Jo saw her coming, and turned her back; Laurie did not see, for he was carefully skating along the shore, sounding the ice, for a warm spell had preceded the cold snap.

'I'll go on to the first bend, and see if it's all right, before we begin to race,' Amy heard him say, as he shot away, looking like a young Russian, in his fur-trimmed coat and cap.

Jo heard Amy panting after her run, stamping her feet, and

blowing her fingers, as she tried to put her skates on; but Jo never turned, and went slowly zigzagging down the river, taking a bitter, unhappy sort of satisfaction in her sister's troubles. She had cherished her anger till it grew strong, and took possession of her, as evil thoughts and feelings always do, unless cast out at once. As Laurie turned the bend, he shouted back, 'Keep near the shore; it isn't safe in the middle.'

Jo heard, but Amy was just struggling to her feet, and did not catch a word. Jo glanced over her shoulder, and the little demon she was harbouring said in her ear, 'No matter whether she heard or not; let her take care of herself.'

Laurie had vanished round the bend; Jo was just at the turn, and Amy, far behind, striking out towards the smoother ice in the middle of the river. For a minute Jo stood still, with a strange feeling at her heart; then she resolved to go on, but something held and turned her round, just in time to see Amy throw up her hands and go down, with the sudden crash of rotten ice, the splash of water and a cry that made Jo's heart stand still with fear. She tried to call Laurie, but her voice was gone; she tried to rush forward, but her feet seemed to have no strength in them; and, for a second, she could only stand motionless, staring, with a terror-stricken face, at the little blue hood above the black water. Something rushed swiftly by her, and Laurie's voice called out, 'Bring a rail; quick, quick!'

How she did it she never knew, but for the next few minutes she worked as if possessed, blindly obeying Laurie, who was quite self-possessed, and, lying flat, held Amy up by his arm and hockey, till Jo dragged a rail from the fence, and together they got the child out, more frightened than hurt.

'Now then, we must walk her home as fast as we can; pile our things on her, while I get off these confounded skates,' cried Laurie, wrapping his coat round Amy, and tugging away at the straps.

Shivering, dripping, and crying, they got Amy home; and, after an exciting time of it, she fell asleep, rolled in blankets, before a hot fire. During the bustle Jo had scarcely spoken, but flown about, looking pale and wild, with her things half off, her dress torn, and her hands cut and bruised by ice, and rails, and refractory buckles. When Amy was comfortably asleep, the house quiet, and Mrs March sitting by the bed, she called Jo to her, and began to bind up the hurt hands.

'Are you sure she is safe?' whispered Jo, looking remorsefully at the golden head, which might have been swept away from her sight for ever, under the treacherous ice.

'Quite safe, dear; she is not hurt, and won't even take cold, I think; you were so sensible in covering and getting her home quickly,' replied her mother cheerfully.

'Laurie did it all; I only let her go. Mother, if she *should* die, it would be my fault,' and Jo dropped down beside the bed, in a passion of penitent tears, telling all that had happened, bitterly condemning her hardness of heart, and sobbing out her gratitude for being spared the heavy punishment which might have come upon her.

'It's my dreadful temper! I try to cure it; I think I have, and then it breaks out worse than ever. Oh, Mother! What shall I do?' cried poor Jo, in despair.

'Watch and pray, dear; never get tired of trying, and never think it is impossible to conquer your fault,' said Mrs March, drawing the blowzy head to her shoulder, and kissing the wet cheek so tenderly, that Jo cried harder than ever.

'You don't know; you can't guess how bad it is! It seems as if I could do anything when I'm in a passion; I get so savage, I could hurt anyone, and enjoy it. I'm afraid I *shall* do something dreadful someday, and spoil my life, and make everybody hate me. Oh, Mother! Help me, do help me!'

'I will, my child; I will. Don't cry so bitterly, but remember this day, and resolve, with all your soul, that you will never know another like it. Jo, dear, we all have our temptations, some far greater than yours, and it often takes us all our lives to conquer them. You think your temper is the worst in the world, but mine used to be just like it.'

'Yours, Mother? Why, you are never angry!' and, for a moment, Jo forgot remorse in surprise.

'I've been trying to cure it for forty years, and have only succeeded in controlling it. I am angry nearly every day of my life, Jo; but I have learned not to show it; and I still hope to learn not to feel it, though it may take me another forty years to do so.'

The patience and the humility of the face she loved so well was a better lesson to Jo than the wisest lecture, the sharpest reproof. She felt comforted at once by the sympathy and confidence given her; the knowledge that her mother had a fault like hers, and tried to mend it, made her own easier to bear, and strengthened her resolution to cure it, though forty years seemed rather a long time to watch and pray to a girl of fifteen.

'Mother, are you angry when you fold your lips tight together, and go out of the room sometimes, when Aunt March scolds, or people worry you?' asked Jo, feeling nearer and dearer to her mother than ever before.

'Yes; I've learned to check the hasty words that rise to my lips, and when I feel that they mean to break out against my will, I just go away a minute, and give myself a little shake, for being so weak and wicked,' answered Mrs March, with a sigh and a smile, as she smoothed and fastened up Jo's dishevelled hair.

'How did you learn to keep still? That is what troubles me – for the sharp words fly out before I know what I'm about; and the more I say the worse I get, till it's a pleasure to hurt people's feelings, and say dreadful things. Tell me how you do it, Marmee, dear.'

'My good mother used to help me – '

'As you do us,' interrupted Jo, with a grateful kiss.

'But I lost her when I was a little older than you are, and for years had to struggle on alone, for I was too proud to confess my weakness to anyone else. I had a hard time, Jo, and shed a good many bitter tears over my failures; for, in spite of my efforts, I never seemed to get on. Then your father came, and I was so happy that I found it easy to be good. But by-and-by, when I had four little daughters round me, and we were poor, then the old trouble began again; for I am not patient by nature, and it tried me very much to see my children wanting anything.'

'Poor Mother! What helped you then?'

'Your father, Jo. He never loses patience, never doubts or complains, but always hopes, and works, and waits so cheerfully, that one is ashamed to do otherwise before him. He helped and comforted me, and showed me that I must try to practise all the virtues I would have my little girls possess, for I was their example. It was easier to try for your sakes than for my own; a startled or surprised look from one of you, when I spoke sharply, rebuked me more than any words could have done; and the love, respect, and confidence of my children was the sweetest reward I could receive for my efforts to be the woman I would have them copy.'

'Oh, Mother! If I'm ever half as good as you, I shall be satisfied,' cried Jo, much touched.

'I hope you will be a great deal better, dear; but you must keep watch over your "bosom enemy", as Father calls it, or it may sadden, if not spoil, your life. You have had a warning; remember it, and try with heart and soul to master this quick temper, before it brings you greater sorrow and regret than you have known today.'

'I will try, Mother; I truly will. But you must help me, remind me, and keep me from flying out. I used to see Father sometimes put his finger on his lips, and look at you with a very kind but sober face; and you always folded your lips tight, or went away. Was he reminding you then?' asked Jo softly.

'Yes; I asked him to help me so, and he never forgot it, but saved me from many a sharp word by that little gesture and kind look.'

Jo saw that her mother's eyes filled, and her lips trembled, as she spoke, and, fearing that she had said too much, she whispered anxiously, 'Was it wrong to watch you, and to speak of it? I didn't mean to be rude, but it's so comfortable to say all I think to you, and feel so safe and happy here.'

'My Jo, you may say anything to your mother, for it is my greatest happiness and pride to feel that my girls confide in me, and know how much I love them.'

'I thought I'd grieved you.'

'No, dear; but speaking of Father reminded me how much I miss him, how much I owe him, and how faithfully I should watch and work to keep his little daughters safe and good for him.'

'Yet you told him to go, Mother, and didn't cry when he went, and never complain now, or seem as if you needed any help,' said Jo, wondering.

'I gave my best to the country I love, and kept my tears till he was gone. Why should I complain, when we both have merely done our duty, and will surely be the happier for it in the end? If I don't seem to need help, it is because I have a better friend even than Father to comfort and sustain me. My child, the troubles and temptations of your life are beginning, and may be many; but you can overcome and outlive them all, if you learn to feel the strength and tenderness of your

Heavenly Father as you do that of your earthly one. The more you love and trust Him, the nearer you will feel to Him, and the less you will depend on human power and wisdom. His love and care never tire or change, can never be taken from you, but may become the source of life-long peace, happiness, and strength. Believe this heartily, and go to God with all your little cares, and hopes, and sins, and sorrows, as freely and confidingly as you come to your mother.'

Jo's only answer was to hold her mother close, and, in the silence which followed, the sincerest prayer she had ever prayed left her heart, without words; for in that sad, yet happy hour, she had learned not only the bitterness of remorse and despair, but the sweetness of self-denial and self-control; and, led by her mother's hand, she had drawn nearer to the Friend who welcomes every child with a love stronger than that of any father, tenderer than that of any mother.

Amy stirred, and sighed in her sleep; and, as if eager to begin at once to mend her fault, Jo looked up with an expression on her face which it had never worn before.

'I let the sun go down on my anger; I wouldn't forgive her, and today, if it hadn't been for Laurie, it might have been too late! How could I have been so wicked?' said Jo, half aloud, as she leaned over her sister.

As if she heard, Amy opened her eyes, and held out her arms, with a smile that went straight to Jo's heart. Neither said a word, but they hugged one another close, in spite of the blankets, and everything was forgiven and forgotten in one hearty kiss.

Charlotte, Her Book
Elizabeth Bartlett

I am Charlotte. I don't say hello
to people and sometimes I bite.
Although I am dead I still jump
out of bed and wake them up at night.

This is my mother. Her hair is blue
and I have drawn her with no eyes
and arms like twigs. I don't do
what I'm told and I tell lies.

This is my father. He has a mouth
under his left ear. I'm fed up
with drawing people, so I scribble
smoke and cover his head right up.

I am a brat kid, fostered out because
my mother is sick in the head,
and I would eat her if I could,
and make her good and dead.

Although I am only four I went away
so soon they hardly knew me,
and stars sprang out of my eyes,
and cold winds blew me.

My mother always says she loves me.
My father says he loves me too.
I love Charlotte. A car ran
over Charlotte. This is her book.

Warning

Jenny Joseph

When I am an old woman I shall wear purple
With a red hat which doesn't go, and doesn't suit me,
And I shall spend my pension on brandy and summer
  gloves
And satin sandals, and say we've no money for butter.
I shall sit down on the pavement when I'm tired
And gobble up samples in shops and press alarm bells
And run my stick along the public railings
And make up for the sobriety of my youth.
I shall go out in my slippers in the rain
And pick the flowers in other people's gardens
And learn to spit.

You can wear terrible shirts and grow more fat
And eat three pounds of sausages at a go
Or only bread and pickle for a week
And hoard pens and pencils and beermats and things in
  boxes.

But now we must have clothes that keep us dry
And pay our rent and not swear in the street
And set a good example for the children.
We will have friends to dinner and read the papers.
But maybe I ought to practice a little now?
So people who know me are not too shocked and
  surprised
When suddenly I am old and start to wear purple.

from Vanity Fair
William Thackeray

While the present century was in its teens, and on one sun-shiny morning in June, there drove up to the great iron gate of Miss Pinkerton's academy for young ladies, on Chiswick Mall, a large family coach, with two fat horses in blazing harness, driven by a fat coachman in a three-cornered hat and wig, at the rate of four miles an hour. A black servant, who reposed on the box beside the fat coachman, uncurled his bandy legs as soon as the equipage drew up opposite Miss Pinkerton's shining brass plate, and, as he pulled the bell, at least a score of young heads were seen peering out of the narrow windows of the stately old brick house. Nay, the acute observer might have recognized the little red nose of good-natured Miss Jemima Pinkerton herself, rising over some geranium pots in the window of that lady's own drawing room.

'It is Mrs Sedley's coach, Sister,' said Miss Jemima. 'Sambo, the black servant, has just rung the bell; and the coachman has a new red waistcoat.'

'Have you completed all the necessary preparations incident to Miss Sedley's departure, Miss Jemima?' asked Miss Pinkerton herself, that majestic lady – the Semiramis of Hammersmith, the friend of Doctor Johnson, the correspon-dent of Mrs Chapone herself.

'The girls were up at four this morning, packing her trunks, Sister,' replied Miss Jemima; 'we have made her a bow-pot.'

'Say a bouquet, Sister Jemima; 'tis more genteel.'

'Well, a booky as big almost as a haystack; I have put up two bottles of the gillyflower-water for Mrs Sedley, and the receipt for making it, in Amelia's box.'

'And I trust, Miss Jemima, you have made a copy of Miss Sedley's account. This is it, is it? Very good – ninety-three pounds, four shillings. Be kind enough to address it to John Sedley, Esquire, and to seal this billet which I have written to his lady.'

In Miss Jemima's eyes an autograph letter of her sister, Miss Pinkerton, was an object of as deep veneration as would have been a letter from a sovereign. Only when her pupils quitted the establishment, or when they were about to be married, and once, when poor Miss Birch died of the scarlet fever, was Miss Pinkerton known to write personally to the parents of her pupils; and it was Jemima's opinion that if anything *could* console Mrs Birch for her daughter's loss, it would be that pious and eloquent composition in which Miss Pinkerton announced the event.

In the present instance Miss Pinkerton's 'billet' was to the following effect:

THE MALL, CHISWICK,
June 15, 18—.

MADAM – After her six years' residence at the Mall, I have the honour and happiness of presenting Miss Amelia Sedley to her parents, as a young lady not un-worthy to occupy a fitting position in their polished and refined circle. Those virtues which characterize the young English gentlewoman, those accomplishments which become her birth and station, will not be found wanting in the amiable Miss Sedley, whose *industry* and *obedience* have endeared her to her instructors, and whose delight-ful sweetness of temper has charmed her *aged* and her *youthful* companions.

In music, in dancing, in orthography, in every variety of embroidery and needlework, she will be found to have realized her friends' *fondest wishes*. In geography there is still much to be desired; and a careful and undeviating use of the backboard, for four hours daily during the next three years, is recommended as necessary to the acquirement of that dignified *deportment* and *carriage* so requisite for every young lady of *fashion*.

In the principles of religion and morality, Miss Sedley will be found worthy of an establishment which has been honoured by the presence of *The Great Lexicographer*, and the patronage of the admirable Mrs Chapone.

In leaving the Mall, Miss Amelia carries with her the hearts of her companions, and the affectionate regards of her mistress, who has the honour to subscribe herself,

Madam,

Your most obliged humble servant,

BARBARA PINKERTON.

P.S. – Miss Sharp accompanies Miss Sedley. It is particularly requested that Miss Sharp's stay in Russell Square may not exceed ten days. The family of distinction with whom she is engaged desire to avail themselves of her services as soon as possible.

This letter completed, Miss Pinkerton proceeded to write her own name and Miss Sedley's in the fly-leaf of a Johnson's Dictionary – the interesting work which she invariably presented to her scholars on their departure from the Mall. On the cover was inserted a copy of 'Lines addressed to a young lady on quitting Miss Pinkerton's school, at the Mall; by the late revered Doctor Samuel Johnson'. In fact, the Lexicographer's name was always on the lips of this majestic woman, and a visit he had paid to her was the cause of her reputation and her fortune.

Being commanded by her elder sister to get 'the Dictionary' from the cupboard, Miss Jemima had extracted two copies of the book from the receptacle in question. When Miss Pinkerton had finished the inscription in the first, Jemima, with rather a dubious and timid air, handed her the second.

'For whom is this, Miss Jemima?' said Miss Pinkerton, with awful coldness.

'For Becky Sharp,' answered Jemima, trembling very much, and blushing over her withered face and neck, as she turned her back on her sister – 'for Becky Sharp: she's going too.'

'MISS JEMIMA!' exclaimed Miss Pinkerton, in the largest capitals. 'Are you in your senses? Replace the Dictionary in the closet, and never venture to take such a liberty in future.'

'Well, Sister, it's only two-and-ninepence, and poor Becky will be miserable if she don't get one.'

'Send Miss Sedley instantly to me,' said Miss Pinkerton. And so venturing not to say another word, poor Jemima trotted off, exceedingly flurried and nervous.

Miss Sedley's papa was a merchant in London, and a man of some wealth; whereas Miss Sharp was an articled pupil, for whom Miss Pinkerton had done, as she thought, quite enough, without conferring upon her at parting the high honour of the Dictionary.

Although schoolmistresses' letters are to be trusted no more or less than churchyard epitaphs; yet, as it sometimes happens that a person departs this life who is really deserving of all the praises the stone-cutter carves over his bones; who *is* a good Christian, a good parent, child, wife, or husband; who actually *does* leave a disconsolate family to mourn his loss; so in academies of the male and female sex it occurs every now and then that the pupil is fully worthy of the praises bestowed by the disinterested instructor. Now, Miss Amelia Sedley was a young lady of this singular species, and deserved not only all that Miss Pinkerton said in her praise, but had many charming qualities which that pompous old Minerva of a woman could not see, from the differences of rank and age between her pupil and herself.

For she could not only sing like a lark, or a Mrs Billington, and dance like Hillisberg or Parisot, and embroider beautifully, and spell as well as the Dictionary itself, but she had such a kindly, smiling, tender, gentle, generous heart of her own, as won the love of everybody who came near her, from Minerva herself down to the poor girl in the scullery, and the one-eyed tart-woman's daughter, who was permitted to vend her wares once a week to the young ladies in the Mall.

She had twelve intimate and bosom friends out of the twenty-four young ladies. Even envious Miss Briggs never spoke ill of her; high and mighty Miss Saltire (Lord Dexter's granddaughter) allowed that her figure was genteel; and as for Miss Swartz, the rich, woolly haired mulatto from St Kitts, on the day Amelia went away, she was in such a passion of tears that they were obliged to send for Dr Floss, and half tipsify her with sal-volatile.

Miss Pinkerton's attachment was, as may be supposed, from the high position and eminent virtues of that lady, calm and dignified; but Miss Jemima had already blubbered several times at the idea of Amelia's departure, and, but for fear of her sister, would have gone off in downright hysterics, like the heiress (who paid double) of St Kitts. Such luxury of grief, however, is only allowed to parlour-boarders. Honest Jemima had all the bills, and the washing, and the mending, and the puddings, and the plate and crockery, and the servants to superintend. But why speak about her? It is probable that we shall not hear of her again from this moment to the end of time, and that when the great filigree iron gates are once closed on her, she and her awful sister will never issue therefrom into this little world of history.

But as we are to see a great deal of Amelia, there is no harm in saying at the outset of our acquaintance that she was one of the best and dearest creatures that ever lived; and a great mercy it is, both in life and in novels, which (and the latter especially) abound in villains of the most sombre sort, that we are to have for a constant companion so guileless and good-natured a person. As she is not a heroine, there is no need to describe her person; indeed I am afraid that her nose was rather short than otherwise, and her cheeks a great deal too round and red for a heroine; but her face blushed with rosy health, and her lips with the freshest of smiles, and she had a pair of eyes, which sparkled with the brightest and honestest good-humour, except indeed when they filled with tears, and that was a great deal too often; for the silly thing would cry over a dead canary-bird, or over a mouse, that the cat haply had seized upon, or over the end of a novel, were it ever so stupid; and as for saying an unkind word to her, were any one hard-hearted enough to do so – why, so much the worse for them. Even Miss Pinkerton, that austere and godlike woman, ceased scolding her after the first time, and though she no more comprehended sensibility than she did Algebra, gave all masters and teachers particular orders to treat Miss Sedley with the utmost gentleness, as harsh treatment was injurious to her.

So that when the day of departure came, between her two customs of laughing and crying, Miss Sedley was greatly puzzled how to act. She was glad to go home, and yet most woefully sad at leaving school. For three days before, little Laura Martin, the orphan, followed her about, like a little dog. She had to make and receive at least fourteen presents, to make fourteen solemn promises of writing every week: 'Send my letters under cover to my grandpapa, the Earl of Dexter,' said Miss Saltire (who, by the way, was rather shabby): 'Never mind the postage, but write every day, you dear darling,' said the impetuous and woolly headed, but generous and affectionate Miss Swartz; and little Laura Martin (who was just in round hand) took her friend's hand and said, looking up in her face wistfully, 'Amelia, when I write to you I shall call you Mamma.' All which details, I have no doubt, Jones, who reads this book at his Club, will pronounce to be excessively foolish, trivial, twaddling, and ultra-sentimental. Yes; I can see Jones at this minute (rather flushed with his joint of mutton and half-pint of wine), taking out his pencil and scoring under the words 'foolish', 'twaddling', etc., and adding to them his own remark of '*quite true*'. Well, he is a lofty man of genius, and admires the great and heroic in life and novels; and so had better take warning and go elsewhere.

Well, then. The flowers, and the presents, and the trunks, and bonnet-boxes of Miss Sedley having been arranged by Mr Sambo in the carriage, together with a very small and weather-beaten old cow's-skin trunk with Miss Sharp's card neatly nailed upon it, which was delivered by Sambo with a grin, and packed by the coachman with a corresponding sneer – the hour for parting came; and the grief of that moment was considerably lessened by the admirable discourse which Miss Pinkerton addressed to her pupil. Not that the parting speech caused Amelia to philosophize, or that it armed her in any way with a calmness, the result of argument; but it was intolerably dull, pompous, and tedious; and, having the fear of her school-mistress greatly before her eyes, Miss Sedley did not venture, in her presence, to give way to any ebullitions of private grief. A seed-cake and a bottle of wine were produced in the drawing room, as on the solemn occasions of the visit of parents, and these refreshments being partaken of, Miss Sedley was at liberty to depart.

'You'll go in and say goodbye to Miss Pinkerton, Becky?' said Miss Jemima to a young lady of whom nobody took any notice, and who was coming down stairs with her own band-box.

'I suppose I must,' said Miss Sharp calmly, and much to the wonder of Miss Jemima; and the latter having knocked at the door, and receiving permission to come in, Miss Sharp advanced in a very unconcerned manner, and said in French, and with a perfect accent, *'Mademoiselle, je viens vous faire mes adieux.'*

Miss Pinkerton did not understand French; she only directed those who did: but biting her lips and throwing up her venerable and Roman-nosed head (on the top of which figured a large and solemn turban), she said, 'Miss Sharp, I wish you a good morning.' As the Hammersmith Semiramis spoke, she waved one hand both by way of adieu, and to give Miss Sharp an opportunity of shaking one of the fingers of the hand which was left out for that purpose.

Miss Sharp only folded her own hands with a very frigid smile and bow, and quite declined to accept the proffered honour; on which Semiramis tossed up her turban more in-dignantly than ever. In fact, it was a little battle between the young lady and the old one, and the latter was worsted. 'Heaven bless you, my child,' said she, embracing Amelia, and scowling the while over the girl's shoulder at Miss Sharp.

'Come away, Becky,' said Miss Jemima, pulling the young woman away in great alarm, and the drawing room door closed upon them for ever.

Then came the struggle and parting below. Words refuse to tell it. All the servants were there in the hall – all the dear friends – all the young ladies – the dancing master who had just arrived; and there was such a scuffling, and hugging, and kissing, and crying, with the hysterical *yoops* of Miss Swartz, the parlour-boarder, from her room, as no pen can depict, and as the tender heart would fain pass over. The embracing was over; they parted – that is, Miss Sedley parted from her friends. Miss Sharp had demurely entered the carriage some minutes before. Nobody cried for leaving *her*.

Sambo of the bandy legs slammed the carriage door on his young weeping mistress. He sprang up behind the carriage. 'Stop!' cried Miss Jemima, rushing to the gate with a parcel.

'It's some sandwiches, my dear,' said she to Amelia. 'You may be hungry, you know; and Becky, Becky Sharp, here's a book for you that my sister – that is, I – Johnson's Dictionary, you know; you mustn't leave us without that. Goodbye. Drive on, coachman. God bless you!'

And the kind creature retreated into the garden, overcome with emotions.

But, lo! and just as the coach drove off, Miss Sharp put her pale face out of the window, and actually flung the book back into the garden.

This almost caused Jemima to faint with terror.

'Well, I never,' said she; 'what an audacious – ' Emotion prevented her from completing either sentence. The carriage rolled away; the great gates were closed; the bell rang for the dancing lesson. The world is before the two young ladies; and so farewell to Chiswick Mall.

On Jessy Watson's Elopement
Marjory Fleming (age 7)

Run of is Jessy Watson fair
Her eyes do sparkel, she's good hair.
But Mrs Leath you shal now be
Now and for all Eternity!

A fragment from the daily Journals of Marjory Fleming (1803–11), born at Kirkcaldy and dying, perhaps of meningitis, when eight and three-quarters. Set as a task by her much-loved cousin and teacher Isabella, the Journals abound in poems, gossip, rebellious, compassionate and quite original thoughts about everything happening around her. (Naomi Lewis.)

from Jane Eyre
Charlotte Brontë

There was no possibility of taking a walk that day. We had been wandering, indeed, in the leafless shrubbery an hour in the morning; but since dinner (Mrs Reed, when there was no company, dined early) the cold winter wind had brought with it clouds so sombre, and a rain so penetrating, that further outdoor exercise was now out of the question.

I was glad of it: I never liked long walks, especially on chilly afternoons: dreadful to me was the coming home in the raw twilight, with nipped fingers and toes, and a heart saddened by the chidings of Bessie, the nurse, and humbled by the consciousness of my physical inferiority to Eliza, John, and Georgiana Reed.

The said Eliza, John, and Georgiana were now clustered round their mama in the drawing room: she lay reclined on a sofa by the fireside, and with her darlings about her (for the time neither quarrelling nor crying) looked perfectly happy. Me, she had dispensed from joining the group; saying, 'She regretted to be under the necessity of keeping me at a distance; but that until she heard from Bessie, and could discover by her own observation, that I was endeavouring in good earnest to acquire a more sociable and childlike disposition, a more attractive and sprightly manner – something lighter, franker, more natural, as it were – she really must exclude me from privileges intended only for contented, happy, little children.'

'What does Bessie say I have done?' I asked.

'Jane, I don't like cavillers or questioners; besides, there is something truly forbidding in a child taking up her elders in that manner. Be seated somewhere; and until you can speak pleasantly, remain silent.'

A small breakfast room adjoined the drawing room. I slipped in there. It contained a bookcase: I soon possessed myself of a volume, taking care that it should be one stored with pictures. I mounted into the window-seat: gathering up my feet, I sat cross-legged, like a Turk; and, having drawn the red moreen curtain nearly close, I was shrined in double retirement.

Folds of scarlet drapery shut in my view to the right hand; to the left were the clear panes of glass, protecting, but not separating me from the drear November day. At intervals, while turning over the leaves of my book, I studied the aspect of that winter afternoon. Afar, it offered a pale blank of mist and cloud; near a scene of wet lawn and storm-beat shrub, with ceaseless rain sweeping away wildly before a long and lamentable blast.

I returned to my book – Bewick's *History of British Birds*: the letterpress thereof I cared little for, generally speaking; and yet there were certain introductory pages that, child as I was, I could not pass quite as a blank. They were those which treat of the haunts of sea-fowl; of 'the solitary rocks and promontories' by them only inhabited; of the coast of Norway, studded with isles from its southern extremity, the Lindeness, or Naze, to the North Cape –

> Where the Northern Ocean, in vast whirls,
> Boils round the naked, melancholy isles

Of farthest Thule; and the Atlantic surge
Pours in among the stormy Hebrides.

Nor could I pass unnoticed the suggestion of the bleak shores of Lapland, Siberia, Spitzbergen, Nova Zembla, Iceland, Greenland, with 'the vast sweep of the Arctic Zone, and those forlorn regions of dreary space – that reservoir of frost and snow, where firm fields of ice, the accumulation of centuries of winters, glazed in Alpine heights above heights, surround the pole and concentre the multiplied rigours of extreme cold'. Of these death-white realms I formed an idea of my own: shadowy, like all the half-comprehended notions that float dim through children's brains, but strangely impressive. The words in these introductory pages connected themselves with the succeeding vignettes, and gave significance to the rock standing up alone in a sea of billow and spray; to the broken boat stranded on a desolate coast; to the cold and ghastly moon glancing through bars of cloud at a wreck just sinking.

I cannot tell what sentiment haunted the quite solitary churchyard, with its inscribed headstone; its gate, its two trees, its low horizon, girdled by a broken wall, and its newly risen crescent, attesting the hour of eventide.

The two ships becalmed on a torpid sea, I believed to be marine phantoms.

The fiend pinning down the thief's pack behind him, I passed over quickly: it was an object of terror.

So was the black horned thing seated aloof on a rock, surveying a distant crowd surrounding a gallows.

Each picture told a story; mysterious often to my undeveloped understanding and imperfect feelings, yet ever profoundly interesting: as interesting as the tales Bessie sometimes narrated on winter evenings, when she chanced to be in good humour; and when, having brought her ironing-table to the nursery hearth, she allowed us to sit about it, and while she got up Mrs Reed's lace frills, and crimped her nightcap borders, fed our eager attention with passages of love and adventure taken from old fairy tales and other ballads; or (as at a later period I discovered) from the pages of *Pamela*, and *Henry, Earl of Moreland*.

With Bewick on my knee, I was then happy: happy at least in my way. I feared nothing but interruption, and that came too soon. The breakfast-room door opened.

'Boh! Madam Mope!' cried the voice of John Reed; then he paused: he found the room apparently empty.

'Where the dickens is she!' he continued. 'Lizzy! Georgy! [calling to his sisters] Joan is not here: tell mama she is run out into the rain — bad animal!'

'It is well I drew the curtain,' thought I; and I wished fervently he might not discover my hiding-place: nor would John Reed have found it out himself; he was not quick either of vision or conception; but Eliza just put her head in at the door, and said at once, 'She is in the window-seat, to be sure, Jack.'

And I came out immediately, for I trembled at the idea of being dragged forth by the said Jack.

'What do you want?' I asked, with awkward diffidence.

'Say, "What do you want, Master Reed?"' was the answer. 'I want you to come here,' and seating himself in an armchair, he intimated by a gesture that I was to approach and stand before him.

John Reed was a schoolboy of fourteen years old; four years older than I, for I was but ten: large and stout for his age, with a dingy and unwholesome skin; thick lineaments in a spacious visage, heavy limbs and large extremities. He gorged himself habitually at table, which made him bilious, and gave him a dim and bleared eye and flabby cheeks. He ought now to have been at school; but his mama had taken him home for a month or two, 'on account of his delicate health'. Mr Miles, the master, affirmed that he would do very well if he had fewer cakes and sweetmeats sent him from home; but the mother's heart turned from an opinion so harsh, and inclined rather to the more refined idea that John's sallowness was owing to over-application and, perhaps, to pining after home.

John had not much affection for his mother and sisters, and an antipathy to me. He bullied and punished me; not two or three times in the week, nor once or twice in the day, but continually: every nerve I had feared him, and every morsel of flesh in my bones shrank when he came near. There were moments when I was bewildered by the terror he inspired, because I had no appeal whatever against either his menaces or his inflictions; the servants did not like to offend their young master by taking my part against him, and Mrs Reed was blind and deaf on the subject: she never saw him strike or heard him abuse me, though he did both now and then in her very presence, more frequently, however, behind her back.

Habitually obedient to John, I came up to his chair: he spent some three minutes in thrusting out his tongue at me as far as he could without damaging the roots: I knew he would soon strike, and while dreading the blow, I mused on the disgusting and ugly appearance of him who would presently deal it. I wonder if he read that notion in my face; for, all at once, without speaking, he struck suddenly and strongly. I tottered, and on regaining my equilibrium retired back a step or two from his chair.

'That is for your impudence in answering Mama awhile since,' he said, 'and for your sneaking way of getting behind curtains, and for the look you had in your eyes two minutes since, you rat!'

Accustomed to John Reed's abuse, I never had an idea of

replying to it; my care was how to endure the blow which would certainly follow the insult.

'What were you doing behind the curtain?' he asked.

'I was reading.'

'Show the book.'

I returned to the window and fetched it thence.

'You have no business to take our books; you are a dependant, Mama says; you have no money; your father left you none; you ought to beg, and not to live here with gentlemen's children like us, and eat the same meals we do, and wear clothes at our mama's expense. Now, I'll teach you to rummage my bookshelves: for they *are* mine; all the house belongs to me, or will do in a few years. Go and stand by the door, out of the way of the mirror and the windows.'

I did so, not at first aware what was his intention; but when I saw him lift and poise the book and stand in act to hurl it, I instinctively started aside with a cry of alarm: not soon enough, however; the volume was flung, it hit me, and I fell, striking my head against the door and cutting it. The cut bled, the pain was sharp: my terror had passed its climax; other feelings succeeded.

'Wicked and cruel boy!' I said. 'You are like a murderer – you are like a slave-driver – you are like the Roman emperors!'

I had read Goldsmith's *History of Rome*, and had formed my opinion of Nero, Caligula, etc. Also I had drawn parallels in silence, which I never thought thus to have declared aloud.

'What! what!' he cried. 'Did she say that to me? Did you hear her, Eliza and Georgiana? Won't I tell Mama? But first – '

He ran headlong at me: I felt him grasp my hair and my shoulder: he had closed with a desperate thing. I really saw in him a tyrant, a murderer. I felt a drop or two of blood from my head trickle down my neck, and was sensible of somewhat pungent suffering: these sensations for the time predominated over fear, and I received him in frantic sort. I don't very well know what I did with my hands, but he called me 'Rat! Rat!' and bellowed out aloud. Aid was near him: Eliza and Georgiana had run for Mrs Reed, who was gone upstairs: she now came upon the scene, followed by Bessie and her maid Abbot. We were parted: I heard the words, 'Dear! dear! What a fury to fly at Master John!' 'Did ever anybody see such a picture of passion!'

Then Mrs Reed subjoined. 'Take her away to the red room, and lock her in there.' Four hands were immediately laid upon me, and I was borne upstairs.

I resisted all the way: a new thing for me, and a circumstance which greatly strengthened the bad opinion Bessie and Miss Abbot were disposed to entertain of me. The fact is, I was a trifle beside myself; or rather *out* of myself, as the French would say: I was conscious that a moment's mutiny had already rendered me liable to strange penalties, and, like any other rebel slave, I felt resolved, in my desperation, to go all lengths.

'Hold her arms, Miss Abbot: she's like a mad cat.'

'For shame! For shame!' cried the lady's-maid. 'What shocking conduct, Miss Eyre, to strike a young gentleman, your benefactress's son! Your young master.'

'Master! How is he my master? Am I a servant?'

'No; you are less than a servant, for you do nothing for your keep. There, sit down, and think over your wickedness.'

They had got me by this time into the apartment indicated by Mrs Reed, and had thrust me upon a stool: my impulse was to rise from it like a spring; their two pair of hands arrested me instantly.

'If you don't sit still, you must be tied down,' said Bessie. 'Miss Abbot, lend me your garters; she would break mine directly.'

161

Miss Abbot turned to divest a stout leg of the necessary ligature. This preparation for bonds, and the additional ignominy it inferred, took a little of the excitement out of me.

'Don't take them off,' I cried; 'I will not stir.'

In guarantee whereof, I attached myself to my seat by my hands.

'Mind you don't,' said Bessie; and when she had ascertained that I was really subsiding, she loosened her hold of me; then she and Miss Abbot stood with folded arms, looking darkly and doubtfully on my face, as incredulous of my sanity.

'She never did so before,' at last said Bessie, turning to the Abigail.

'But it was always in her,' was the reply. 'I've told Missis often my opinion about the child, and Missis agreed with me. She's an underhand little thing: I never saw a girl of her age with so much cover.'

Bsssie answered not; but ere long, addressing me, she said, 'You ought to be aware, miss, that you are under obligations to Mrs Reed: she keeps you: if she were to turn you off, you would have to go to the poorhouse.'

I had nothing to say to these words: they were not new to me: my very first recollections of existence included hints of the same kind. This reproach of my dependence had become a vague sing-song in my ear: very painful and crushing, but only half intelligible. Miss Abbot joined in.

'And you ought not to think yourself on an equality with the Misses Reed and Master Reed, because Missis kindly allows you to be brought up with them. They will have a great deal of money, and you will have none: it is your place to be humble, and to try to make yourself agreeable to them.'

'What we tell you is for your good,' added Bessie, in no harsh voice; 'you should try to be useful and pleasant, then, perhaps, you would have a home here; but if you become passionate and rude, Missis will send you away, I am sure.'

'Besides,' said Miss Abbot, 'God will punish her: He might strike her dead in the midst of her tantrums, and then where would she go? Come, Bessie, we will leave her: I wouldn't have her heart for anything. Say your prayers, Miss Eyre, when you are by yourself; for if you don't repent, something bad might be permitted to come down the chimney and fetch you away.'

They went, shutting the door, and locking it behind them.

The red room was a square chamber, very seldom slept in, I might say never, indeed, unless when a chance influx of visitors at Gateshead Hall rendered it necessary to turn to account all the accommodation it contained: yet it was one of the largest and stateliest chambers in the mansion. A bed supported on massive pillars of mahogany, hung with curtains of deep red damask, stood out like a tabernacle in the centre; the two large windows, with their blinds always drawn down, were half-shrouded in festoons and falls of similar drapery; the carpet was red; the table at the foot of the bed was covered with a crimson cloth; the walls were a soft fawn colour with a blush of pink in it; the wardrobe, the toilet-table, the chairs were of darkly polished old mahogany. Out of these deep surrounding shades rose high, and glared white, the piled-up mattresses and pillows of the bed, spread with a snowy Marseilles counterpane. Scarcely less prominent was an ample cushioned easy-chair near the head of the bed, also white, with a footstool before it; and looking, as I thought, like a pale throne.

This room was chill, because it seldom had a fire; it was silent, because remote from the nursery and kitchen; solemn, because it was known to be so seldom entered. The housemaid alone came here on Saturdays, to wipe from the mirrors and the furniture a week's quiet dust: and Mrs Reed herself, at far intervals, visited it to review the contents of a certain secret drawer in the wardrobe, where were stored divers parchments, her jewel-casket, and a miniature of her deceased husband; and in those last words lies the secret of the red room – the spell which kept it so lonely in spite of its grandeur.

Mr Reed had been dead nine years: it was in this chamber he breathed his last; here he lay in state; hence his coffin was borne by the undertaker's men; and, since that day, a sense of dreary consecration had guarded it from frequent intrusion.

My seat, to which Bessie and the bitter Miss Abbot had left me riveted, was a low ottoman near the marble chimney-piece; the bed rose before me; to my right hand there was the high, dark wardrobe, with subdued, broken reflections varying the gloss of its panels; to my left were the muffled windows; a great looking-glass between them repeated the vacant majesty of the bed and room. I was not quite sure whether they had locked the door; and when I dared move, I got up and went to see. Alas! yes: no jail was ever more secure. Returning, I had to cross before the looking-glass; my fascinated glance involuntarily explored the depth it revealed. All looked colder and darker in that visionary hollow than in reality: and the strange little figure there gazing at me, with a white face and arms specking the gloom, and glittering eyes of fear moving where all else was still, had the effect of a real spirit: I thought it like one of the tiny phantoms, half-fairy, half-imp, Bessie's evening stories represented as coming out of lone, ferny dells in moors, and appearing before the eyes of belated travellers. I returned to my stool.

Superstition was with me at that moment; but it was not yet her hour for complete victory: my blood was still warm; the mood of the revolted slave was still bracing me with its bitter vigour; I had to stem a rapid rush of retrospective thought before I quailed to the dismal present.

All John Reed's violent tyrannies, all his sisters' proud in-
difference, all his mother's aversion, all the servants' partiality,
turned up in my disturbed mind like a dark deposit in a turbid
well. Why was I always suffering, always browbeaten, always
accused, forever condemned? Why could I never please? Why
was it useless to try to win anyone's favour? Eliza, who was
headstrong and selfish, was respected. Georgiana, who had a
spoiled temper, a very acrid spite, a captious and insolent
carriage, was universally indulged. Her beauty, her pink
cheeks and golden curls, seemed to give delight to all who
looked at her, and to purchase indemnity for every fault. John
no one thwarted, much less punished; though he twisted the
necks of the pigeons, killed the little pea-chicks, set the dogs
at the sheep, stripped the hothouse vines of their fruit, and
broke the buds off the choicest plants in the conservatory: he
called his mother 'old girl', too; sometimes reviled her for her
dark skin, similar to his own; bluntly disregarded her wishes;
not unfrequently tore and spoiled her silk attire; and he was
still 'her own darling'. I dared commit no fault: I strove to fulfil
every duty; and I was termed naughty and tiresome, sullen
and sneaking, from morning to noon, and from noon to night.

My head still ached and bled with the blow and fall I had
received: no one had reproved John for wantonly striking me;
and because I had turned against him to avert further
irrational violence, I was loaded with general opprobrium.

'Unjust! – unjust!' said my reason, forced by the agonizing
stimulus into precocious though transitory power: and
Resolve, equally wrought up, instigated some strange
expedient to achieve escape from insupportable oppression –
as running away, or, if that could not be effected, never eating
or drinking more, and letting myself die.

What a consternation of soul was mine that dreary afternoon! How all my brain was in tumult, and all my heart in

insurrection! Yet in what darkness, what dense ignorance, was the mental battle fought! I could not answer the ceaseless inward question – *why* I thus suffered; now, at the distance of – I will not say how many years, I see it clearly.

I was a discord in Gateshead Hall: I was like nobody there; I had nothing in harmony with Mrs Reed or her children, or her chosen vassalage. If they did not love me, in fact, as little did I love them. They were not bound to regard with affection a thing that could not sympathize with one amongst them; a heterogeneous thing, opposed to them in temperament, in capacity, in propensities; a useless thing, incapable of serving their interest, or adding to their pleasure; a noxious thing, cherishing the germs of indignation at their treatment, of contempt of their judgement. I know that had I been a sanguine, brilliant, careless, exacting, handsome, romping child – though equally dependent and friendless – Mrs Reed would have endured my presence more complacently; her children would have entertained for me more of the cordiality of fellow-feeling; the servants would have been less prone to make me the scapegoat of the nursery.

Daylight began to forsake the red room; it was past four o'clock, and the beclouded afternoon was tending to drear twilight. I heard the rain still beating continuously on the staircase window, and the wind howling in the grove behind the hall; I grew by degrees cold as a stone, and then my courage sank. My habitual mood of humiliation, self-doubt, forlorn depression, fell damp on the embers of my decaying ire. All said I was wicked, and perhaps I might be so; what thought had I been but just conceiving of starving myself to death? That certainly was a crime: and was I fit to die? Or was the vault under the chancel of Gateshead church an inviting bourne? In such vault I had been told did Mr Reed lie buried; and led by this thought to recall his idea, I dwelt on it with gathering dread. I could not remember him; but I knew that he was my own uncle – my mother's brother – that he had taken me when a parentless infant to his house; and that in his last moments he had required a promise of Mrs Reed that she would rear and maintain me as one of her own children. Mrs Reed probably considered she had kept this promise; and so she had, I dare say, as well as her nature would permit her; but how could she really like an interloper not of her race, and unconnected with her, after her husband's death, by any tie? It must have been most irksome to find herself bound by a hard-wrung pledge to stand in the stead of a parent to a strange child she could not love, and to see an uncongenial alien permanently intruded on her own family group.

A singular notion dawned upon me. I doubted not – never doubted – that if Mr Reed had been alive he would have treated me kindly; and now, as I sat looking at the white bed and overshadowed walls – occasionally also turning a fascinated eye towards the dimly gleaming mirror – I began to recall what I had heard of dead men, troubled in their graves by the violation of their last wishes, revisiting the earth to punish the perjured and avenge the oppressed; and I thought Mr Reed's spirit, harassed by the wrongs of his sister's child, might quit its abode – whether in the church vault or in the unknown world of the departed – and rise before me in this chamber. I wiped my tears and hushed my sobs, fearful lest any sign of violent grief might waken a preternatural voice to comfort me, or elicit from the gloom some haloed face, bending over me with strange pity. This idea, consolatory in theory, I felt would be terrible if realized: with all my might I endeavoured to stifle it – I endeavoured to be firm. Shaking my hair from my eyes, I lifted my head and tried to look boldly round the dark room; at this moment a light gleamed on the wall. Was it, I asked myself, a ray from the moon penetrating some aperture in the blind? No; moonlight was still, and this stirred; while I gazed, it glided up to the ceiling and quivered over my head. I can now conjecture readily that this streak of light was, in all likelihood, a gleam from a lantern carried by someone across the lawn: but then, prepared as my mind was for horror, shaken as my nerves were by agitation, I thought the swift darting beam was a herald of some coming vision from another world. My heart beat thick, my head grew hot; a sound filled my ears, which I deemed the rushing of wings; something seemed near me; I was oppressed, suffocated: endurance broke down; I rushed to the door and shook the lock in desperate effort. Steps came running along the outer passage; the key turned, Bessie and Abbot entered.

'Miss Eyre, are you ill?' said Bessie.

'What a dreadful noise! It went quite through me!' exclaimed Abbot.

'Take me out! Let me go into the nursery!' was my cry.

'What for? Are you hurt? Have you seen something?' again demanded Bessie.

'Oh! I saw a light, and I thought a ghost would come.' I had now got hold of Bessie's hand, and she did not snatch it from me.

'She has screamed out on purpose,' declared Abbot, in some disgust. 'And what a scream! If she had been in great pain one would have excused it, but she only wanted to bring us all here: I know her naughty tricks.'

'What is all this?' demanded another voice peremptorily; and Mrs Reed came along the corridor, her cap flying wide, her gown rustling stormily. 'Abbot and Bessie, I believe I gave orders that Jane Eyre should be left in the red room till I came to her myself.'

'Miss Jane screamed so loud, ma'am,' pleaded Bessie.

'Let her go,' was the only answer. 'Loose Bessie's hand,

child: you cannot succeed in getting out by these means, be assured. I abhor artifice, particularly in children; it is my duty to show you that tricks will not answer: you will now stay here an hour longer, and it is only on condition of perfect submission and stillness that I shall liberate you then.'

'Oh Aunt! Have pity! Forgive me! I cannot endure it – let me be punished some other way! I shall be killed if – '

'Silence! This violence is all most repulsive,' and so, no doubt, she felt it. I was a precocious actress in her eyes; she sincerely looked on me as a compound of virulent passions, mean spirit, and dangerous duplicity.

Bessie and Abbot having retreated, Mrs Reed, impatient of my now frantic anguish and wild sobs, abruptly thrust me back and locked me in, without farther parley. I heard her sweeping away; and soon after she was gone, I suppose I had a species of fit: unconsciousness closed the scene.

'No Coward Soul is Mine'
Emily Brontë

No coward soul is mine,
No trembler in the world's storm-troubled sphere!
I see Heaven's glories shine,
And Faith shines equal, arming me from Fear

O God within my breast,
Almighty ever-present Deity!
Life, that in me hast rest,
As I, Undying Life, have power in thee!

Vain are the thousand creeds
That move men's hearts, unutterably vain;

Worthless as withered weeds,
Or idlest froth amid the boundless main,

To waken doubt in one
Holding so fast by thy infinity,
So surely anchored on
The steadfast rock of Immortality.

With wide-embracing love
Thy spirit animates eternal years,
Pervades and broods above,
Changes, sustains, dissolves, creates, and rears.

Though earth and moon were gone,
And suns and universes ceased to be,
And thou wert left alone,
Every Existence would exist in thee.

There is not room for Death,
Nor atom that his might could render void;
Since thou art Being and Breath
And what thou art may never be destroyed.

I may, I might, I must
Marianne Moore

If you will tell me why the fen
appears impassable, I then
will tell you why I think that I
can get across it if I try.

170

Long Ago and Far Away

The Inquisitive Girl
Nathaniel Hawthorne

Long, long ago, when this old world was still very young, everyone was happy, no one was ever ill or naughty, and people did not know what trouble meant.

In those old days there lived a boy who had neither father nor mother. That he might not be lonely, a little girl, who like himself had no father or mother, was sent from a far country to live with him and be his playmate. This child's name was Pandora.

The first thing that Pandora saw, when she came to the cottage where the boy lived, was a large wooden box. 'What have you got in that box?' she asked.

'That is a secret,' he answered, 'and you must not ask any questions about it; the box was left here for safety, and I do not know what is in it.'

'But who gave it to you and where did it come from?'

'That is a secret too,' answered the boy.

'How tiresome!' exclaimed Pandora, pouting. 'I wish the great ugly box were out of the way,' and she looked very cross.

'Come along, and let us play games,' said the boy; 'we will not think any more about it,' and they ran out to play with the other children, and for a time Pandora forgot all about the box.

But when she came back to the cottage, there it was in front of her, and she began to say to herself, 'Whatever can be inside it? I wish I just knew who brought it!'

'Do tell me?' she said, turning to the boy. 'I know I cannot be happy till you tell me all about it.'

'How can I tell you, Pandora?' he said. 'I do not know any more than you do.'

'Well, you could open it, and we could see for ourselves!'

But the boy looked so shocked at the very idea of opening a box that had been given to him in trust, that Pandora saw she had better not suggest such a thing again.

'At least you can tell me how it came here,' she said.

'It was left at the door,' answered the boy, 'just before you came, by a person dressed in a very strange cloak; he had a cap that seemed to be partly made of feathers. It looked exactly as if he had wings.'

'What kind of a staff had he?' asked Pandora.

'Oh, the most curious staff you ever saw!' cried the boy; 'it seemed like two serpents twisted round a stick.'

'I know him,' said Pandora. 'It was Mercury, and he brought me here as well as the box. I am sure he meant the box for me, and perhaps there are pretty clothes in it for us to wear, and toys for us both to play with.'

'It may be so,' answered the boy, turning away, 'but until Mercury comes back and tells us that we may open it, neither of us has any right to lift the lid,' and he went out of the cottage.

'What a stupid boy he is!' muttered Pandora, 'I do wish he had a little more spirit.' Then she stood gazing at the box. She had called it ugly, but it was really a very handsome box, and would have been an ornament in any room. The box was not fastened with a lock and key like most boxes, but with a strange knot of gold cord. There never was a knot so strangely tied. It seemed to have no end and no beginning, but was twisted so cunningly, with so many ins and outs, that not even the cleverest fingers could undo it.

Pandora looked closely at the knot to see how it was made. 'I really believe,' she said to herself, 'that I begin to see how it

174

is done; I am sure I could tie it up again after undoing it. There could be no harm in that; I need not open the box even if I undo the knot.'

And the longer she looked at it the longer she wanted to try. So she took the gold cord in her fingers and looked at it closely. But at that moment she gave the knot a little shake, and the gold cord undid itself as if by magic, and there was the box without any fastening.

'This is the strangest thing I have ever known,' said Pandora, trembling. 'Now, can I possibly tie it up again?'

She tried once or twice, but the knot would not come right; it had untied itself so suddenly she could not remember at all how the cord had been twisted together. So there was nothing to be done but to let the box remain as it was until the boy should come home.

'But,' thought Pandora, 'when he finds the knot untied he will know that I have done it; how shall I ever make him believe that I have not looked into the box?'

And then the naughty thought came into her head that, as the boy would believe that she had looked into the box, she might as well have a little peep.

'Yes, I must just peep,' said Pandora; 'only one little peep, and the lid will be shut down as safely as ever. There cannot really be any harm in one little peep.'

When the boy came back to the cottage what do you think he saw? The naughty little girl had put her hand on the lid of the box and was just going to open it. The boy saw this quite well, and if he had cried out at once it would have given Pandora such a fright she would have let go the lid. But he was very naughty too. Although he had said very little about the box, he was quite as curious as Pandora was to see what was inside. If they really found anything pretty or of value in it, he meant to take half of it for himself. So that he was quite

175

as naughty and nearly as much to blame as the little girl.

When Pandora raised the lid the cottage had grown very dark, for a black cloud now covered the sun, and a heavy peal of thunder was heard. But Pandora was too busy and excited to notice either. She lifted the lid, and at once a swarm of creatures with wings flew out of the box, and a minute after she heard the boy crying loudly, 'Oh, I am stung, I am stung! You naughty Pandora, why did you open this dreadful box?'

Pandora let the lid fall with a crash, and started up to find out what had happened to her playmate. The thunder-cloud had made the room so dark that she could scarcely see. She heard a loud buzz-buzzing, as if a great many huge flies had flown in, and soon she saw a crowd of ugly little shapes darting about, with wings like bats and with long stings in their tails.

It was one of these that had stung the boy, and it was not long before Pandora herself began to scream with pain and fear.

Now I must tell you that these ugly creatures with stings, which had escaped from the box, were evil tempers and a great many kinds of cares; and there were more than a hundred and fifty sorrows, and there were many pains. In fact all the sorrows and worries that hurt people in the world today had been shut up in the magic box, and given to the boy and Pandora to keep safely.

That was in order that the happy children in the world might never be troubled by them. If only these two had obeyed Mercury, and had left the box alone as he had told them, all would have gone well. But you see what mischief they had done. The winged troubles flew out at the window, and went all over the world; and they made people so unhappy that no one smiled for a great many days.

Meanwhile Pandora and the boy remained in the cottage;

they were very sad and in great pain, which made them both cross.

Suddenly they heard a gentle tap-tap inside the box. 'What can that be?' said Pandora, raising her head, and again came the tap-tap. It sounded like the knuckles of a tiny hand knocking lightly on the inside of the box.

'Who are you?' asked Pandora.

A sweet little voice came from inside, 'Only lift the lid, and you will see.'

But Pandora was afraid to lift the lid again. She looked across to the boy, but he was so angry that he took no notice. Pandora sobbed, 'No, no, I am afraid; there are so many troubles with stings flying about that we do not want any more.'

'Ah, but I am not one of those,' the sweet voice said. 'They are no friends of mine. Come, come, dear Pandora, I am sure you will let me out.'

The voice sounded so kind and cheerful that it made Pandora feel better even to listen to it. The boy too had heard the voice. He stopped crying. Then he came forward, and said, 'Let me help you, Pandora, as the lid is very heavy.'

So this time both the children opened the box and out flew a bright, smiling little fairy who brought light and sunshine with her. She flew to the boy, and with her finger touched his brow where the trouble had stung him, and at once the pain was gone. Then she kissed Pandora, and her hurt was better at once.

'Pray, who are you, kind fairy?' Pandora asked.

'I am called Hope,' was the answer. 'I was shut up in the box so that I might be ready to comfort people when the family of troubles got loose in the world.'

'What lovely wings you have! They are just like a rainbow. And will you stay with us,' asked the boy, 'for ever and ever?'

'Yes,' said Hope, 'I shall stay with you as long as you live. Sometimes you will not be able to see me, and you may think I am dead, but you will find that I come back again and again when you have given up expecting me, and you must always trust my promise that I will never really leave you.'

'Yes, we do trust you,' cried both children. And all the rest of their lives Pandora and the boy did trust the sweet fairy, even when the troubles came back and buzzed about their heads and left bitter stings of pain.

At such times they would remember whose fault it was that the troubles had ever come into the world at all, and they would wait till sweet Hope with her rainbow wings came back to heal and comfort them.

Sword Song
Rosemary Sutcliffe

[from *Song for a Dark Queen*]

I am Cadwan of the Harp. I am the Singer of Songs and the Teller of Tales. There are, there were, many harpers among the Iceni; but I am Harper to the Queen herself; to the Lady Boudicca, as I was when I was young, to her mother before her.

That was long ago, before ever the Red Crests came, in the days when the enemy were the Catuvellauni, the Cats of War.

Five lifetimes ago, ever since they hurled their spears against the first Red Crests who came following Julius Caesar, and the Red Crests went away again in a hurry over the Great Water, the Catuvellauni have followed the conqueror's path. And the names of their kings – Cassivellaunus, Tasciovanus, Cunobelin – have been names that women use to frighten their naughty children. Many tribes, they overcame. Less than one lifetime ago, when Cunobelin was first a king, he overran the Trinovantes whose borders marched with ours in the south, and made his new Strong Place where their old one had been, at Dun Camulus, the Dun of the War God, less than a day's riding across our frontier line.

So always, from the first that I remember, we have known that one day, soon or late, it would be our turn. We prayed to the Lord of Battle, that our spears might be stronger than the spears of the Catuvellauni when that day came. We watched our borders and built great turf banks where the fens and the forest left us open to attack; and the women added the names of Cunobelin's two sons to those they used for frightening naughty children, though they were but cubs themselves as yet. 'Togodumnos will catch you!' they said, and 'If you do that again, Caratacus will creep in and snatch you out of your beds one dark night!'

And always, there was unquiet along our borders; a small flurrying warfare of slave and cattle raiding at the full of the moon.

A day in hawthorn time came when the Lady Boudicca was six years old, and the king her father had moved down to his summer steading with all his household, as he often did at that time of year, to see how the foals on the southern runs were shaping. And in the lag end of the night, a man on a sweating horse brought word of raiders within our borders, loose in the grazing land between the forest and the fens. Then the king and his sword-companions came out from sleep, calling for spears and horses, and there were flaring torches and the trampling of war-ponies brought from the stables, and a yelping of horns to summon the fighting men from round about, just as I had known it all a score and a score of times before.

But after all was quiet again, when the king and his war-band were away in a green dawn with the marsh birds calling, and the hawthorn blossom showing curd pale in the darkness of the hedge around the Royal Garth, it was found that the Lady Boudicca was not in her bed in the women's quarters.

Then there began to be another kind of uproar. Maybe there would have been less if the queen her mother had been yet alive. But Rhun, her nurse, was ever like a hen with one chick and a hawk hovering over; a thing I have noticed more than once among women who rear a child some other woman bore, and have no child of their own. And soon, all the women of the household were in full cry, scurrying here and there, crying and calling, 'Boudicca! Boudicca! – Stop hiding, I can see you! – Come out from there, child of blackness! – Where are you, little bird?' And the slaves were sent flying to look in this place and that, in the foaling pens, along the fringes of the oak woods, in every pool of marsh water lest she be lying drowned among the reeds.

I knew better than that. I hitched up my harp in its embroidered mare's-skin bag – no harper worth the name is willingly parted from his harp, nor leaves her unguarded where even a friendly hand may come too near – and I set off along the way that the king and his companions had followed.

The way ran along the rich grazing country between the wide salt marshes, and the tawny wind-shaped oak woods that are the outriders of the dark forest inland. Three times I asked horse herdsmen if they had seen a girl-child go by; and the first two had seen no one since the war-band passed in the dawn: but the third man said, 'A while back. She was dripping with mud and water as though she had fallen into a stream.'

'And you did not think to stop her?' I said.

He scratched one ear. 'Na. She would be from one of the

180

villages round, I thought. She seemed to know where she was going, well enough.'

'That would be her,' I said, and pressed on.

There are many winding waters, poplar and willow fringed, among the horse-runs, and soon the way would turn inland; and I did not care to think of her once she came among the trees. The forest is good for a hunting party that knows its way, but not for one small girl-child alone. So I pushed on as fast as might be. But I had to stop and search as I went, and the sun was far to the west of noon, when I found her at last, not far short of the forest verge. She was sitting among the roots of an ancient willow tree beside one of the slow-flowing streams that vein and dapple all this countryside with winding brightness and sky-reflecting pools. And she forlorn as a fledgling thrush new-fallen from the nest.

She had walked until she could walk no more. There was blood on one of her feet, and her hair was matted with mud; and the mud had dried into a mask on her face, save where the tracks of tears cut through it. At first I thought she was asleep; but when I drew near, she turned, showing her teeth like a small wild thing at the nearing of danger. Then, seeing that it was I, she loosened with a little sigh; and squatting down beside her, I saw that the tear tracks were still wet.

'This is a long way that you are from home,' I said, 'and you with a cut foot.'

And she said, 'They would not take me. Still my father says I am too young. I thought maybe they would take me this time – now that I am nearly seven.'

'And so you followed them.'

'I thought if I followed them all the way, they would not send me back alone.'

'But they rode swift as the wind on their war-ponies, and you have walked the soles off your feet,' I said. 'And one of them is cut and bleeding. So we will bathe it here in the stream, and then we will go home for this time. Truly the world is full of sorrow.'

She tipped up her head and looked at me, proud as any brave in his first warpaint, and let another tear run into her mouth rather than wipe it away.

'I am not crying,' she said.

'Surely you are not crying. It is just the wind that has got into your eyes.'

'I never cry. I am the Royal Daughter of the Iceni, and one day I shall be queen!'

I lifted her down the bank, where the sun-streaks dappled through the willow leaves, and began to bathe her foot. 'I shall hurt you,' I said, 'but you will not be minding that.'

She shook her head; and looking up, I saw that her grief was grown smaller: a little.

'Now we will go home. See, I will carry you; and I will make you a song to shorten the way.'

'Make me a sword,' she said. 'Old Nurse made me a sword out of two sticks, but she bound it together with wool, and it broke. Make me a sword, and then we will go home.'

I thought of the hunting and calling that would still be going on, and the rings of search spreading wider and wider. And I was thinking it would do small harm to let them spread a little wider yet. It would not take long. I have always been a man of my hands, as well as a harper. I made her a sword of a thick white willow rod split with my dagger, with a short piece laid cross-wise to give it shoulders and mark off the hilt from the blade. But with what should I bind it? It must not break as Rhun's had done. I pulled round the harp-bag from my shoulder and drew out a spare harpstring of red horsehair, the thickest string that yields the deepest note. Good harpstrings are not easily come by; but it was passably strong. She was

182

watching me, her chin almost resting on my arm, as I cut the length I needed. 'See,' I said, 'I am binding your sword with harp-song, so that it will never break. Let you give me three hairs from your head to use also, that it may be like your father's great sword that has goldwork in the hilt.'

She pulled me out three hairs and gave them to me, and I dipped them in the water to rid them of mud, and twisted them together with the harpstring, and bound her sword, and gave it to her.

She looked at it, and sighed. She had known that it could be only a toy sword made of willow wood; but her heart had hoped for something more. 'One day I shall have a real sword,' she said; and then, 'You could make me a real song, now.'

She was growing a little sleepy, even then.

'Surely I will make you a real song,' I told her, and picked her up, muffling my cloak about her, for a small mean wind was blowing up off the marshes, and a silvery haze dimming the westering sun. And I set out, back the way that we had come. 'I will make you the song I promised you for home-going. And one day, when you have a great sword like the king your father's, I will make you a great song of the Victories of a Queen. But now, I will make you only a little song, to match with your little sword.'

And I sang to her as we went along, taking the words as they came into my head:

'Listen now, for your sword is singing,
"I am the proud one, I that am sword to a Queen.
The sun flames not more brightly than my hilt,
The night cannot outshine my blade's dark sheen.
The earth shall tremble at our passing;
We will make the warhosts scatter, she and I."
But now the light fades

And the wild duck home are winging,
And sleep falls like dew from the quiet sky.
"Sleep now," says your sword,
"Sleep now, you and I."'

By the time I had done, her head was growing heavy in the hollow of my shoulder.

So I carried her home to the household that was like a disturbed ants' nest in the dusk, more than any other thing that I can call to mind. Rhun the nurse came running to meet me with a white face that looked as though she had not slept for a hundred years. And I put Boudicca into her arms, still in her sleep holding to the plaything sword that I had made for her.

'Here she is,' I said, 'she had followed the war-band. Take better care of her another time.'

Little Fan

James Reeves

'I don't like the look of little Fan, Mother,
    I don't like her looks a little bit.
Her face – well, it's not exactly different,
    But there's something wrong with it.

'She went down to the sea-shore yesterday,
    And she talked to somebody there,
Now she won't do anything but sit
    And comb out her yellowy hair.

'Her eyes are shiny and she sings, Mother,
    Like nobody ever sang before.

Perhaps they gave her something queer to eat,
  Down by the rocks on the shore.

'Speak to me, speak, little Fan dear,
  Aren't you feeling very well?
Where have you been and what are you singing,
  And what's that seaweedy smell?

'Where did you get that shiny comb, love,
  And those pretty coral beads so red?
Yesterday you had two legs, I'm certain,
  But now there's something else instead.

'I don't like the looks of little Fan, Mother,
  You'd best go and close the door.
Watch now, or she'll be gone for ever
  To the rocks by the brown sandy shore.'

The Blue Beard

[folk tale]

There was once upon a time a man who had several fine
houses both in town and country, a good deal of silver and
gold plate, embroider'd furniture, and coaches gilt all over
with gold. But this same man had the misfortune to have a
Blue Beard, which made him so frightfully ugly that all the
women and girls ran away from him.

One of his neighbours, a lady of quality, had two daughters
who were perfect beauties. He desired of her one of them in
marriage, leaving to her the choice of which of them she would
bestow upon him. They would neither of them have him, and
sent him backwards and forwards from one another, being

resolved never to marry a man that had a Blue Beard. That which moreover gave them the greater disgust and aversion, was that he had already been marry'd to several wives, and nobody ever knew what were become of them.

The Blue Beard, to engage their affection, took them with my lady their mother, and three or four other ladies of their acquaintance, and some young people of the neighbourhood, to one of his country seats, where they stayed full eight days. There was nothing now to be seen but parties of pleasure, hunting of all kinds, fishing, dancing, feasts and collations. Nobody went to bed, they passed the night in rallying and playing upon one another: In short, everything so well succeeded, that the youngest daughter began to think, that the master of the house had not a Beard so very Blue, and that he was a very civil gentleman.

As soon as they returned home the marriage was concluded. About a month afterwards the Blue Beard told his wife that he was obliged to take a journey into a distant country for six weeks at least, about an affair of very great consequence, desiring her to divert herself in his absence, send for her friends and acquaintance, carry them into the country, if she pleased, and make good cheer wherever she was: Here, said he, are the keys of the two great rooms that hold my best and richest furniture; these are of my silver and gold plate, which is not to be made use of every day; these open my strongboxes, which hold my gold and silver money; these my caskets of jewels; and this is the master-key that opens all my apartments: But for this little one here, it is the key of the closet at the end of the great gallery on the ground floor. Open them all, go into all and every one except that little closet, which I forbid you, and forbid you in such a manner, that if you happen to open it, there is nothing but what you may expect from my just anger and resentment. She promised to observe everything he order'd her, who, after having embraced her, got into his coach and proceeded on his journey.

Her neighbours and good friends did not stay to be sent for by the new married lady, so great was their impatience to see all the rich furniture of her house, not daring to come while the husband was there, because of his Blue Beard which frighten'd them. They ran through all the rooms, closets, wardrobes, which were all so rich and fine that they seemed to surpass one another. After that, they went up into the two great rooms where were the best and richest furniture; they could not sufficiently admire the number and beauty of the tapestry, beds, couches, cabinets, stands, tables and looking-glasses, in which you might see yourself from head to foot; some of them were framed with glass, others with silver and silver gilt, the finest and most magnificent as ever were seen: They never ceased to extol and envy the happiness of their friend, who in the meantime no ways diverted herself in looking upon all these rich things, because of the impatience she had to go and open the closet of the ground floor. She was so much pressed by her curiosity, that without considering that it was very uncivil to leave her company, she went down a back pair of stairs, and with such an excessive haste, that she had like to have broken her neck two or three times.

Being come to the closet door, she stopt for some time, thinking upon her husband's orders, and considering what unhappiness might attend her were she disobedient; but the temptation was so strong she could not overcome it: She took then the little key and opened it in a very great trembling. But she could see nothing distinctly, because the windows were shut; after some moments she began to observe that the floor was all covered over with clotted blood, on which lay the bodies of several dead women ranged against the walls. (These were all the wives that the Blue Beard had married and murder'd one after another.) She thought that she should have died for fear, and the key that she pulled out of the lock fell out of her hand. After having somewhat recover'd her surprise, she took up the key, locked the door and went upstairs into her chamber to recover herself, but she could not, so much was she frightened. Having observed that the key of the closet was stain'd with blood, she tried two or three times to wipe it off, but the blood would not come out; in vain did she wash it and even rub it with soap and sand, the blood still remained, for the key was a Fairy, and she could never quite make it clean; when the blood was gone off from one side, it came again on the other.

The Blue Beard returned from his journey the same evening, and said he had received letters upon the road, informing him that the affair he went about was finished to his advantage. His wife did all she could to convince him she was extremely glad of his speedy return. The next morning he asked for the keys, which she returned, but with such a trembling hand, that he easily guess'd what had happen'd. What is the matter, said he, that the key of the closet is not amongst the rest? I must certainly, said she, have left it above upon the table. Do not fail, said the Blue Beard, of giving it to me presently. After several goings backwards and forwards she was forced to bring him the key. The Blue Beard having very attentively consider'd it, said to his wife, how comes this blood upon the key? I don't know, said the poor woman paler than death. You don't know, replied the Blue Beard, I know very well, you were resolv'd to go into the closet, were you not? Very well, madam, you shall go in, and take your place amongst the ladies you saw there.

Upon this she threw herself at her husband's feet, and begged his pardon with all the signs of a true repentance, and that she would never more be disobedient. She would have melted a rock, so beautiful and sorrowful was she; but the Blue

Beard had a heart harder than the hardest rock! You must die, madam, said he, and that presently. Since I must die, said she, looking upon him with her eyes all bathed in tears, give me some little time to say my prayers. I give you, said the Blue Beard, a quarter of an hour, but not one moment more.

When she was alone, she called out to her sister, and said to her, Sister Anne, for that was her name, go up, I desire thee, upon the top of the tower, and see if my brothers are not coming, they promised me that they would come today, and if thou seest them, give them a sign to make haste. Her sister Anne went up upon the top of the tower, and the poor afflicted lady cried out from time to time, *Anne, Sister Anne, dost thou see nothing coming?* And Sister Anne said, *I see nothing but the sun that makes a dust, and the grass that grows green.* In the mean while the Blue Beard, holding a great cutlass in his hand, cried out as loud as he could to his wife, Come down presently, or I'll come up to you. One moment longer, if you please, said his wife, and immediately she cried out very softly, *Anne, Sister Anne, dost thou see nothing coming?* And Sister Anne said, *I see nothing but the sun that makes a dust, and the grass that grows green.* Come down quickly, cried the Blue Beard, or I'll come up to you. I am coming, answer'd his wife, and then she cried, *Anne, Sister Anne, dost thou see nothing coming?* I see, replied Sister Anne, a great dust that comes on this side here. *Are they my brothers?* Alas! no, my dear sister, I see a flock of sheep. Will you not come down? cried the Blue Beard. One moment longer, said his wife, and then she cried out, *Anne, Sister Anne, dost thou see nothing coming?* I see, said she, two horsemen coming, but they are yet a great way off. God be praised, said she immediately after, they are my brothers; I have made them a sign as well as I can to make haste. The Blue Beard cried out now so loud, that he made the whole house tremble.

The poor lady came down and threw herself at his feet all

in tears with her hair about her shoulders: This signifies
nothing, says the Blue Beard, you must die; then taking hold
of her hair with one hand, and holding up the cutlass with the
other, he was going to cut off her head. The poor lady turning
about to him, and looking at him with dying eyes, desired him
to afford her one little moment to recollect herself. No, no, said
he, recommend thyself to God; for at this very instant there
was such a loud knocking at the gate, that the Blue Beard stopt
short of a sudden: They open'd the gate, and immediately
enter'd two horsemen, who drawing their swords, ran directly
to the Blue Beard. He knew them to be his wife's brothers, one
a dragoon, the other a musketeer, so that he ran away immediately to save himself: but the two brothers pursued him
so close, that they overtook him before he could get to the steps
of the porch, when they ran their swords through his body
and left him dead.

The poor lady was almost as dead as her husband, and had
not strength enough to rise and embrace her brothers. The Blue
Beard had no heirs, and so his wife became mistress of all his
estate. She made use of one part of it to marry her sister Anne
to a young gentleman who had loved her a long while, another
part to buy captains' commissions for her brothers, and the
rest to marry herself to a very honest gentleman, who made
her forget the ill time she had pass'd with the Blue Beard.

Translated by Robert Samber

The Woman of Water
Adrian Mitchell

There once was a woman of water
Refused a Wizard her hand.

So he took the tears of a statue
And the weight from a grain of sand
And he squeezed the sap from a comet
And the height from a cypress tree
And he drained the dark from midnight
And he charmed the brains from a bee
And he soured the mixture with thunder
And stirred it with ice from hell
And the woman of water drank it down
And she changed into a well.

There once was a woman of water
Who was changed into a well
And the well smiled up at the Wizard
And down down down that old Wizard fell . . .

The Highwayman
Alfred Noyes

1

The wind was a torrent of darkness among the gusty trees,
The moon was a ghostly galleon tossed upon cloudy seas,
The road was a ribbon of moonlight over the purple moor,
And the highwayman came riding –
     Riding – riding –
The highwayman came riding, up to the old inn-door.

He'd a French cocked-hat on his forehead, a bunch of lace at
  his chin,
A coat of the claret velvet, and breeches of brown doeskin:
They fitted with never a wrinkle; his boots were up to the
  thigh!

And he rode with a jewelled twinkle,
     His pistol butts a-twinkle,
His rapier hilt a-twinkle, under the jewelled sky.

Over the cobbles he clattered and clashed in the dark inn-
     yard,
And he tapped with his whip on the shutters, but all was
     locked and barred:
He whistled a tune to the window, and who should be
     waiting there
But the landlord's black-eyed daughter,
     Bess, the landlord's daughter,
Plaiting a dark red love-knot into her long black hair.

And dark in the dark old inn-yard a stable-wicket creaked
Where Tim, the ostler, listened; his face was white and
     peaked,
His eyes were hollows of madness, his hair like mouldy hay;
But he loved the landlord's daughter,
     The landlord's red-lipped daughter:
Dumb as a dog he listened, and he heard the robber say –

'One kiss, my bonny sweetheart, I'm after a prize tonight,
But I shall be back with the yellow gold before the morning
     light.
Yet if they press me sharply, and harry me through the day,
Then look for me by moonlight,
     Watch for me by moonlight:
I'll come to thee by moonlight, though Hell should bar the
     way.'

2

He did not come in the dawning; he did not come at noon;
And out of the tawny sunset, before the rise o' the moon,

When the road was a gypsy's ribbon, looping the purple
  moor,
A red-coat troop came marching –
      Marching – marching –
King George's men came marching, up to the old inn-door.

They said no word to the landlord, they drank his ale
  instead;
But they gagged his daughter and bound her to the foot of
  her narrow bed.
Two of them knelt at her casement, with muskets at the side!
There was death at every window;
      And Hell at one dark window;
For Bess could see, through her casement, the road that *he*
  would ride.

They had tied her up to attention, with many a sniggering
  jest:
They had bound a musket beside her, with the barrel
  beneath her breast!
'Now keep good watch!' and they kissed her.
      She heard the dead man say –
Look for me by moonlight;
      Watch for me by moonlight;
I'll come to thee by moonlight, though Hell should bar the way!

She twisted her hands behind her; but all the knots held
  good!
She writhed her hands till her fingers were wet with sweat
  or blood!
They stretched and strained in the darkness, and the hours
  crawled by like years;
Till, now, on the stroke of midnight,
      Cold, on the stroke of midnight,

The tip of one finger touched it! The trigger at least was
  hers!

The tip of one finger touched it; she strove no more for the
  rest!
Up, she stood up to attention, with the barrel beneath her
  breast,
She would not risk their hearing: she would not strive again;
For the road lay bare in the moonlight,
        Blank and bare in the moonlight;
And the blood of her veins in the moonlight throbbed to her
  Love's refrain.

Tlot-tlot, in the frosty silence! *Tlot-tlot* in the echoing night!
Nearer he came and nearer! Her face was like a light!
Her eyes grew wide for a moment; she drew one last deep
  breath,
Then her finger moved in the moonlight,
        Her musket shattered the moonlight,
Shattered her breast in the moonlight and warned him –
  with her death.

He turned; he spurred him westward; he did not know who
  stood
Bowed with her head o'er the musket, drenched with her
  own red blood!
Not till the dawn he heard it, and slowly blanched to hear
How Bess, the landlord's daughter,
        The landlord's black-eyed daughter,
Had watched for her Love in the moonlight; and died in the
  darkness there.

Back, he spurred like a madman, shrieking a curse to the
  sky,
With the white road smoking behind him, and his rapier

brandished high!
Blood-red were his spurs i' the golden noon; wine-red was
his velvet coat;
When they shot him down on the highway,
    Down like a dog on the highway,
And he lay in his blood on the highway, with the bunch of
lace at his throat.

*

*And still of a winter's night, they say, when the wind is in the
trees,*
When the moon is a ghostly galleon tossed upon cloudy seas,
When the road is a ribbon of moonlight over the purple moor,
A highwayman comes riding —
        Riding — riding —
A highwayman comes riding, up to the old inn-door.

Over the cobbles he clatters and clangs in the dark inn-yard;
*And he taps with his whip on the shutters, but all is locked and
barred:*
*He whistles a tune to the window, and who should be waiting
there*
But the landlord's black-eyed daughter,
        Bess, the landlord's daughter,
Plaiting a dark red love-knot into her long black hair.

The Little Mermaid

Hans Christian Andersen

Far out in the wide sea, where the water is as blue as the loveliest cornflower, and where it is very, very deep, dwell the Mer-people.

Now you must not imagine that there is nothing but sand below: no, indeed, far from it! Trees and plants of wonderful beauty grow there. Their stems and leaves are so light that they are waved to and fro by the slightest motion of the water, almost as if they were living beings.

Fishes, great and small, glide in and out among the branches, just as birds fly about among our trees.

Where the water is deepest, stands the palace of the Mer-king. The walls of this palace are of coral, and the high, pointed windows are of amber; the roof, however, is made of mussel shells, which, as the billows pass over them, are always opening and shutting.

This looks very pretty, for each mussel shell contains a number of glittering pearls, any one of which would be a costly ornament in the crown of a king in the upper world.

The Mer-king had been for many years a widower; his old mother managed the household for him. She was very proud of her high birth and station, and for this reason she wore twelve oysters on her tail, whilst the other dwellers of the sea were allowed only six.

In every other way she won great praise, especially for the affection she showed to the six little princesses, her grand-daughters. These were all very beautiful.

The youngest was, however, the most lovely; her skin was

as soft and delicate as a rose leaf, her eyes were of as deep a blue as the sea. But, like all other mermaids, she had no feet, and her body ended in a tail like that of a fish.

The whole day long the children used to play in the palace, where beautiful flowers grew out of the walls on all sides around them. When the great amber windows were opened, fishes would swim into the rooms as swallows fly into ours.

But the fishes were bolder than the swallows; they swam straight up to the little princesses, ate from their hands, and allowed themselves to be caressed.

In front of the palace there was a large garden full of fiery red and dark blue trees. The sand that formed the soil of the garden was of a bright blue colour and a strangely beautiful blue was spread over the whole. When the waters were quite still, the sun might be seen looking like a purple flower.

Each of the little princesses had her own plot in the garden, where she might plant and sow at her pleasure. One chose hers to be made in the shape of a whale; another preferred the form of a mermaid; but the youngest had hers quite round like the sun, and planted in it only those flowers that were red, as the sun seemed to her.

She was a very quiet and thoughtful child. Whilst her sisters were adorning themselves with all sorts of gay things that came out of a ship which had been wrecked, she asked for nothing but a beautiful white marble statue of a boy, which had been found in it.

She put the statue in her garden, and planted a red weeping-willow by its side. The tree grew up quickly, and let its long boughs fall upon the bright blue ground.

Nothing pleased the little princess more than to hear about the world of human beings living above the sea.

She made her old grandmother tell her everything she knew about ships, towns, men, and land animals, and was specially

197

pleased when she heard that the flowers of the upper world had a pleasant smell – for the flowers of the sea are scentless.

Her grandmother told her the woods were green, and the fishes fluttering among the branches were of various gay colours, and that they could sing with a loud, clear voice. The old lady meant birds, but she called them fishes, because her grandchildren, having never seen a bird, would not otherwise have understood her.

'When you have reached your fifteenth year,' added she, 'you will be allowed to rise to the surface of the sea; you will then sit by moonlight in the clefts of the rocks, see the ships sail by, and learn about towns and men.'

The next year the eldest of the sisters reached this happy age, but the others – alas! The second sister was a year younger than the eldest, the third a year younger than the second, and so on; the youngest had still five whole years to wait till that joyful time should come when she also might rise to the surface of the water and see what was going on in the upper world.

However, the eldest promised to tell the others of everything she might see, when the first day of her being of age arrived; for the grandmother told them little, and there was so much that they wished to hear.

But none of all the sisters longed so keenly for the day when she should be free from childish rules as the youngest.

Many a night she stood by the open window, looking up through the clear blue water, whilst the fishes were leaping and playing around her. She could see the sun and the moon; their light was pale, but they seemed larger than they do to those who live in the upper world. If a shadow passed over them, she knew it must be either a whale, or a ship sailing by full of human beings.

The day had now come when the eldest princess was allowed to rise up to the surface of the sea.

When she came home, she had a thousand things to tell. Her chief pleasure had been to sit upon a sandbank in the moonlight, looking at the large town which lay on the coast.

There she saw lights beaming like stars, and heard music playing. She had heard the noise of men and carriages in the distance; she had seen the high church towers, had listened to the ringing of the bells; and, just because she could not go there, she longed the more after all these things.

How eagerly did her youngest sister listen to her story!

And when she next stood at night-time by her open window, gazing upward through the blue waters, she fancied she could hear the church bells ringing.

Next year the second sister was allowed to swim wherever she pleased. She rose to the surface of the sea just when the sun was setting. This sight so delighted her that she said it was more beautiful than anything else she had seen above the waters.

'The whole sky seemed tinged with gold,' said she, 'and I cannot tell you about the beauty of the clouds: now red, now violet, they glided over me. But still more swiftly flew over the water a flock of white swans, just where the sun was setting.'

It was now time for the third sister to visit the upper world. She was the boldest of the six, and ventured up a river.

On its shore she saw green hills covered with woods and vineyards, and houses and castles. She heard the birds singing, and the sun shone so strongly that she had to plunge below again and again in order to cool her burning face.

In a little bay she met with a number of children, who were bathing and jumping about. She would have joined in their gambols, but the children fled back to land in fear, and a little black animal barked at her so fiercely that she herself was frightened at last, and swam back to the sea.

She could not forget the pretty children, who, although they had no fins, were swimming about in the river.

The fourth sister was not so bold; she remained in the open sea, and said, on coming home, she thought nothing could be more beautiful. She had seen ships sailing by, so far off that they looked like seagulls, and she had watched the merry dolphins gambolling in the water.

The year after, the fifth sister reached her fifteenth year. Her birthday happened at a different season from that of her sisters.

It was winter, the sea was of a green colour, and icebergs were floating on its surface. These, she said, looked like pearls and were much larger than the church towers in the land of human beings.

She sat down upon one of these pearls and let the wind play with her long hair; but the sailors in the ships hoisted their sails in terror, and sailed away as quickly as possible.

The first time that either of these sisters rose out of the sea, she was quite charmed at the sight of so many new and beautiful things.

Soon they grew tired of them and liked their own home better than the upper world, for there only did they find everything agreeable.

Many an evening would the five sisters rise hand in hand from the floor of the ocean. Their voices were far sweeter than any human voice, and when a storm was coming on, they would swim in front of the ships and sing songs, telling the sailors not to be afraid.

The mariners, however, did not understand their words. They fancied the song was only the whistling of the wind.

Whilst the sisters were swimming at evening time, the youngest would remain alone in her father's palace, looking up after them. She would have wept, but mermaids cannot weep, and so, when they are troubled, they suffer much more than human beings do.

'Oh! if I were but fifteen,' sighed she; 'I know that I should love the upper world and its people so much.'

At last the time she had so longed for came.

'Well, now it is your turn,' said the grandmother; 'come here that I may adorn you like your sisters.'

And she wound around her hair a wreath of white lilies, whose every petal was the half of a pearl. Then she ordered eight large oysters to fasten themselves to the princess's tail, in token of her high rank.

The princess would have given up all this show and changed her heavy crown for the red flowers of her garden, but she dared not do so.

'Farewell,' said she; and she rose from the sea, light as a flake of foam.

When, for the first time in her life, she came to the surface of the water, the sun had just sunk below the horizon. The clouds were beaming with bright golden and rosy hues, and the sea as smooth as a looking-glass.

A large ship with three masts lay on the still waters; and the sailors were quietly seated about the ladders of the vessel. Music and song came from the deck, and after it grew dark, hundreds of lamps, all on a sudden, burst forth into light.

The little mermaid swam close up to the captain's cabin and every now and then, when the ship was raised by the motion of the water, she could look through the clear window panes.

She saw within many richly dressed men; the handsomest among them was a young prince with large, black eyes.

He could not certainly be more than sixteen years old, and it was in honour of his birthday that a grand party was being held. The crew were dancing on the deck, and when the young prince came among them a hundred rockets were sent up into the air. The rockets made the little mermaid so afraid that for some minutes she plunged beneath the water.

However, she soon raised her little head again, and then it seemed as if all the stars were falling down upon her. Such a fiery shower she had never seen before. It was so light in the ship that everything could be seen clearly.

Oh! how happy the young prince was! He shook hands with the sailors, laughed and jested with them, whilst sweet notes of music broke the silence of night.

It was now late but the little mermaid could not tear herself away from the ship and the handsome young prince. She remained looking through the cabin window, rocked to and fro by the waves.

Soon there was a foaming in the sea and the ship began to move on faster. The sails were spread, and the waves rose high, and thick clouds gathered over the sky.

The sailors saw that a storm was coming on. The great vessel was tossed about on the stormy ocean like a light boat, and the waves rose to a great height.

To the little mermaid this seemed most delightful, but the ship's crew thought very differently. The vessel cracked and the stout masts bent under the force of the waves.

For a minute the ship was tossed to and fro; then the mainmast broke, as if it had been a reed; the ship turned over, and was filled with water.

The little mermaid now saw that the crew was in danger.

But at the same time it became pitch dark, so that she could not see anything. Presently, however, a dreadful flash of lightning showed her the whole of the wreck.

Her eyes sought the young prince – the same instant the ship sank to the bottom. At first she was delighted, thinking that the prince must now come to her abode, but she soon remembered that men cannot live in water.

'Die! No, he must not die!'

She swam through the wreckage with which the water was strewn, with no fear of danger. At last she found the prince keeping his head above water with great difficulty. He had already closed his eyes, and must surely have been drowned, had not the little mermaid come to his rescue.

She seized hold of him and kept him above water, and the current bore them on together.

Towards morning the storm was hushed, but there was no trace of the ship. The sun rose like fire out of the sea; his beams seemed to restore colour to the prince's cheeks, but his eyes were still closed.

The mermaid kissed his high forehead and stroked his wet hair away from his face. He looked like the marble statue in her garden. She kissed him again, and wished with all her heart that he might recover.

She now saw the dry land with its mountains glittering with snow. A green wood stretched along the coast, and near the wood stood a chapel or convent – she could not be sure which.

The sea here formed a little bay, in which the water was quite smooth but very deep, and under the cliffs there were dry firm sands. Hither swam the little mermaid with the prince seemingly dead.

She laid him upon the warm sand, and took care to place his head high, and to turn his face to the sun.

The bells began to ring in the large, white building which stood before her, and a number of young girls came to walk in the garden.

The mermaid went away from the shore, hid herself behind some stones, and covered her head with foam, so that her little face could not be seen. From there she watched the prince.

It was not long before one of the young girls came forward. Soon she ran back to call her sisters to the place.

The little mermaid saw that the prince revived, and that all around smiled kindly and joyfully upon him. For her, however, he looked not; he knew not that it was she who had saved him.

When the prince was taken into the house, she felt so sad that she plunged at once beneath the water, and returned to her father's palace.

If she had before been quiet and thoughtful, she now grew still more so. Her sisters asked her what she had seen in the upper world, but she made no answer. Many an evening she rose to the place where she had left the prince. She saw the snow melt on the mountains and the fruits ripen in the garden, but the prince she never saw.

She always came back to her home in sorrow. Her only pleasure was to sit in her little garden, gazing on the beautiful statue so like the prince.

At last, being unable to hide her sorrow any longer, she let one of her sisters into her secret. Her sister soon told it to the other princesses, and they to some of their friends.

Among them was a young mermaid who remembered the prince, for she also had seen the festivities in the ship. She knew also in what country the prince lived, and the name of its king.

'Come, little sister!' said the princesses; and they rose together, arm-in-arm, out of the water, just in front of the prince's palace.

This palace was built of bright yellow stones, with a flight of white marble steps leading from it down to the sea. Through the clear glass of the high windows one might look into grand rooms hung with silken curtains and with fine paintings on the walls.

It was a real treat to the little royal mermaids to behold so splendid an abode. They gazed through the windows of one of the largest rooms, and in the centre saw a fountain playing. The sunbeams fell dancing on the water and brightening the pretty plants which grew around it.

The little mermaid now knew where her beloved prince dwelt, and henceforth she went there almost every evening. She often went nearer the land than her sisters had ventured, and even swam up the narrow channel that flowed under the marble balcony.

Here, on a bright moonlight night, she would watch the young prince, who believed himself alone.

Sometimes she saw him sailing on the water in a gaily painted boat with many-coloured flags waving above. She would then hide among the green reeds which grew on the banks, listening to his voice. If anyone in the boat heard the rustling of her long silver veil, which was caught now and then by the light breeze, they only fancied it was a swan flapping his wings.

There were many things that she wished to hear explained, but her sisters could not give her any proper answers. She had to ask the old queen-mother, who knew a great deal about the upper world, which she used to call 'the country above the sea'.

'Do men, when they are not drowned, live for ever?' she asked one day. 'Do they not die as we do, who live at the bottom of the sea?'

'Yes,' was the grandmother's reply; 'they must die like us, and their life is much shorter than ours. We live to the age of three hundred years, but when we die we become foam on the sea, and are not allowed even to share a grave among those that are dear to us.

'We have no souls, so we can never live again, and are like the grass which, when once cut down, is withered for ever. Human beings have souls that go on living; and as we rise out of the water to admire the homes of man, they go to glorious unknown dwellings in the skies, which we are not allowed to see.'

'Why have *we* not souls?' asked the little mermaid. 'I would willingly give up my three hundred years to be a human being for only one day so that I could go to that heavenly world above.'

'You must not think of that,' answered her grandmother; 'it is much better as it is: we live longer and are far happier than human beings.'

'So I must die, and be dashed like foam over the sea. Tell me, dear grandmother, are there no means by which I may get a soul?'

'No!' replied the old lady. 'It is true that if thou couldst make a human being love thee with all his heart and promise to be always faithful to thee, then his soul would flow into thine.

'But that can never be! For what in our eyes is the most beautiful part of our body – our tail – the people of the earth think hideous. To be handsome to them, the body must have two clumsy props which they call legs.'

The little mermaid sighed and looked sadly at the scaly part of her form.

That evening a court ball was held in the palace.

It was far more splendid than any that the earth has ever seen. The walls of the ball-room were of crystal, very thick, but yet very clear. Hundreds of large mussel-shells were planted along them in rows; some of these shells were rose-coloured, some green as grass, but all sent forth a bright, dazzling light.

They also shone through the glassy walls so as to light up the waters around for a great space, and made the scales of the fishes appear crimson and purple, silver and gold-coloured.

Through the centre of the ball-room flowed a bright, clear stream, on the surface of which danced mermen and mermaids to the music of their own sweet voices – voices far sweeter than those of the dwellers upon earth.

The little princess sang more sweetly than any other, and they clapped their hands in praise of her.

She was pleased at this, for she knew well that there was neither on earth nor in the sea a more beautiful voice than hers. But her thoughts soon returned to the world above her: she could not forget the handsome prince.

At last she stole away from her father's palace, and whilst all was joy within, she sat alone, lost in thought, in her little neglected garden.

On a sudden she heard the tones of horns over the water far away in the distance.

'Now he is going out to hunt,' she said to herself, 'he whom I love more than my father and my mother, and to whom I would so gladly trust the happiness of my life. Whilst my sisters are still dancing in the palace, I will go to the enchantress, the only person who is able to advise and help me.'

So the little mermaid left the garden, and went to the foaming whirlpool beyond which dwelt the enchantress.

She had never been this way before, neither flowers nor sea-grass bloomed along her path. She had to go across a stretch of bare gray sand till she reached the whirlpool, whose waters were like mill-wheels, tearing everything they could see along with them.

She had to make her way through this horrible place, in order to arrive at the house of the enchantress. Her house stood in a wood, and a strange abode it was.

All the trees and bushes were like hundred-headed serpents, having long, slimy arms with fingers of worms, instead of branches. Whatever they seized they fastened upon, so that it could not loosen itself from their grasp.

The little mermaid stood still for a minute looking at this horrible wood. Her heart beat with fear, and she would certainly have turned back had she not remembered the prince.

This gave her new courage.

She bound up her long waving hair, crossed her arms over her bosom, and swifter than a fish can glide through the water, she passed through the wood.

When she got safely through this wood of horrors, she arrived at a slimy place, where huge, fat snails were crawling about. In the midst of this place stood a house built of the bones of people who had been drowned. Here sat the witch stroking a toad in the same manner as some persons would pet a bird.

'I know well what you ask of me,' said she to the little princess. 'Your wish is foolish enough, but you shall have it, though it will be sure to bring trouble to you, my fairest princess. You wish to get rid of your tail and to have instead two stilts like those of human beings, because you wish a young prince to fall in love with you, and that you may have a soul. Is it not so?'

While the witch spoke these words, she laughed so loudly that her pet toad and snails fell from her lap.

'You come just at the right time,' continued she; 'had you come after sunset, I could not have helped you before another year.

'I will give you a drink with which you must swim to land. You must sit down upon the shore and swallow it, and then your tail will shrink up to the things men call legs.

'This change will, however, be very painful; you will feel as though a sharp knife passed through your body. All who look on you after you have been thus changed will say that you are the loveliest child of earth they have ever seen. You will keep your graceful ways, and no dancer will move so lightly. But every step you take will cause you pain almost too much to bear – it will seem to you as if you were walking on the sharp edges of swords – and your blood will flow. Can you suffer all this? If so, I will give you your wish.'

'Yes, I will,' answered the princess, with a faltering voice; for she remembered her dear prince, and the soul which, through her suffering, she might win.

'Only remember,' said the witch, 'that you can never again become a mermaid, when once you have got human form. You may never come back to your sisters, and your father's palace; and unless you win so much of the prince's love that he shall leave father and mother for you, you will never get the soul you seek.

'The day after he is married to another, will see your death. Your heart will break with sorrow and you will be changed to foam on the sea.'

'Still I will try,' said the little mermaid, pale and trembling.

'Besides all this, I must be paid, and it is no slight thing that I wish for my trouble. Thou hast the sweetest voice of all the dwellers in the sea, and thou thinkest to charm the prince with it; this voice, however, I ask as my payment.'

'But if you take my voice from me,' said the princess, 'what have I left with which to charm the prince?'

'Thy graceful form and speaking eyes,' replied the witch. 'With such as these, it will be easy to win a vain human heart. Well, now! Hast thou lost courage? Put out thy little tongue, that I may cut it off, and take it for myself in return for my magic drink.'

'Be it so!' said the princess, and the witch took up her pot in order to mix the drink.

The magic drink, at length, clear as pure water, was ready.

'Here it is,' said the witch to the princess, cutting out her tongue at the same moment. The poor little mermaid was now dumb: she could neither sing nor speak.

'If the trees should attempt to seize you, as you pass through my little grove,' said the witch, 'you have only to sprinkle some of this magic drink over them, and their arms will burst into a thousand pieces.'

But the princess had no need of this advice, for the branches drew hastily back as soon as they saw the bright phial, that glittered in her hand like a star. Thus she passed safely through the wood and over the moor.

She now looked once again at her father's palace; the lamps were out, and all the family were asleep. She would not go in, for she could not speak if she did; she was about to leave her home for ever. Her heart was ready to break with sorrow at the thought. She stole into the garden, plucked a flower from the bed of each of her sisters, kissed her hand again and again, and then rose through the dark blue waters to the world above.

The sun had not yet risen when she reached the prince's palace and went up the marble steps. The moon still shone in the sky when the little mermaid drank of the wonderful liquid contained in her phial. She felt it run through her like a sharp knife, and she fell down in a faint.

When the sun rose she awoke, and felt a burning pain in all her limbs; but – she saw standing close to her the handsome young prince. His coal-black eyes were fixed upon her. Full of shame, she cast down her own, and saw, instead of the long fish-like tail, two slender legs.

The prince asked who she was, and how she had got there. In reply she smiled and gazed upon him with her bright blue eyes, for alas! she could not speak.

He then led her by the hand into the palace. She found that the witch had told her true; she felt as though she were walking on the edges of sharp swords, but she bore the pain willingly. On she passed, light as a gentle breeze, and all who saw her wondered at her graceful movements.

When she went into the palace, rich clothes of muslin and silk were brought to her, and she was lovelier than all who dwelt there, but she could neither speak nor sing. Some female slaves, gaily dressed, sang before the prince and his royal parents. One of them sang to the prince, who clapped his hands with pleasure at her clear, sweet voice.

This made the little mermaid very sad, for she knew that she used to sing far better than the young slave.

'Alas!' thought she, 'if he did but know that, for his sake, I have given away my voice for ever.'

The slaves began to dance; our lovely little mermaiden then arose, stretched out her soft white arms, and tripped gracefully about the room. Every motion showed more and more the perfect elegance of her figure.

All were charmed, and especially the young prince, who called her his dear little foundling. And she danced again and again, although every step cost her great pain.

The prince then said she should always be with him, and a suit of male apparel was made for her, so that she might go along with him in his rides.

Together they went through the sweet-smelling woods, where green boughs brushed against their shoulders, and the birds sang merrily among the fresh leaves. With him she climbed up steep mountains, and although her tender feet bled, she only smiled and followed her dear prince to the tops of the mountains.

During the night she would, when all in the palace were at rest, walk down the marble steps, in order to cool her feet in the deep waters. She would then think of those loved ones who dwelt in the lower world.

One night, as she was thus bathing her feet, her sisters

swam together to the spot, arm-in-arm and singing, but alas! so mournfully! She signed to them, and they at once knew her and told her how great was the mourning in her father's house for her loss.

From this time the sisters paid her a visit every night; and once they brought with them the old grandmother, who had not seen the upper world for a great many years. Their father, the Mer-king, with his crown on his head, also came: but these two old people did not dare come near enough to land to be able to speak to her.

The little mermaiden became dearer and dearer to the prince every day; but he only looked upon her as a sweet, gentle child, and the thought of making her his wife never entered his head. And yet his wife she must be, ere she could have a soul; his wife she must be or she would change into foam, and be driven over the billows of the sea!

'Dost thou not love me above all others?' her eyes seemed to ask, as he kissed her lovely brow.

'Yes,' the prince would say; 'thou art dearer to me than any other, for no one is as good as thou art. And thou art so like a young maiden whom I have seen but once, and may never see again.

'I was on board a ship which was wrecked by a sudden tempest; the waves threw me on the shore near a holy temple, where there lived a number of young girls. The youngest of them found me on the shore, and saved my life. I saw her only once, and her alone can I love. But she belongs to the holy temple, and thou who art so like her hast been given to me to take her place. Never will we be parted!'

'Alas! he does not know that it was I who saved his life,' thought the little mermaiden, sighing deeply. 'I carried him over the wild waves into the bay where the holy temple stood. I sat behind the rocks, waiting till someone should come. I saw the pretty maiden approach, whom he loves more than me,' and again she heaved a deep sigh, for she could not weep.

'So the prince is going to be married to the beautiful daughter of the king of the next country,' said the courtiers, 'that is why he is having that splendid ship fitted out. It is said that he wishes to travel, but he is really going to see the princess.'

The little mermaiden smiled at this news, for she knew what the prince meant to do better than anyone else.

'I must go,' he said to her; 'I must see the beautiful princess; but my parents will not make me marry her. She cannot be so like the beautiful girl in the temple as thou art; and if I had to choose, I should prefer thee, my little silent foundling, with the speaking eyes.'

'Thou art not afraid of the sea, art thou, my sweet silent child?' asked he tenderly, as they stood together in the splendid ship which was to take them to the country of the neighbouring king. And then he told her of the storms that sometimes stir the waters and of the strange fishes that live in the deep. But she smiled at his words, for she knew better than any child of earth what went on down in the ocean.

At night-time, when the moon shone brightly, and when all on board were fast asleep, she sat and looked down into the sea. It seemed to her that she saw her father's palace, and her grandmother's silver crown.

She then saw her sisters rise out of the water, looking sad and stretching out their hands towards her. She nodded to them and smiled, but just then the cabin boy came near, so the sisters plunged beneath the water.

The next morning the ship entered the harbour of the king's capital. Bells were rung and trumpets sounded. Every day some new entertainment was given; balls and parties followed each other.

The princess, however, was not yet in the town, for she had been sent to a distant school to be taught all the royal virtues.

At last she came home to the palace. When the little mermaid saw her, she said to herself that she had never before seen so beautiful a creature.

'It is herself!' cried the prince, when they met; 'it is she who saved my life, when I lay on the seashore!' and he pressed his blushing bride to his beating heart.

'Oh, I am all too happy!' said he to his dumb foundling. 'What I never dared to hope for has come to pass. Thou must join in my happiness, for thou lovest me more than all others who are always with me.'

And the little mermaid kissed his hand in silent sorrow. It seemed to her as if her heart was breaking already, and yet it was not near his marriage day, which must see her death.

Again the church bells rang, whilst heralds rode through the streets of the capital, to tell the people of the coming bridal celebration. Flames burned in silver candlesticks on all the altars; and bride and bridegroom joined hands in marriage.

The little mermaid, clad in silk and cloth-of-gold, stood behind the princess, and held the train of the bridal dress. But her ear heard nothing of the solemn music and her eye saw nothing of the wedding. She thought only that she would soon die, and remembered that she had lost both this world and the next.

That very same evening, bride and bridegroom went on board the ship. Flags waved in the breeze and with the favourable wind the ship glided lightly over the blue waters. As soon as it was dark, coloured lamps were hung out, and dancing began on the deck. The little mermaid was thus reminded of what she had seen the first time she rose to the upper world.

She joined in the dance, hovering lightly as a bird over the ship's boards. All praised her, for never had she danced with more charming grace. She no longer felt the pain of her little feet; the grief her heart suffered was much greater.

It was the last evening she might see him, for whose sake she had left her home and all her family, had given away her beautiful voice, and suffered daily fearful pain. A long night, in which she might neither think nor dream, awaited her. All was joy in the ship; and she, her heart filled with thoughts of death, smiled and danced with the others till past midnight.

All was now still; the steersman alone stood at the ship's wheel. The little mermaid leaned her white arms on the side of the ship and looked towards the east, watching for the dawn. She well knew that the first sunbeam would see her death.

She saw her sisters rise out of the sea. Their faces were deadly pale, and their long hair no more fell over their shoulders – it had all been cut off.

'We have given it to the witch,' said they, 'to get her to help thee, so that thou mayest not die. She has given to us a penknife: here it is! Before the sun rises, thou must plunge it into the prince's heart; and when his warm blood trickles down upon thy feet, they will again be changed to a fish-like tail.

'Thou wilt once more become a mermaid, and wilt live thy full three hundred years, ere thou changest to foam on the sea. But hasten! either he or thou must die before sunrise.'

At these words they sighed deeply and plunged into the sea.

The little mermaid drew aside the purple curtains where lay the bride and bridegroom; bending over them she kissed the prince's forehead, and then glancing at the sky, she saw that the dawning light became every moment brighter. The prince's lips murmured the name of his bride – he was dreaming of her, and her only, whilst the fatal penknife trembled in the hand of the unhappy mermaid.

All at once she threw the penknife far out into the sea. The waves rose like bright, blazing flames around where it fell.

With eyes fast becoming dim and fixed, she looked once more at her beloved prince; then plunged from the ship into the sea, and felt her body slowly but surely changing into foam.

The sun rose from his watery bed; his beams fell so softly and warmly upon her that our little mermaid scarcely felt she was dying.

She still saw the bright sun, and the white sails of the ship, and the bright red clouds in the sky.

And now again all were awake and rejoicing in the ship. The prince, with his pretty bride, had missed her, and they looked sadly down on the foamy waters, as if they knew she had plunged into the sea.

Unseen, our little mermaid leaped up and kissed the bridegroom's forehead, smiled upon him, and then, turning her head, she sped out of sight across the surface of the sea. And, for the first time in her life, her eyes were wet with tears.

The Wraggle Taggle Gipsies
Anonymous

There were three gipsies a-come to my door,
And down-stairs ran this a-lady, O!
One sang high, and another sang low,
And the other sang, Bonny, bonny Biscay, O!

Then she pulled off her silk-finished gown
And put on hose of leather, O!
The ragged, ragged rags about our door –

She's gone with the wraggle taggle gipsies, O!

It was late last night, when my lord came home,
Enquiring for his a-lady, O!
The servants said, on every hand:
'She's gone with the wraggle taggle gipsies, O!'

'O saddle to me my milk-white steed,
Go and fetch me my pony, O!
That I may ride and seek my bride,
Who is gone with the wraggle taggle gipsies, O!'

O he rode high and he rode low,
He rode through woods and copses too,
Until he came to an open field,
And there he espied his a-lady, O!

'What makes you leave your house and land?
What makes you leave your money, O?
What makes you leave your new-wedded lord;
To go with the wraggle taggle gipsies, O!'

'What care I for my house and my land?
What care I for my money, O?
What care I for my new-wedded lord?
I'm off with the wraggle taggle gipsies, O!'

'Last night you slept on a goose-feather bed,
With the sheet turned down so bravely, O!
And tonight you'll sleep in a cold open field,
Along with the wraggle taggle gipsies, O!'

'What care I for a goose-feather bed,
With the sheet turned down so bravely, O?
For tonight I shall sleep in a cold open field,
Along with the wraggle taggle gipsies, O!'

Bridal Morning

Anonymous

The maidens came
When I was in my mother's bower;
  I had all that I would.
    The bailey beareth the bell away
    The lily, the rose, the rose I lay.

The silver is white, red is the gold;
The robes they lay in fold.
    The bailey beareth the lull away;
    The lily, the rose, the rose I lay.

And thro the glass window shines the sun.
How should I love, and I so young?
    The bailey beareth the lull away;
    The lily, the rose, the rose I lay.

Young

Anne Sexton

A thousand doors ago
when I was a lonely kid
in a big house with four
garages and it was summer
as long as I could remember,
I lay on the lawn at night,
clover wrinkling under me,
the wise stars bedding over me,
my mother's window a funnel
of yellow heat running out,
my father's window, half shut,
an eye where sleepers pass,
and the boards of the house
were smooth and white as wax
and probably a million leaves
sailed on their strange stalks
as the crickets ticked together
and I, in my brand new body,
which was not a woman's yet,
told the stars my questions
and thought God could really see
the heat and the painted light,
elbows, knees, dreams, goodnight.

The Princess in the Suit of Leather

[Russian folk tale]

Neither here nor elsewhere lived a king who had a wife whom he loved with all his heart and a daughter who was the light of his eyes. The princess had hardly reached womanhood when the queen fell ill and died. For one whole year the king kept vigil, sitting with bowed head beside her tomb. Then he summoned the matchmakers, elderly women wise in the ways of living, and said, 'I wish to marry again. Here is my poor queen's anklet. Find me the girl, rich or poor, humble or well-born, whose foot this anklet will fit. For I promised the queen as she lay dying that I would marry that girl and no other.'

The matchmakers travelled up and down the kingdom looking for the king's new bride. But search and search as they would, they could not find a single girl around whose ankle the jewel would close. The queen had been such that there was no woman like her. Then one old woman said, 'We have entered the house of every maiden in the land except the house of the king's own daughter. Let us go to the palace.'

When they slipped the anklet on to the princess's foot, it suited as if it had been made to her measure. Out of the seraglio went the women at a run, straight into the king's presence, and said, 'We have visited every maiden in your kingdom, but none was able to squeeze her foot into the late queen's anklet. None, that is, except the princess your daughter. She wears it as easily as if it were her own.' A wrinkled matron spoke up: 'Why not marry the princess? Why give her to a stranger and deprive yourself?' The words were hardly spoken when the king summoned the *qadi* to pen the papers for the marriage. To the princess he made no mention of his plan.

Now there was a bustle in the palace as the jewellers, the clothiers, and the furnishers came to outfit the bride. The princess was pleased to know that she was to be wed. But who her husband was she had no inkling. As late as the 'night of the entering', when the groom first sees the bride, she remained in ignorance even though the servants with their whispers were busy around her, combing and pinning and making her beautiful. At last the minister's daughter, who had come to admire her in her finery, said, 'Why are you frowning? Were not women created for marriage with men? And is there any man whose standing is higher than the king's?'

'What is the meaning of such talk?' cried the princess.

'I won't tell you,' said the girl, 'unless you give me your golden bangle to keep.' The princess pulled off the bracelet, and the girl explained how everything had come about so that the bridegroom was no other than the princess's own father.

The princess turned whiter than the cloth on her head and trembled like one who is sick with the forty-day fever. She rose to her feet and sent away all who were with her. Then, knowing only that she must escape, she ran on to the terrace and leaped over the palace wall, landing in a tanner's yard which lay below. She pressed a handful of gold into the tanner's palm and said, 'Can you make me a suit of leather to hide me from head to heels, showing nothing but my eyes? I want it by tomorrow's dawn.'

The poor man was overjoyed to earn the coins. He set to work with his wife and children. Cutting and stitching through the night they had the suit ready, before it was light enough to know a white thread from a dark. Wait a little! And here comes our lady, the princess. She put on the suit – such a

221

strange spectacle that anyone looking at her would think he was seeing nothing but a pile of hides. In this disguise she left the tanner and lay down beside the city gate, waiting for the day.

Now to return to my lord the king. When he entered the bridal chamber and found the princess gone, he sent his army into the city to search for her. Time and again a soldier would stumble upon the princess lying at the gate and ask, 'Have you seen the king's daughter?' And she would reply:

> 'My name is Juleidah for my coat of skins,
> My eyes are weak, my sight is dim,
> My ears are deaf, I cannot hear.
> I care for no one far or near.'

When it was day and the city gate was unbarred, she shuffled out until she was beyond the walls. Then she turned her face away from her father's city and fled.

Walking and running, one foot lifting her and one foot setting her down, there was a day when, with the setting of the sun, the princess came to another city. Too weary to travel a step farther, she fell to the ground. Now her resting place was in the shadow of the wall of the women's quarters, the harem of the sultan's palace. A slave girl, leaning from the window to toss out the crumbs from the royal table, noticed the heap of skins on the ground and thought nothing of it. But when she saw two bright eyes staring out at her from the middle of the hides, she sprang back in terror and said to the queen, 'My lady, there is something monstrous crouching under our window. I have seen it, and it looks like nothing less than an Afreet!'

'Bring it up for me to see and judge,' said the queen.

The slave girl went down shivering with fear, not knowing which was the easier thing to face, the monster outside or her mistress's rage should she fail to do her bidding. But the princess in her suit made no sound when the slave girl tugged at a corner of the leather. The girl took courage and dragged her all the way into the presence of the sultan's wife.

Never had such an astonishing creature been seen in that country. Lifting both palms in amazement, the queen asked her servant, 'What is it?' and then turned to the monster and asked, 'Who are you?' When the heap of skins answered –

> 'My name is Juleidah for my coat of skins,
> My eyes are weak, my sight is dim,
> My ears are deaf, I cannot hear.
> I care for no one far or near.'

- how the queen laughed at the quaint reply! 'Go bring food and drink for our guest,' she said, holding her side. 'We shall keep her to amuse us.'

When Juleidah had eaten, the queen said, 'Tell us what you can do, so that we may put you to work about the palace.'

'Anything you ask me to do, I am ready to try,' said Juleidah.

Then the queen called, 'Mistress cook! Take this broken-winged soul into your kitchen. Maybe for her sake God will reward us with His blessings.'

So now our fine princess was a kitchen skivvy, feeding the fires and raking out the ashes. And whenever the queen lacked company and felt bored, she called Juleidah and laughed at her prattle.

One day the *wazir* sent word that all the sultan's harem was invited to a night's entertainment in his house. All day long there was a stir of excitement in the women's quarters. As the queen prepared to set out in the evening, she stopped by Juleidah and said, 'Won't you come with us tonight? All the servants and slaves are invited. Aren't you afraid to stay alone?' But Juleidah only repeated her refrain:

'My ears are deaf, I cannot hear.
I care for no one far or near.'

One of the serving girls sniffed and said, 'What is there to make her afraid? She is blind and deaf and wouldn't notice an Afreet even if he were to jump on top of her in the dark!' So they left.

In the women's reception hall of the *wazir*'s house there was dining and feasting and music and much merriment. Suddenly, at the height of the talk and enjoyment, such a one entered that they all stopped in the middle of the word they were speaking. Tall as a cypress, with a face like a rose and the silks and jewels of a king's bride, she seemed to fill the room with light. Who was it? Juleidah, who had shaken off her coat of leather as soon as the sultan's harem had gone. She had followed them to the *wazir*'s, and now the ladies who had been so merry began to quarrel, each wanting to sit beside the newcomer.

When dawn was near, Juleidah took a handful of gold sequins from the fold of her sash and scattered them on the floor. The ladies scrambled to pick up the bright treasure. And while they were occupied, Juleidah left the hall. Quickly, quickly she raced back to the palace kitchen and put on the coat of leather. Soon the others returned. Seeing the heap of hides on the kitchen floor, the queen poked it with the toe of her red slipper and said, 'Truly, I wish you had been with us to admire the lady who was at the entertainment.' But Juleidah only mumbled, 'My eyes are weak, I cannot see . . .' and they all went to their own beds to sleep.

When the queen woke up next day, the sun was high in the sky. As was his habit, the sultan's son came in to kiss his mother's hand and bid her good morning. But she could talk only of the visitor at the *wazir*'s feast. 'O my son,' she sighed, 'it was a woman with such a face and such a neck and such a form that all who saw her said, "She is the daughter of neither a king nor a sultan, but of someone greater yet!"' On and on the queen poured out her praises of the woman, until the prince's heart was on fire. Finally his mother concluded, 'I wish I had asked her father's name so that I could engage her to be your bride.' And the sultan's son replied, 'When you return tonight to continue your entertainment, I shall stand outside the *wazir*'s door and wait until she leaves. I'll ask her then about her father and her station.'

At sunset the women dressed themselves once more. With the folds of their robes smelling of orange blossom and incense and their bracelets chinking on their arms, they passed by Juleidah lying on the kitchen floor and said, 'Will you come with us tonight?' But Juleidah only turned her back on them. Then as soon as they were safely gone, she threw off her suit of leather and hurried after them.

In the *wazir*'s hall the guests pressed close around Juleidah, wanting to see her and ask where she came from. But to all their questions she gave no answer, whether yes or no, although she sat with them until the dawning of the day. Then she threw a fistful of pearls on the marble tiles, and while the women pushed one another to catch them, she slipped away as easily as a hair is pulled out of the dough.

Now who was standing at the door? The prince, of course. He had been waiting for this moment. Blocking her path, he grasped her arm and asked who her father was and from what land she came. But the princess had to be back in her kitchen or her secret would be known. So she fought to get away, and in the scuffle, she pulled the prince's ring clean off his hand.

'At least tell me where you come from!' he shouted after her as she ran. 'By Allah, tell me where!'

And she replied, 'I live in a land of paddles and ladles.'

Then she fled into the palace and hid in her coat of hides.

In came the others, talking and laughing. The prince told his mother what had taken place and announced that he intended to make a journey. 'I must go to the land of the paddles and ladles,' he said.

'Be patient, my son,' said the queen. 'Give me time to prepare your provisions.'

Eager as he was, the prince agreed to delay his departure for two days – 'But not one hour more!'

Now the kitchen became the busiest corner of the palace. The grinding and sieving, the kneading and the baking began and Juleidah stood watching.

'Away with you,' cried the cook, 'this is no work for you!'

'I want to serve the prince our master like the rest!' said Juleidah.

Willing and not willing to let her help, the cook gave her a piece of dough to shape. Juleidah began to make a cake, and when no one was watching, she pushed the prince's ring inside it. And when the food was packed Juleidah placed her own little cake on top of the rest.

Early on the third morning the rations were strapped into the saddlebags, and the prince set off with his servants and his men. He rode without slackening until the sun grew hot. Then he said, 'Let us rest the horses while we ourselves eat a mouthful.' A servant, seeing Juleidah's tiny loaf lying on top of all the rest, flung it to one side.

'Why did you throw that one away?' asked the prince.

'It was the work of the creature Juleidah; I saw her make it,' said the servant. 'It is as misshapen as she is.'

The prince felt pity for the strange halfwit and asked the servant to bring back her cake. When he tore open the loaf, look, his own ring was inside! The ring he lost the night of the *wazir*'s entertainment. Understanding now where lay the land

226

of ladles and paddles, the prince gave orders to turn back.

When the king and queen had greeted him, the prince said, 'Mother, send me my supper with Juleidah.'

'She can barely see or even hear,' said the queen. 'How can she bring your supper to you?'

'I shall not eat unless Juleidah brings the food,' said the prince. So when the time came, the cooks arranged the dishes on a tray and helped Juleidah lift it on to her head. Up the stairs she went, but before she reached the prince's room she tipped the dishes and sent them crashing to the floor.

'I told you she cannot see,' the queen said to her son.

'And I will only eat what Juleidah brings,' said the prince.

The cooks prepared a second meal, and when they had balanced the loaded tray upon Juleidah's head, they sent two slave girls to hold her by either hand and guide her to the prince's door.

'Go,' said the prince to the two slaves, 'and you, Juleidah, come.'

Juleidah began to say,

'My eyes are weak, my sight is dim,
I'm called Juleidah for my coat of skins,
My ears are deaf, I cannot hear,
I care for no one far or near.'

But the prince told her, 'Come and fill my cup.' As she approached, he drew the dagger that hung at his side and slashed her leather coat from collar to hem. It fell into a heap upon the floor – and there stood the maiden his mother had described, one who could say to the moon, 'Set that I may shine in your stead.'

Hiding Juleidah in a corner of the room, the prince sent for the queen. Our mistress cried out when she saw the pile of skins upon the floor. 'Why, my son, did you bring her death upon your neck? The poor thing deserved your pity more than your punishment!'

'Come in, Mother,' said the prince. 'Come and look at our Juleidah before you mourn her.' And he led his mother to where our fine princess sat revealed, her fairness filling the room like a ray of light. The queen threw herself upon the girl and kissed her on this side and on that, and bade her sit with the prince and eat. Then she summoned the *qadi* to write the paper that would bind our lord the prince to the fair princess, after which they lived together in the sweetest bliss.

Now we make our way back to the king, Juleidah's father. When he entered the bridal chamber to unveil his own daughter's face and found her gone, and when he had searched the city in vain for her, he called his minister and his servants and dressed himself for travel. From country to country he journeyed, entering one city and leaving the next, taking with him in chains the old woman who had first suggested to him that he marry his own daughter. At last he reached the city where Juleidah was living with her husband the prince.

Now, the princess was sitting in her window when they entered the gate, and she knew them as soon as she saw them. Straightway she sent to her husband urging him to invite the strangers. Our lord went to meet them and succeeded in detaining them only after much pressing, for they were impatient to continue their quest. They dined in the prince's guest hall, then thanked their host and took leave with the words, 'The proverb says: "Have your fill to eat, but then up, on to your feet!"' – while he delayed them further with the proverb, 'Where you break your bread, there spread out your bed!'

In the end the prince's kindness forced the tired strangers to lie in his house as guests for the night. 'But why did you single out these strangers?' the prince asked Juleidah.

'Lend me your robes and headcloth and let me go to them,' she said. 'Soon you will know my reasons.'

Thus disguised, Juleidah sat with her guests. When the coffee cups had been filled and emptied, she said, 'Let us tell stories to pass the time. Will you speak first, or shall I?'

'Leave us to our sorrows, my son,' said the king her father. 'We have not the spirit to tell tales.'

'I'll entertain you, then, and distract your mind,' said Juleidah. 'There once was a king . . .' she began, and went on to tell the history of her own adventures from the beginning to the end. Every now and then the old woman would interrupt and say, 'Can you find no better story than this, my son?' But Juleidah kept right on, and when she had finished she said, 'I am your daughter the princess, upon whom all these troubles fell through the words of this old sinner and daughter of shame!'

In the morning they flung the old woman over a tall cliff into the *wadi*. Then the king gave half his kingdom to his daughter and the prince, and they lived in happiness and contentment until death, the parter of the truest lovers, divided them.

Eskimo Occasion
Judith Rodriguez

I am in my Eskimo-hunting-song mood,
Aha!
The lawn is tundra   the car will not start
the sunlight is an avalanche   we are avalanche-struck at
    our breakfast
struck with sunlight through glass   me and my spoon-fed
    daughters

out of this world in our kitchen.

I will sing the song of my daughter-hunting,
Oho!
The waves lay down   the ice grew strong
I sang the song   of dark water under ice
the song of winter fishing   the magic for seal rising
among the ancestor-masks.

I waited by water to dream new spirits,
Hoo!
The water spoke   the ice shouted
the sea opened   the sun made young shadows
they breathed my breathing   I took them from deep water
I brought them fur-warmed home.

I am dancing the years of the two great hunts,
Ya-hay!
It was I who waited   cold in the wind-break
I stamp like the bear   I call like the wind of the thaw
I leap like the sea spring-running.   My sunstruck daughters
    splutter
and chuckle and bang their spoons:

Mummy is singing at breakfast and dancing!
So big!

Ghost Dance
Susan Price

In a place far distant from where you are now grows an oak
tree by a lake.

Round the oak's trunk is a chain of golden links.

Tethered to the chain is a learned cat, and this most learned of all cats walks round and round the tree continually.

As it walks one way, it sings songs.

As it walks the other, it tells stories.

This is one of the stories the cat tells.

I tell (says the cat) of the Northlands, where, in the long, dark winter, the white snow falls out of the black, black sky. Soft, silent it falls through the branches of the pines and birch, and mounts, thin flake on thin flake, until the snow lies ten cold feet deep, and the silence is frozen to the darkness.

This (says the cat) is the land where that white, sharp-backed horse, North Wind, carries Granddad Frost swiftly through the trees. The old man breathes to the left and right, and what his breath touches is blasted and withered, and his rasping voice whispers, 'Are you cold, children? Are you cold?'

I tell (says the cat) of a gyrfalcon flying – a bird the colour of snow in darkness, flying above snow and through darkness. It turned in sweeping circles, it gyred, and its sickle-winged shadow scudded before it over the moonlit snow far beneath.

The gyrfalcon looked down and saw a flat circle of the Earth tipped up to its gaze. A circle of Earth gleaming white, but marked with black rocks, with black trees, and all growing smaller as the falcon gyred upwards; all growing greater as it spun down. The only sounds the falcon hears are the soft huff of wind under its wings, and its own cry, thin and sharp as wire drawn from ice: *Keeee-ya! Keeee-ya!*

A gyrfalcon's eyes can outstare the sun, and now they pierced the winter darkness. It saw a tree, and its eyes stared, and saw the cones in its branches; and stared, and saw each needle leaf. And stared, and saw the mice running up the trunk.

Its eyes stared down, and saw the rocks; and stared and saw the cracks in the rocks; and stared and saw the voles that hid there. It stared down and saw the fox making tracks across the snow. It saw the fish beneath the ice.

It wheeled in the sky and looked down and saw the tents of the reindeer people, and the reindeer, and the wolves following, and the ever-hungry glutton hurrying among the trees. It saw the snow-rabbit and the lynx and the bear.

But of all these things, trees and people, deer and wolves, fish and lynx, fox and bear, the gyrfalcon saw fewer, far fewer than before. And it saw bloodied places in the snow, and twisted, frozen bodies in traps; and the cut stumps of trees. *Keeee-ya! Keeee-ya!*

Then the gyrfalcon's eyes sharpened on what it searched for, and it wheeled in the cold sky and circled down. Below, a small line of men, black against the snow, slid on skis through the pines. Lower the falcon gyred, and lower, staring on the men.

I'll tell of the men (says the cat). They were hunters, and hungry. The snow was so deep that they were raised high among the tree branches and skimmed through them like birds. All of them looked like fat old men, with their round bodies and their white beards – but their fatness was the thick, warm padding of their clothes; and their beards were not white with age, but with ice frozen to the hair. All of them skied with their heads ducked low, to keep their faces from the scraping of the wind-blown ice, and they gripped bows in their mittened hands, and wore hoods or tall caps with flaps to cover their ears. Quivers of arrows rustled and thumped at their sides, but no game. They had caught nothing.

They peered from side to side as they went, for the wind carried a load of ice-crystals that rattled and crackled in the cold air, and made a shifting white, grey, ice-blue veil before their eyes. The wind would drop, and let the ice fall, crackling, to the snow, and the black trees would stand out clear against the white, the silver stars bright against the black. But then the wind would lift up the ice and snow once more, and the stars dimmed, and the trees would seem to shrink or grow, or even to leave the Earth and walk, when seen through that shifting, icy cloud.

A whiteness swooped at the men and they skidded to a halt, snow spurting from their skis. They ducked and cried out as the gyrfalcon came swinging towards them again. With up-raised wings, it dropped from the sky into the snow, and turned into – what? Too small for a man. A boy?

The figure straightened from a crouch and stood before them, its booted feet denting the frozen surface of the snow. The hunters reached to their quivers for arrows, and fitted them to their bowstrings.

A lad – or a girl. A girl, or a lad, who had dropped out of a tree – or out of the sky. A lad, or a girl, alone, so far from any camp or settlement – and dressed, in this cold and darkness, as if for a stroll on a summer evening. Boots, yes, hide boots like theirs, embroidered and patterned; but above the boots only a tunic and breeches of thin reindeer hide, stitched with brass rings, with tiny mirrors that flashed a dimmed white light, with bunches of tiny bones and bunches of white feathers. But no gloves and no hat – the stranger's long black hair blew about in the wind, and was quickly turning white with snow, as if this youngster were growing old in moments.

The hunters knew that no one living could endure such cold, dressed so lightly. They dared not take their eyes from the creature to look at each other, but all of them feared, in their own minds, that this was the ghost of one frozen to death, searching for others to soothe to freezing death in the snow.

The stranger came closer and, in the light reflected from the

233

snow, they could see the face of one of their own people. But it could have been the face of a pretty boy or a handsome girl. The stranger stretched out a naked hand and placed it on the arm of the hunters' leader.

'Are you cold, Uncle?' the stranger asked, just as Frost is said to ask. The voice was that of a boy, but croaking and quiet, as if the cold had withered it. 'I've been sent to find you.'

The hunters looked at each other, hoping one of them would know what to do. Some bent their bows further, ready to send an arrow into the ghost. Their leader, with the stranger's hand still on his wrist, looked into the boy-girl's face and asked, 'Who sent you to find us?'

'My grandmother.' The hoarse voice seemed surprised. 'Are you not searching for a shaman? I'm sent to bring you to her.'

The hunters gasped, sending puffs of their white breath into the darkness before their faces – breath which froze into icicles on their beards. They drew back from the stranger – all but the leader, who stood as if the hand on his wrist held him to the spot. Those with bent bows hastily let them down, took the arrows from the strings and put them back into their quivers as if no thought of shooting at the shaman's grandchild had been in their minds. It is never wise to offend a shaman. But they were not made happy by the stranger's words.

'Go with this forest ghost? Too dangerous!'

'We must! Haven't we proved a shaman can't be found by looking? Haven't we looked and looked and never found a trace of one?'

'It's an ice-devil! It will breathe in our faces and freeze us to death!'

The leader, still standing face to face with the stranger, said, 'How can we tell if we can trust you?'

In the hoarse voice that seemed always about to choke into silence, the young stranger said, 'If my grandmother meant to hurt you, Uncle, she could have done it without sending me within reach of your arrows. If I had meant to hurt you, I could have done it before you ever saw me.'

The leader nodded. 'Go on. I'll follow.' He slithered around on his skis and said to his friends, 'You can stay here, or go home, if you like.'

'I'll come!' said one.

'And I,' said another, shamefaced; and the rest grumbled that they would come too.

The young stranger gave a wide, white smile, turned and ran away over the snow. The frozen surface crunched and creaked beneath the running steps, but did not break; and the hunters pushed with their bows and slid swiftly after on their skis as the running figure vanished in the snow-mist and waveringly reappeared.

The runner leaped, spread arms that feathered and beat and lifted – and the white gyrfalcon was flying, sweeping high and circling and swooping down to flash white before their faces. *Keeee-ya!* It led them, a moon-white bird, through the black trees, over the white snow, under the black sky.

The hunters followed, skimming over the snow, the leaders intent on keeping the bird in sight. Those who came behind, with less to think of, were more nervous, and looked back into the cold and dark. The wind followed them, whispering, in the rattle and rustle of its shaken ice-crystals, 'Are you cold, my children? Are you cold?'

The falcon led them through the trees, through the snow-grey darkness and wind, to a snow-covered mound among the pines. But thin stripes of yellow light poked from the mound and fell across the snow, and they saw that it was a small house, with snow piled high on its roof and plastered to its sides, until it seemed a house built of snow planks, with snow carving, snow shutters and snow sills – a house roofed

235

with snow shingles. Only the smoking stove-pipe poking from the roof was free of snow.

But, though the snow was so deep, the door of the house was above the frozen surface. The hunters sent frightened looks to each other. They feared that the house door was raised above the snow because, beneath the snow, hidden, were crouched a pair of giant chicken-legs. In all the stories they had ever heard, shamans lived in houses that walked on chicken-legs. And, indeed, as they slid nearer the house through the stinging grey mist, they heard a soft crooning, clucking noise, like that of a sleepy chicken.

The gyrfalcon wheeled around and about the little house, screaming its shrill, cold cry, and then dropped to the snow, and turned as it dropped into that pretty boy or handsome girl.

The hunters stopped, jostling into each other, those behind peering over the shoulders of those before. They had all heard, and told, stories of shamans, and to be there, in front of a shaman's hut, was frightening, like finding the gingerbread cottage.

'Come in from the cold,' said the shaman's grandchild.

The leader slid over to the house, and took off his skis. With hissings and scrapings of wooden runners over ice, the others joined him. They stuck the skis, and their bows, upright in the snow around the house, and they hung back, to let their leader be the first to follow the shaman's grandchild into the little house.

Once their leader had stepped through the outer door, the others crowded after, afraid to be left outside, and the small, dark space between the double doors was full of pushing and shoving until the inner door was opened and let them into the hut's single room.

It was a wooden room, a gold and cream and white room of

236

split wood, and its air was hung with a thin, glimmering curtain of candlelight, all dusty with wood-scented dust. In the corners, shadows hung down from the ceiling like thick cobwebs. On the walls hung lutes, rattles, flutes and a big, oval drum, its skin painted with red signs which drew the stares of all the hunters. They knew it for a ghost drum, the very badge of a shaman. The light of the candles made white flares in the polish of the instruments, and deep shadows between them and the walls.

The stove had made the room so hot that the hunters sweated in their heavy clothes and tugged off their caps and mittens and opened the fronts of their coats. The shaman's grandchild knelt to help the leader off with his boots, and the other men leaned on each other as they kicked off their own boots. The shaman's grandchild collected all their coats and hats from them, throwing them into a heap on a chest against the wall.

In the centre of the room was a wooden table, set about with wooden benches and stools, and the table was crammed with dishes of black bread and jugs of vodka, bowls of dried fish and cheese and fruit. The hunters looked at it all, mouths watering, but too shy to ask if the food was for them. They had all been taught that a guest should be given a seat, food, drink and warmth before being asked a single question, but they had not expected a shaman to be so welcoming.

'Sit, Uncles, eat,' said the shaman's grandchild, and the hunters clambered over benches and hooked stools to them with their feet. Before their backsides were on the wood, their hands were reaching for the food and putting it into their mouths. They were hungry.

At the other end of the room was a small bed-closet, with wooden doors that could be closed against draughts. The doors were carved with interlacing lines, and hearts, and deer nibbling at trees whose branches were full of flowers and birds. One of the closet doors stood open, and the shaman's grandchild went over to this open door, and sat on the bed.

The hunters' leader looked up, his mouth full of bread and fish, and saw the other door of the bed-closet swing open. In the deep shadows within the bed sat someone small and hunched, peering out at them. A little, thin hand, twisted with knots of veins, reached out into the candlelight and took the hand of the youngster who sat on the end of the bed.

The hunters' leader raised his glass of vodka to the old woman in the bed, whom he could hardly see. 'To you, Grandmother! Thank you for this welcome! Long life and good luck to you!'

From within the bed's deep shadows came an old, cracked laugh. A scraping voice, almost worn away by age and use, said, 'The long life I have had, son; the luck I have made – but I thank you for your good wishes. Eat all you want – it's cold outside! And while you eat, tell me why you search for a shaman.'

'Here,' said the hunters' leader and, standing, he pulled free something that was tucked under his belt. He threw it to the youngster. 'Show your granny that. Can she say what kind of animal it came from?'

The thing was a small hide, oval in shape, and covered with a long, fine hair. The youngster turned it over and over, and stroked the long hair, puzzled.

The old voice from within the bed said, 'Put it on your head, little pancake, then you will see – it's the skin and hair from a man's head.'

The leader of the hunters nodded. 'My brother's scalp.'

The youngster dropped the scalp to the floor. 'No, no,' chided the old voice. 'You don't throw your shirt from you, that's made of reindeer skin. The scalp's only skin and hair, the same.'

'Reindeer don't kill and skin each other!' said the youngster.

From inside the bed came the harsh laugh. 'Only because they can't hold a knife!'

The leader of the hunters picked up the scalp and tucked it in his belt again. 'It was done by the Czar's hunters. Have you heard of the Czar, Grandmother, who says he owns all this land and even says he owns us?'

The old voice answered, sounding amused, 'I have heard some mention of this Czar.'

'Grandmother, the Czar has been sending his people into our Northlands – more and more of his people. They fish the rivers and lakes, they hunt our animals, they cut down the trees – '

'They're killing the land, Grandmother!' said another man.

The old woman's voice came whispering through the haze of candlelight and wood-dust. 'So my little daughter has been telling me.' Her ugly old hand pulled out a long strand of the girl's black hair. 'Such startling news to bring an old woman – that woodcutters are felling trees, that hunters are killing animals, and fishers are killing fish! Such shocks will be the death of me!'

The youngster, the handsome girl, said, 'Grandmother, I – ' but was quiet at once when the old woman held up a skinny hand.

There was a silence in the hot, crowded little hut. They heard the fire hissing in the stove, and the house crooning to itself.

'Grandmother,' said the hunters' leader, 'it is true that we all live by killing each other. It's the way the world turns. But always before, the hunters have left alive enough animals and trees to fill the land again; always we have sung the ghost songs, to send the ghosts safely to the Ghost World. But these hunters of the Czar, Grandmother – they don't know the ghost songs and they mean to leave nothing alive!'

'And it's not only the beavers, the foxes, the wolves they kill, either,' said another man, and others joined in.

'No – they kill our reindeer, Grandmother! Do we go to the Czar's house and steal his gold?'

There were shouts of angry agreement, and the stamping of feet.

'Yes, killed our reindeer – and when we've tried to stop them – '

'Then they've killed us!'

Another laugh came from within the bed. 'And have you never killed men of another tribe, to take their reindeer? Men have always killed each other.'

The men's excitement died away into silence. They even stopped eating.

'That's true, Grandmother,' said the leader. 'But listen – the Czar's hunters use nets of mesh so small they empty the rivers of fish, young and old. Big catches this year, none next. They cut down whole lands of trees. They catch birds in traps and they steal the eggs. And we, we who have always lived here, and hunted here, and kept our bargain with the animals – we must steal from the Czar's traps if we're to eat. And then the Czar's hunters say we are stealing from him, and shoot us!'

The old shaman said, 'A sorry story, my sons. Why do you bring it to me?'

The men had nothing to say to that. They put down their glasses. They stared at each other, and looked towards the darkness of the bed-closet.

The lass said quietly, 'They want you to help them, Granny.'

'And how do they think I can help?'

'Granny, my dream – '

'Shh, shh,' said the old woman, and the lass was quiet. 'Listen to me, all of you.' The shaman leaned forward in her bed, so that the candlelight fell on her, and, for the first time,

240

the hunters saw her. She was more than old. She was a skeleton covered with wrinkled leather, worn thin. The flesh sagged from her brittle bones: the skin was crossed, re-crossed and crumpled with many, many lines, both deep and fine. Age had pulled down her lower lids to show the red linings, and her eyes would not properly close. Her lips sagged away from her brown teeth, and her mouth dribbled at its ever-damp corners. A beard and moustache of fine silver hairs hung from her chin and upper lip, while her head was almost bald. Age had made her so horrible that some of the men winced at the sight of her, but the lass sitting on the bed held the old woman's hand and watched her, as she spoke, with respect and love.

'I pitied you your wanderings in this cold,' said the shaman, 'so I sent out my little falcon to find you and bring you here. And now I tell you, eat all you can, and then go back to your homes, to your people. There is no such help as you seek.'

The lass said, 'The Northlands are dying, Granny.'

'I have lived too long, more than three hundred years,' said the shaman, gasping, for she was running out of breath. 'In that time I have heard many cries of, "Save us, the world is coming to an end!" But the world never was ending. It was only changing. The world must change, always, because to be unchanging is to be nothing. Even the dead change. But living things fear change and death.' She leaned from her bed towards the hunters. 'Listen to me! Neither I nor any shaman will halt this change for you, even if we could. Go back to your homes and people.' And the ancient woman lay back in the shadows of her bed-closet. They could hear her breath gasping and tearing.

The men sat at the table, not eating any more, and hanging their heads. The shadows lowered from the corners of the ceiling, and the candlelight shimmered thinly over the walls and figures like fiery water.

In the quiet came the lass's voice. 'Grandmother, I had a dream, a strong dream. I saw men coming into the Northlands, and they were all on leashes, and these leashes were all held in the hands of a man who sat on a heap of – '

'Little daughter,' said the old woman, with hardly enough breath to speak the words, and the lass stopped speaking at once. 'You are not a shaman yet. A witch – a good witch – but no shaman. So be quiet now.' The lass lowered her head. Her long black hair fell forward, starred with its white beads, and hid her face.

'You see how it is with me,' gasped the ancient woman after a while. 'I am the only shaman who will hear you, but even if I would help you, I could not. You see my little daughter here, my apprentice?' She tried to heave herself up, and the lass quickly rose and went to sit at her pillow, to lift up the old woman and support her against her own shoulder. 'Three hundred years of life my own grandmother gave me when I became a shaman – and three hundred years I waited for the birth of my apprentice. I should have gone into the Ghost World long ago, but I could not leave my daughter alone . . . So on I have gone, and on, until I am nothing but clotted dust clinging to bones. My legs will not hold me up; my spine is both bent and unbending. This is my last act as a shaman before going into the Ghost World – to spare you the labour of searching any further for a shaman's help. The shamans will not help you, my sons. There is no help to give. All things must change.'

'But – ' began the leader of the men.

'But they are killing the Northlands!' rasped the old woman. 'If that is true, then you must live with the death, or you must die with it, that is all. I am going to rest now. I have a long journey ahead of me. You may eat all you want. You may even stay to see me go to the Ghost World, if you wish. Lay me down now,' she said to the lass, and the youngster carefully laid her down in the bed, before standing and closing the door of the bed-closet, to keep out draughts and the light.

The leader of the hunters stood and said, 'We shall go now.' The other men rose from their places, and they began to pull on their boots, and throw their coats and hats to each other.

'Stay, Uncles – eat more,' said the lass, but the men would not look at her or answer. They stamped their feet into their boots, pulled on their mittens, fastened coats, and they went to the door, opened it and crowded through.

A cold wind, thin but sharp, blew into the warmth of the little room, and crept round and round its corners, chilling it, as the door stayed open for the men to struggle out. But then the door clapped shut, and the draught died.

The lass went over to the window and opened a shutter a little, looking out into the grey snow-mist. She saw the shapes of the men, dim in the grey, quickly growing darker, and then vanishing altogether. She felt sadness when she could no longer see them; and she thought of them struggling home through the cold, and having nothing to tell, at the end, but how they had failed.

But they also vanish from this story (says the cat). I have no more to tell of them.

The lass returned to the bed-closet, where the hard breathing of the old shaman could be heard through the doors. She kicked a stool against the closet and sat there, dejectedly hanging her head, so her face was hidden behind her long black hair.

The door of the bed-closet was pushed open, creaking, and the voice of the old shaman said, 'You think me cruel, little daughter, but I have learned – pull one thread, and that thread pulls others, and those others pull still more. You cannot change one thing alone; you will always change many things, and you cannot tell what might become of that – it may be worse than what you tried to cure.'

The lass said, 'Grandmother, I have dreamed this same dream many times. A man – the Czar – sits on a mound of cut tree-trunks and furs and carcasses of men and animals, and in his hands he holds the leashes of many men who come here, into the Northlands. And these men, they hunt and they fish and they cut down trees. They take it all back to the Czar and make a bigger mound for him to sit on – but he sends more hunters and more, until there is nothing left beneath the stars here but snow and tree-stumps. And then they begin making more mounds, here in the Northlands, and more mounds, and more; and people come from the South to live on these mounds . . . But there are no northern people left and the only animals are rats and mice and fleas . . . And the new people are lonely, lonely and sick, like animals in a cage . . .'

'A true dream,' said the shaman.

'But these hunters, Grandmother – the Czar holds them on leashes. They come at his orders. The Czar can order them to heel.'

'Do you think they would obey him?'

'Many would, Granny! And I am only a witch – I couldn't guard the whole of the Northlands – but I could spell one man. The Czar is only a man, isn't he? I could bind him with spells and make him call his men back. And you could do it easily, Granny. I would have to go to the Czar's city, but you, you could walk into his dreams without leaving your bed. Granny – '

The old shaman sighed with a sound like sheets tearing. 'All things must change, all things must die. I will not speak one word or sing one note to stop it.'

The lass jumped to her feet angrily and said, 'Then why

244

have I been given this dream? What use are shamans, and what use is being a shaman?'

She lost some of her anger when the old shaman laughed at her. 'Shamans are no use, little pancake. Shamans are like the dreamers in the Ghost World, who dream the shamans and everything else. What use are the Northlands? What use are the reindeer people? What use are trees and fish and falcons?' She lay back in her bed and gasped for breath, and the lass sat on her stool again. Then the old woman asked, 'Is my pyre built? Tonight I must go.'

The lass left her stool and threw herself down on the bed by the old woman. She lowered her head to her grandmother's shoulder, as if lying against her, as she had done when younger – but the old woman was too frail for that now: mere clotted dust and brittle bone. The lass was afraid to break her and held her weight a hair's breadth above the ancient body. The old woman put her hand on the lass's head and stroked her fingers through strands of the long black hair, enjoying, for the last time, the way its warm smoothness snagged on her fingers, both soft and coarse, like raw silk.

'You don't want me to go,' she said. 'But I've stayed too long already, and if I stay longer I shall break into pieces and blow away in the wind, and everything I was will be lost and gone. I wish . . . But what use is wishing? Still, I wish that I could have taught you the ways of the Ghost World, and made you a shaman – ' Her whispering voice choked, either from weariness and lack of breath or from grief. 'When you have seen the smoke rise for me, go to my sister in the East . . . She will teach you what I've not had time to teach, and bring you to me in the Ghost World. I will be waiting for you. I will give you your three hundred years of life.'

The lass sat up, but her head hung and her long hair hid her face. 'You're going . . . And the land will die . . .'

The old shaman felt water fall from under the hair on to her face and arms. 'Shingebiss,' she said, using the lass's true name, 'I don't want to die, but I must. The land must die, everything must die. It is sad – but many things are sad, and if we wept for all the sad things, we would weep the seas full and flood the Earth – and when the Earth was nothing but one great drowning sea, then that would be so sad, we would have to weep again!' Breathlessly, painfully, she laughed.

Shingebiss's head hung lower, and she shook, but not with laughter.

The old shaman said, 'Now take me to my pyre.'

Shingebiss put on her heavy coat and hat and mittens, which she had not needed before when she had been clothed in warm feathers. She opened the doors of the bed-closet wide, and she went over to the house doors, and opened them, and propped them open with stools. A cold, cold wind blew into the house, and the hanging shadows climbed further down the walls as candles were blown out.

Then Shingebiss stooped over the bed and lifted the old shaman in her arms. The old woman was heavy, but Shingebiss was strong, and the weight was not too heavy. She carried the old woman across the room, and out through the door.

Out from the warmth and candlelight of the house, into the darkness, the cold, of deep winter. The wind shrilled at the house corners and struck as keen across their faces as a sharp knife-blade. The sky above was immense and black and high, freezing with stars. The white of the snow, broken by the blackness of the trees, stretched away into a grey fog of twilight, and then into deeper and deeper darkness until it met the black of the sky. Under Shingebiss's feet the frozen crust of the snow crunched and sometimes let her sink to her ankles, but held her up. The ice glittered against the white snow; the distant stars glittered against the black sky.

The pyre was close to the little house, among the trees. It had been built of bundles of branches, and its top was spread with a blanket, on which a thin layer of snow had fallen. With a last heave of her back and shoulders, Shingebiss lifted the old woman on to the pyre, and carefully laid her down. Then she ran back over the snow to the little house, and brought back the shaman's ghost drum, which she put into her hands, and a flask of drink, and a lump of smoked reindeer meat, which she laid beside the old woman.

And again Shingebiss ran back to the house, but this time she brought back, in a clay pot, fire from the stove. She climbed up on to the pyre and sat, holding the pot between her mittens, and looking at her grandmother. The freezing wind lifted her long strands of black hair and scoured her face, but still she sat there.

'Put the fire to the wood now, Shingebiss,' said the old woman.

'I'm afraid, Granny. What if I never become a shaman?'

'You are sure to, my clever lass.'

'But if I don't – how will we find each other in Iron Wood?'

The old woman reached up one arm and caught one of the long, flying plaits. Gently, she pulled Shingebiss's head down towards her and said, 'Shingebiss, there is always reason to be afraid – but whenever you poke your nose out of doors, little daughter, pack courage and leave fear at home. Do as I tell you. Go to my sister in the East, and learn from her to be a shaman. Don't love these Northlands too much, Shingebiss. Don't go to the Czar thinking you can spell him as you would a simple, sane man of the North.' She let go of the plait and held her apprentice's mittened hand while she panted for breath. 'He is only a man, the Czar – but he has a mind like broken glass, reflecting many things and all of them crookedly. I have watched him in my scrying mirror. To try spelling him would be like plunging your hand into a box of sharp knives and hooks.' She tugged Shingebiss, weakly, towards her. 'It would be dangerous to try, and if you are killed before you are made a shaman, then the Ghost World Gate will open for you only once. You will lose yourself in Iron Wood, and even if I found you there, you would not know me. Go to my sister in the East – but now get down and set the fire to the wood. I am cold up here. I want the fire!'

Shingebiss bent over and kissed her face. There were sharp spikes in the old woman's moustache and beard, which pricked, but the worn old skin was so soft that she could hardly feel it. Once the kiss was given, there was nothing more to do or say. Shingebiss climbed down and set the fire to twigs in the bundles.

The cold was fierce, freezing, but dry. The twigs soon caught and blazed in the darkness. And they set light to the branches, and soon the fire leaped and roared through the bundles. Shingebiss stood back from the heat and watched the glory of the flames burning on the ice against the dark.

The old, old woman lying on the pyre was silent for a while, but soon Shingebiss heard her voice lifted above the sound of the flames and wind. She was singing a song even older than she was herself: a song which told of the journey from this world to the Ghost World, the ways which must be taken, the dangers which must be faced. As she sang, her voice weakened and faded, seeming to come from further and further away. The last words were unheard. She was at the Gate.

The pyre burned, casting flickering flares of light over the snow and drawing back to itself long shadows. The heat drove Shingebiss further away and, though it warmed her face, made the wind at her back yet more stiffeningly, cripplingly cold. Sparks, burning red, flew high against the black and silver of the sky, and the snow glared red as if stained with spilt blood. The good stink of the burning wood half choked her and drove her further off.

Shingebiss stood staring at the beauty of the fire, but, in her mind, she was the gyrfalcon again, gyring, flying. The gyrfalcon can outstare the sun. It can look down from the wing and see every pine needle, every mouse.

It can see more: it can see the harm done and the harm still to be done. It sees the trees dwindle away to cut stumps, and the city walls rear up through the snow-mist. It sees the roads dividing up the open land, leading to more cities, and it sees the foxes, the wolves, turning into fur hats and coats. It sees the traps set and the hunts riding; it hears the screams and sees the snow redden, and not with firelight. Foxes, mice, rats, fleas – these might live in cities. But not wolves, bear, lynx, beaver. Not trees.

And what use is it to be a shaman, if a shaman will do nothing?

Crippled with cold, she limped away from the dying fire into the glowing silver mist of darkness, moon and snowlight, striped and barred with the blackness of tree-trunks. All around her trees had been draped in strange cloaks and covers of snow; drifts had been blown into wind-smoothed curves, and over all glittered the hard frost.

The wind tore itself on the corners of the little house as she came to the door, and in the wind the voice of old Frost whispered, 'Are you cold, child? Are you cold?'

In the house Shingebiss found her skis, and filled a pack with food. Down from the wall she took her bow and quiver of arrows. That was all she would need for her journey to the Czar's city. She was no shaman, and never would be one. She needed no ghost drum.

Before she left she poured water on the fire in the stove and raked out the embers, so the house would die quickly. She sang it the ghost song, to tell it which way to travel, on its chicken-legs, to find her grandmother in Iron Wood.

The Ballad of Mulan

[Written in northern China, 6th century AD]

Click, click, for ever click, click;
Mulan sits at the door and weaves.
Listen, and you will not hear the shuttle's sound,
But only hear a girl's sobs and sighs.
'Oh, tell me, lady, are you thinking of your love,
Oh tell me, lady, are you longing for your dear?'
'Oh no, oh no, I am not thinking of my love,
Oh no, oh no, I am not longing for my dear.
But last night I read the battle-roll;
The Khan has ordered a great levy of men.
The battle-roll was written in twelve books,
And in each book stood my father's name.
My father's sons are not grown men,
And of all my brothers, none is older than me.
Oh let me to the market to buy saddle and horse,
And ride with the soldiers to take my father's place.'
In the eastern market she's bought a gallant horse,
In the western market she's bought saddle and cloth.
In the southern market she's bought snaffle and reins,
In the northern market she's bought a tall whip.
In the morning she stole from her father's and mother's
    house;
At night she was camping by the Yellow River's side.

She could not hear her father and mother calling to her by
    her name,
But only the voice of the Yellow River as its waters swirled
    through the night.
At dawn they left the River and went on their way;
At dusk they came to the Black Water's side.
She could not hear her father and mother calling to her by
    her name,
She could only hear the muffled voices of foreign horsemen
    riding on the hills of Yen.
A thousand leagues she tramped on the errands of war,
Frontiers and hills she crossed like a bird in flight.
Through the northern air echoed the watchman's tap;
The wintry light gleamed on coats of mail.
The captain had fought a hundred fights, and died;
The warriors in ten years had won their rest.
They went home, they saw the Emporor's face;
The Son of Heaven was seated in the Hall of Light.
The deeds of the brave were recorded in twelve books;
In prizes he gave a hundred thousand cash.
Then spoke the Khan and asked her what she would take.
'Oh, Mulan asks not to be made
        A Counsellor at the Khan's court;
I only beg for a camel that can march
        A thousand leagues a day,
        To take me back to my home.'

When her father and mother heard that she had come,
They went out to the wall and led her back to the house.
When her little sister heard that she had come,
She went to the door and rouged her face afresh.
When her little brother heard that his sister had come,
He sharpened his knife and darted like a flash

Towards the pigs and sheep.
She opened the gate that leads to the eastern tower,
She sat on her bed that stood in the western tower.
She cast aside her heavy soldier's cloak,
And wore again her old-time dress.
She stood at the window and bound her cloudy hair;
She went to the mirror and fastened her yellow combs.
She left the house and met her messmates in the road;
Her messmates were startled out of their wits.
They had marched with her for twelve years of war
And never known that Mulan was a girl.
For the male hare sits with its legs tucked in,
And the female hare is known for her bleary eye;
But set them both scampering side by side,
And who so wise could tell you 'This is he?'

                                    Translated by Arthur Waley

Vasilisa the Priest's Daughter

[Russian folk tale]

In a certain land, in a certain kingdom, there was a priest named Vasily who had a daughter named Vasilisa Vasilyevna. She wore man's clothes, rode horseback, was a good shot with the rifle, and did everything in a quite unmaidenly way, so that only very few people knew that she was a girl; most people thought that she was a man and called her Vasily Vasilyevich, all the more so because Vasilisa Vasilyevna was very fond of vodka, and this, as is well known, is entirely unbecoming to a maiden. One day, King Barkhat (for that was the name of the king of that country) went to hunt game, and he met Vasilisa Vasilyevna. She was riding horseback in man's clothes and was also hunting. When he saw her, King Barkhat asked his servants: 'Who is that young man?'

One servant answered him: 'Your Majesty, that is not a man, but a girl; I know for a certainty that she is the daughter of the priest Vasily and that her name is Vasilisa Vasilyevna.'

As soon as the king returned home he wrote a letter to the priest Vasily asking him to permit his son Vasily Vasilyevich to come to visit him and eat at the king's table. Meanwhile he himself went to the little old back-yard witch and began to question her as to how he could find out whether Vasily Vasilyevich was really a girl. The little old witch said to him: 'On the right side of your chamber hang up an embroidery frame, and on the left side a gun; if she is really Vasilisa Vasilyevna, she will first notice the embroidery frame; if she is Vasily Vasilyevich, she will notice the gun.' King Barkhat followed the little old witch's advice and ordered his servants to hang up an embroidery frame and a gun in his chamber.

As soon as the king's letter reached Father Vasily and he showed it to his daughter, she went to the stable, saddled a grey horse with a grey mane, and went straight to King Barkhat's palace. The king received her; she politely said her prayers, made the sign of the cross as is prescribed, bowed low to all four sides, graciously greeted King Barkhat, and entered the palace with him. They sat together at table and began to drink heady drinks and eat rich viands. After dinner, Vasilisa Vasilyevna walked with King Barkhat through the palace chambers; as soon as she saw the embroidery frame she began to reproach King Barkhat: 'What kind of junk do you have here, King Barkhat? In my father's house there is no trace of such womanish fiddle-faddle, but in King Barkhat's palace womanish fiddle-faddle hangs in the chambers!' Then she politely said farewell to King Barkhat and rode home. The king had not found out whether she was really a girl.

And so two days later – no more – King Barkhat again sent a letter to the priest Vasily, asking him to send his son Vasily Vasilyevich to the palace. As soon as Vasilisa Vasilyevna heard about this, she went to the stable, saddled a grey horse with a grey mane, and rode straight to King Barkhat's palace. The king received her. She graciously greeted him, politely said her prayers to God, made the sign of the cross as is prescribed, and bowed low to all four sides. King Barkhat had been advised by the little old back-yard witch to order kasha cooked for supper and to have it stuffed with pearls. The little old witch had told him that if the youth was really Vasilisa Vasilyevna he would put the pearls in a pile, and if he was Vasily Vasilyevich he would throw them under the table.

Suppertime came. The king sat at table and placed Vasilisa Vasilyevna on his right hand, and they began to drink heady drinks and eat rich viands. Kasha was served after all the other dishes, and as soon as Vasilisa Vasilyevna took a spoonful of it and discovered a pearl, she flung it under the table together with the kasha and began to reproach King Barkhat. 'What kind of trash do they put in your kasha?' she said. 'In my father's house there is no trace of such womanish fiddle-faddle, yet in King Barkhat's house womanish fiddle-faddle is put in the food!' Then she politely said farewell to King Barkhat and rode home. Again the king had not found out whether she was really a girl, although he badly wanted to know.

Two days later, upon the advice of the little old witch, King Barkhat ordered that his bath be heated; she had told him that if the youth really was Vasilisa Vasilyevna he would refuse to go to the bath with him. So the bath was heated.

Again King Barkhat wrote a letter to the priest Vasily, telling him to send his son Vasily Vasilyevich to the palace for a visit. As soon as Vasilisa Vasilyevna heard about it, she went to the stable, saddled her grey horse with the grey mane, and galloped straight to King Barkhat's palace. The king went out to receive her on the front porch. She greeted him civilly and entered the palace on a velvet rug; having come in, she politely said her prayers to God, made the sign of the cross as is prescribed, and bowed very low to all four sides. Then she sat at table with King Barkhat, and began to drink heady drinks and eat rich viands.

After dinner the king said: 'Would it not please you, Vasily Vasilyevich, to come with me to the bath?'

'Certainly, Your Majesty,' Vasilisa Vasilyevna answered, 'I have not had a bath for a long time and should like very much to steam myself.'

So they went together to the bathhouse. While King Barkhat undressed in the anteroom, she took her bath and left. So the king did not catch her in the bath either. Having left the bath-house, Vasilisa Vasilyevna wrote a note to the king and ordered the servants to hand it to him when he came out. And this note ran: 'Ah, King Barkhat, raven that you are, you could not surprise the falcon in the garden! For I am not Vasily Vasilyevich, but Vasilisa Vasilyevna.' And so King Barkhat got nothing for all his trouble; for Vasilisa Vasilyevna was a clever girl, and very pretty too!

The Pangs of Love
Jane Gardam

It is not generally known that the good little mermaid of Hans Christian Andersen, who died for love of the handsome prince and allowed herself to dissolve in the foam of the ocean, had a younger sister, a difficult child of very different temper.

She was very young when the tragedy occurred, and was only told it later by her five elder sisters and her grandmother, the Sea King's mother with the twelve important oyster shells in her tail. They spent much of their time, all these women, mourning the tragic life of the little mermaid in the Sea King's palace below the waves, and a very dreary place it had become in consequence.

'I don't see what she did it for,' the seventh little mermaid used to say. 'Love for a man – ridiculous,' and all the others would sway on the tide and moan, 'Hush, hush – you don't know how she suffered for love.'

'I don't understand this "suffered for love",' said the seventh mermaid. 'She sounds very silly and obviously spoiled her life.'

'She may have spoiled her life,' said the Sea King's mother,

256

'but think how good she was. She was given the chance of saving her life, but because it would have harmed the prince and his earthly bride she let herself die.'

'What had he done so special to deserve that?' asked the seventh mermaid.

'He had *done* nothing. He was just her beloved prince to whom she would sacrifice all.'

'What did he sacrifice for her?' asked Signorina Settima.

'Not a lot,' said the Sea King's mother, 'I believe they don't on the whole. But it doesn't stop us loving them.'

'It would me,' said the seventh mermaid. 'I must get a look at some of this mankind, and perhaps I will then understand more.'

'You must wait until your fifteenth birthday,' said the Sea King's mother. 'That has always been the rule with all your sisters.'

'Oh, shit,' said the seventh mermaid (she was rather coarse). 'Times change. I'm as mature now as they were at fifteen. Howsabout tomorrow?'

'I'm sure I don't know what's to be done with you,' said the Sea King's mother, whose character had weakened in later years. 'You are totally different from the others and yet I'm sure I brought you all up the same.'

'Oh no you didn't,' said the five elder sisters in chorus, 'she's always been spoiled. We'd never have dared talk to you like that. Think if our beloved sister who died for love had talked to you like that.'

'Maybe she should have done,' said the dreadful seventh damsel officiously, and this time in spite of her grandmother's failing powers she was put in a cave for a while in the dark and made to miss her supper.

Nevertheless, she was the sort of girl who didn't let other people's views interfere with her too much, and she could argue like nobody else in the sea, so that in the end her grand-mother said, 'Oh for goodness' sake then – go. Go now and don't even wait for your *fourteenth* birthday. Go and look at some men and don't come back unless they can turn you into a mermaid one hundredth part as good as your beloved foamy sister.'

'Whoops,' said Mademoiselle Sept, and she flicked her tail and was away up out of the Sea King's palace, rising through the coral and the fishes that wove about the red and blue seaweed trees like birds, up and up until her head shot out into the air and she took a deep breath of it and said, 'Wow!'

The sky, as her admirable sister had noticed, stood above the sea like a large glass bell, and the waves rolled and lifted and tossed towards a green shore where there were fields and palaces and flowers and forests where fish with wings and legs wove about the branches of green and so forth trees, singing at the tops of their voices. On a balcony sticking out from the best palace stood, as he had stood before his marriage when the immaculate sister had first seen him, the wonderful prince with his chin resting on his hand as it often did of an evening – and indeed in the mornings and afternoons, too.

'Oh, help!' said the seventh mermaid, feeling a queer twisting around the heart. Then she thought, 'Watch it.' She dived under water for a time and came up on a rock on the shore, where she sat and examined her sea-green fingernails and smoothed down the silver scales of her tail.

She was sitting where the prince could see her and after a while he gave a cry and she looked up. 'Oh,' he said, 'how you remind me of someone. I thought for a moment you were my lost love.'

'Lost love,' said the seventh mermaid. 'And whose fault was that? She was my sister. She died for love of you and you never gave her one serious thought. You even took her along on your honeymoon like a pet toy. I don't know what she saw in you.'

'I always loved her,' said the prince. 'But I didn't realize it until too late.'

'That's what they all say,' said Numera Septima. 'Are you a poet? They're the worst. Hardy, Tennyson, Shakespeare, Homer. Homer was the worst of all. And he hadn't a good word to say for mermaids.'

'Forgive me,' said the prince, who had removed his chin from his hand and was passionately clenching the parapet. 'Every word you speak reminds me more and more – '

'I don't see how it can,' said the s.m., 'since for love of you and because she was told it was the only way she could come to you, she let them cut out her tongue, the silly ass.'

'And your face,' he cried, 'your whole aspect, except of course for the tail.'

'She had that removed, too. They told her it would be agony and it was, so my sisters tell me. It shrivelled up and she got two ugly stumps called legs – I dare say you've got them under that parapet. When she danced, every step she took was like knives.'

'Alas, alas!'

'Catch me getting rid of my tail,' said syedmaya krasavitsa, twitching it seductively about, and the prince gave a great spring from the balcony and embraced her on the rocks. It was all right until halfway down but the scales were cold and prickly. Slimy, too, and he shuddered.

'How dare you shudder,' cried La Septième. 'Go back to your earthly bride.'

'She's not here at present,' said the p., 'she's gone to her mother for the weekend. Won't you come in? We can have dinner in the bath.'

The seventh little mermaid spent the whole weekend with

259

the prince in the bath, and he became quite frantic with desire by Monday morning because of the insurmountable problem below the mermaid's waist. 'Your eyes, your hair,' he cried, 'but that's about all.'

'My sister did away with her beautiful tail for love of you,' said the s.m., reading a volume of Descartes over the prince's shoulder as he lay on her sea-green bosom. 'They tell me she even wore a disgusting harness on the top half of her for you, and make-up and dresses. She was the saint of mermaids.'

'Ah, a saint,' said the prince. 'But without your wit, your spark. I would do anything in the world for you.'

'So what about getting rid of your legs?'

'Getting rid of my *legs*?'

'Then you can come and live with me below the waves. No one has legs down there and there's nothing wrong with any of us. As a matter of fact, aesthetically we're a very good species.'

'Get rid of my *legs*?'

'Yes – my grandmother, the Sea King's mother, and the Sea Witch behind the last whirlpool who fixed up my poor sister, silly cow, could see to it for you.'

'Oh, how I love your racy talk,' said the prince. 'It's like nothing I ever heard before. I should love you even with my eyes shut. Even at a distance. Even on the telephone.'

'No fear,' said the seventh m., 'I know all about this waiting by the telephone. All my sisters do it. It never rings when they want it to. It has days and days of terrible silence and they all roll about weeping and chewing their handkerchieves. You don't catch me getting in that condition.'

'Gosh, you're marvellous,' said the prince, who had been to an old-fashioned school, 'I'll do anything – '

'The legs?'

'Hum. Ha. Well – the legs.'

'Carry me back to the rocks,' said the seventh little mermaid, 'I'll leave you to think about it. What's more I hear a disturbance in the hall which heralds the return of your wife. By the way, it wasn't your wife, you know, who saved you from drowning when you got shipwrecked on your sixteenth birthday. It was my dear old sister once again. "She swam among the spars and planks which drifted on the sea, quite forgetting they might crush her. Then she ducked beneath the water, and rising again on the billows managed at last to reach you who by now" (being fairly feeble in the muscles I'd guess, with all the stately living) "was scarcely able to swim any longer in the raging sea. Your arms, your legs" (ha!) "began to fail you and your beautiful eyes were closed and you must surely have died if my sister had not come to your assistance. She held your head above the water and let the billows drive her and you together wherever they pleased."'

'What antique phraseology.'

'It's a translation from the Danish. Anyway, "when the sun rose red and beaming from the water, your cheeks regained the hue of life but your eyes remained closed. My sister kissed –"

('No!')

' " – your lofty handsome brow and stroked back your wet locks . . . She kissed you again and longed that you might live." What's more if you'd only woken up then she could have spoken to you. It was when she got obsessed by you back down under the waves again that she went in for all this tongue and tail stuff with the Sea Witch.'

'She was an awfully nice girl,' said the prince, and tears came into his eyes – which was more than they ever could do for a mermaid however sad, because as we know from H.C. Andersen, mermaids can never cry which makes it harder for them.

'The woman I saw when I came on to the beach,' said the prince, 'was she who is now my wife. A good sort of woman but she drinks.'

'I'm not surprised,' said the seventh mermaid. 'I'd drink if I was married to someone who just stood gazing out to sea thinking of a girl he had allowed to turn into foam,' and she flicked her tail and disappeared.

'Now then,' she thought, 'what's to do next?' She was not to go back, her grandmother had said, until she was one hundredth part as good as the little m. her dead sister, now a spirit of air, and although she was a tearaway and, as I say, rather coarse, she was not altogether untouched by the discipline of the Sea King's mother and her upbringing. Yet she could not say that she exactly yearned for her father's palace with all her melancholy sisters singing dreary stuff about the past. Nor was she too thrilled to return to the heaviness of water with all the featherless fishes swimming through the amber windows and butting into her, and the living flowers growing out of the palace walls like dry rot. However, after flicking about for a bit, once coming up to do an inspection of a fishing boat in difficulties with the tide and enjoying the usual drop-jawed faces, she took a header home into the front room and sat down quietly in a corner.

'You're back,' said the Sea King's mother. 'How was it? I take it you now feel you are a hundredth part as good as your sainted sister?'

'I've always tried to be good,' said the s.m., 'I've just tried to be rationally good and not romantically good, that's all.'

'Now don't start again. I take it you have seen some men?'

'I saw the prince.'

At this the five elder sisters set up a wavering lament.

'Did you feel for him – '

'Oh, feelings, feelings,' said the seventh and rational

262

mermaid, 'I'm sick to death of feelings. He's good-looking, I'll give you that, and rather sweet-natured and he's having a rough time at home, but he's totally self-centred. I agree that my sister must have been a true sea-saint to listen to him dripping on about himself all day. He's warm-hearted though, and not at all bad in the bath.'

The Sea King's mother fainted away at this outspoken and uninhibited statement, and the five senior mermaids fled in shock. The seventh mermaid tidied her hair and set off to find the terrible cave of the Sea Witch behind the last whirlpool, briskly pushing aside the disgusting polypi, half plant, half animal, and the fingery seaweeds that had so terrified her dead sister on a similar journey.

'Aha,' said the Sea Witch, stirring a pot of filthy black bouillabaisse, 'you, like your sister, cannot do without me. I suppose you also want to risk body and soul for the human prince up there on the dry earth?'

'Good afternoon, no,' said the seventh mermaid. 'Might I sit down?' (For even the seventh mermaid was polite to the Sea Witch.) 'I want to ask you if, when the prince follows me down here below the waves, you could arrange for him to live with me until the end of time?'

'He'd have to lose his legs. What would he think of that?'

'I think he might consider it. In due course.'

'He would have to learn to sing and not care about clothes or money or possessions or power – what would he think of that?'

'Difficult, but not impossible.'

'He'd have to face the fact that if you fell in love with one of your own kind and married him he would die and also lose his soul as your sister did when he wouldn't make an honest woman of her.'

'It was not,' said the seventh mermaid, 'that he wouldn't

make an honest woman of her. It just never occurred to him. After all – she couldn't speak to him about it. You had cut out her tongue.'

'Aha,' said the s.w., 'it's different for a man, is it? Falling in love, are you?'

'Certainly not,' said Fräulein Sieben. 'Certainly not.'

'Cruel then, eh? Revengeful? Or do you hate men? It's very fashionable.'

'I'm not cruel. Or revengeful. I'm just rational. And I don't hate men. I think I'd probably like them very much, especially if they are all as kind and as beautiful as the prince. I just don't believe in falling in love with them. It is a burden and it spoils life. It is a mental illness. It killed my sister and it puts women in a weak position and makes us to be considered second class.'

'They fall in love with us,' said the Sea Witch. 'That's to say, with women. So I've been told. Sometimes. Haven't you read the sonnets of Shakespeare and the poems of Petrarch?'

'The sonnets of Shakespeare are hardly all about one woman,' said the bright young mermaid. 'In fact some of them are written to a man. As for Petrarch [there was scarcely a thing this girl hadn't read], he only saw his girl once, walking over a bridge. They never exactly brushed their teeth together.'

'Well, there are the Brownings.'

'Yes. The Brownings were all right,' said the mermaid. 'Very funny looking though. I don't suppose anyone else ever wanted them.'

'You are a determined young mermaid,' said the Sea Witch. 'Yes, I'll agree to treat the prince if he comes this way. But you must wait and see if he does.'

'Thank you, yes I will,' said the seventh mermaid. 'He'll come,' and she did wait, quite confidently, being the kind of girl well-heeled men do run after because she never ran after them, very like Elizabeth Bennet.

So, one day, who should come swimming down through the wonderful blue water and into the golden palaces of the Sea King and floating through the windows like the fish and touching with wonder the dry-rot flowers upon the walls, but the prince, his golden hair floating behind him and his golden hose and tunic stuck tight to him all over like a wet-suit, and he looked terrific.

'Oh, princess, sweet seventh mermaid,' he said, finding her at once (because she was the sort of girl who is always in the right place at the right time). 'I have found you again. Ever since I threw you back in the sea I have dreamed of you. I cannot live without you. I have left my boozy wife and have come to live with you for ever.'

'There are terrible conditions,' said the seventh mermaid. 'Remember. The same conditions which my poor sister accepted in reverse. You must lose your legs and wear a tail.'

'This I will do.'

'You must learn to sing for hours and hours in unison with the other mermen, in wondrous notes that hypnotize simple sailors up above and make them think they hear faint sounds from Glyndebourne or Milan.'

'As to that,' said the prince, 'I always wished I had a voice.'

'And you must know that if I decide that I want someone more than you, someone of my own sort, and marry him, you will lose everything, as my sister did – your body, your immortal soul and your self-respect.'

'Oh well, that's quite all right,' said the prince. He knew that no girl could ever prefer anyone else to him.

'*Right*,' said the mermaid. 'Well, before we go off to the Sea Witch, let's give a party. And let me introduce you to my mother and sisters.'

Then there followed a time of most glorious celebration, similar only to the celebration some years back for the prince's wedding night when the poor little mermaid now dead had had to sit on the deck of the nuptial barque and watch the bride and groom until she had quite melted away. Then the cannons had roared and the flags had waved and a royal bridal tent of cloth-of-gold and purple and precious furs had been set upon the deck and when it grew dark, coloured lamps had been lit and sailors danced merrily and the bride and groom had gone into the tent without the prince giving the little mermaid a backward glance.

Now, beneath the waves the sea was similarly alight with glowing corals and brilliant sea-flowers and a bower was set up for the seventh mermaid and the prince and she danced with all the mermen who had silver crowns on their heads and St Christophers round their necks, very trendy like the South of France, and they all had a lovely time.

And the party went on and on. It was beautiful. Day after day and night after night and anyone who was anyone was there, and the weather was gorgeous – no storms below or above and it was exactly as Hans Christian Andersen said: 'a wondrous blue tint lay over everything; one would be more inclined to fancy one was high up in the air and saw nothing but sky above and below than that one was at the bottom of the sea. During a calm, too, one could catch a glimpse of the sun. It looked like a crimson flower from the cup of which, light streamed forth.' The seventh mermaid danced and danced, particularly with a handsome young merman with whom she seemed much at her ease.

'Who is that merman?' asked the prince. 'You seem to know him well.'

'Oh – just an old friend,' said the seventh m., 'he's always been about. We were in our prams together.' (This was not true.

The seventh m. was just testing the prince. She had never bothered with mermen even in her pram.)

'I'm sorry,' said the prince, 'I can't have you having mermen friends. Even if there's nothing in it.'

'We must discuss this with the Sea Witch,' said the seventh mermaid, and taking his hand she swam with him out of the palace and away and away through the dreadful polypi again. She took him past the last whirlpool to the cave where the Sea Witch was sitting eating a most unpleasant-looking type of caviare from a giant snail shell and stroking her necklace of sea snakes.

'Ha,' said the Sea Witch, 'the prince. You have come to be rid of your legs?'

'Er – well – '

'You have come to be rid of your earthly speech, your clothes and possessions and power?'

'Well, it's something that we might discuss.'

'And you agree to lose soul and body and self-respect if this interesting mermaid goes off and marries someone?'

There was a very long silence and the seventh mermaid closely examined some shells round her neck, tiny pale pink oyster shells each containing a pearl which would be the glory of a Queen's crown. The prince held his beautiful chin in his lovely, sensitive hand. His gentle eyes filled with tears. At last he took the mermaid's small hand and kissed its palm and folded the sea-green nails over the kiss (he had sweet ways) and said, 'I must not look at you. I must go at once,' and he pushed off. That is to say, he pushed himself upwards off the floor of the sea and shot up and away and away through the foam, arriving home in time for tea and early sherry with his wife, who was much relieved.

It was a very long time indeed before the seventh little

mermaid returned to the party. In fact the party was all but over. There was only the odd slithery merman twanging a harp of dead fisherman's bones and the greediest and grubbiest of the deep-water fishes eating up the last of the sandwiches. The Sea King's old mother was asleep, her heavy tail studded with important oyster shells coiled round the legs of her throne.

The five elder sisters had gone on somewhere amusing.

The seventh mermaid sat down at the feet of her grandmother and at length the old lady woke up and surveyed the chaos left over from the fun. 'Hello, my child,' she said. 'Are you alone?'

'Yes. The prince has gone. The engagement's off.'

'My dear – what did I tell you? Remember how your poor sister suffered. I warned you.'

'Pooh – I'm not suffering. I've just proved my point. Men aren't worth it.'

'Maybe you and she were unfortunate,' said the Sea King's mother. 'Which men you meet is very much a matter of luck, I'm told.'

'No – they're all the same,' said the mermaid who by now was nearly fifteen years old. 'I've proved what I suspected. I'm free now – free of the terrible pangs of love which put women in bondage, and I shall dedicate my life to freeing and instructing other women and saving them from humiliation.'

'Well, I hope you don't become one of those frowsty little women who don't laugh and have only one subject of conversation,' said the Sea Witch. 'It is a mistake to base a whole philosophy upon one disappointment.'

'Disappointment – pah!' said the seventh mermaid. 'When was I ever negative?'

'And I hope you don't become aggressive.'

'When was I ever aggressive?' said Senorita Septima ferociously.

'That's a good girl then,' said the Sea King's mother, 'So now – unclench that fist.'

from The Book of Genesis

[Chapter 3]

Now the serpent was more subtil than any beast of the field which the Lord God had made. And he said unto the woman, Yea, hath God said, Ye shall not eat of every tree of the garden?

And the woman said unto the serpent, We may eat of the fruit of the trees of the garden:

But of the fruit of the tree which is in the midst of the garden, God hath said, Ye shall not eat of it, neither shall ye touch it, lest ye die.

And the serpent said unto the woman, Ye shall not surely die:

For God doth know that in the day ye eat thereof, then your eyes shall be opened, and ye shall be as gods, knowing good and evil.

And when the woman saw that the tree was good for food, and that it was pleasant to the eyes, and a tree to be desired to make one wise, she took of the fruit thereof, and did eat, and gave also unto her husband with her; and he did eat.

And the eyes of them both were opened, and they knew that they were naked; and they sewed fig leaves together, and made themselves aprons.

And they heard the voice of the Lord God walking in the garden in the cool of the day: and Adam and his wife hid themselves from the presence of the Lord God amongst the trees of the garden.

And the Lord God called unto Adam, and said unto him, Where art thou?

And he said, I heard thy voice in the garden, and I was afraid, because I was naked; and I hid myself.

And he said, Who told thee that thou wast naked? Hast thou eaten of the tree, whereof I commanded thee that thou shouldest not eat?

And the man said, The woman whom thou gavest to be with me, she gave me of the tree, and I did eat.

Eve to Her Daughters
Judith Wright

It was not I who began it.
Turned out into draughty caves,
hungry so often, having to work for our bread,
hearing the children whining,
I was nevertheless not unhappy.
Where Adam went I was fairly contented to go.
I adapted myself to the punishment: it was my life.

But Adam, you know . . . !
He kept on brooding over the insult,
over the trick They had played on us, over the scolding.
He had discovered a flaw in himself
and he had to make up for it.
Outside Eden the earth was imperfect,
the seasons changed, the game was fleet-footed,
he had to work for our living, and he didn't like it.

He even complained of my cooking
(it was hard to compete with Heaven).

So, he set to work.
The earth must be made a new Eden
with central heating, domesticated animals,
mechanical harvesters, combustion engines,
escalators, refrigerators,
and modern means of communication
and multiplied opportunities for safe investment
and higher education for Abel and Cain
and the rest of the family.
You can see how his pride had been hurt.

In the process he had to unravel everything,
because he believed that mechanism
was the whole secret – he was always mechanical-
   minded.
He got to the very inside of the whole machine
exclaiming as he went, So this is how it works!
And now that I know how it works, why, I must have
   invented it.
As for God and the Other, they cannot be demonstrated,
and what cannot be demonstrated
doesn't exist.
You see, he had always been jealous.

Yes, he got to the centre
where nothing at all can be demonstrated.
And clearly he doesn't exist; but he refuses
to accept the conclusion.
You see, he was always an egotist.

It was warmer than this in the cave;
there was none of this fall-out.

I would suggest, for the sake of the children,
that it's time you took over.
But you are my daughters, you inherit my own faults of
     character;
you are submissive, following Adam
even beyond existence.
Faults of character have their own logic
and it always works out.
I observed this with Abel and Cain.

Perhaps the whole elaborate fable
right from the beginning
is meant to demonstrate this; perhaps it's the whole
     secret.
Perhaps nothing exists but our faults?

But it's useless to make
such a suggestion to Adam.
He has turned himself into God,
who is faultless, and doesn't exist.

Acknowledgements

We would like to thank the following authors, publishers and agents for their kind permission to reproduce copyright material.

VIVIEN ALCOCK: John Johnson Ltd for 'How Does Your Garden Grow?' from *Beware! Beware!* ed. Jean Richardson (Hamish Hamilton, 1987), © Vivien Alcock. ELIZABETH BARTLETT: the author for 'Charlotte, Her Book', reprinted from *Two Women Dancing: New and Selected Poems*, edited by Carol Rumens (Bloodaxe Books, 1995). DAVID BOWIE: EMI Publishing Ltd, 127 Charing Cross Road, London WC2 (37.5%), Chrysalis Music Limited, The Chrysalis Building, Bramley Road, London W10 (25%) and Jones Music America administration by RZO Music Publishing Inc. for the USA and Canada and by RZO Music Ltd for the World excluding the USA and Canada (37.5%), for lines from *Rebel Rebel*. Words and Music by David Bowie © 1974 All rights reserved. International copyright secured. PETRONELLA BREINBURG: HarperCollins Publishers for 'Suddenly There Came a Crack in the Ice' from *School's O.K.*, edited by Josie Karavasil and Roy Blatchford. CHARLES CAUSLEY: David Higham Associates Ltd for 'What Has Happened to Lulu?' from *Collected Poems* (Macmillan). HELEN CRESSWELL: A. M. Heath & Co Ltd for the extract from *Lizzie Dripping Runs Away*, © Helen Cresswell. ANDREW DAVIES: The Agency (London Ltd) for the extract from *Danger: Marmalade At Work* © Andrew Davies; all rights reserved, enquiries to The Agency (London) Ltd, 24 Pottery Lane, London W11 4LZ fax: 0171 727 9037. ANTONIA FOREST: the author for the extract from *Autumn Term* (Faber and Faber Ltd). JANE GARDAM: David Higham Associates Ltd for the extracts from *Long Way from Verona* and *The Pangs of Love and Other Stories* (Abacus). PAULETTE JILES: the author for 'Paper Matches'. JENNY JOSEPH: John Johnson Ltd for 'Warning' from *Selected Poems* (Bloodaxe Books), copyright © Jenny Joseph, 1992. TIM KENNEMORE: Faber and Faber Ltd for the extract from *Here Tomorrow Gone Today*. GENE KEMP: Faber and Faber Ltd for the quotation from *Jason Bodger and the Priory Ghost*. NAOMI LEWIS: the author for the footnote to 'On Jesse Watson's Elopement' by Marjory Fleming from *Messages* (Faber and Faber Ltd). JAN MARK: Viking Kestrel (1980) for 'Charming' from *Nothing To Be Afraid Of*, © Jan Mark, 1977, 1980. WILLIAM MAYNE: David Higham Associates Ltd for the extract from *It* (Hamish Hamilton, 1977). ADRIAN MITCHELL: Peters, Fraser & Dunlop for 'The Woman of Water' from *Balloon Lagoon* (Orchard Books, 1997). MARIANNE MOORE: Faber and Faber Ltd for 'I may, I might, I must' from *The Complete Poems* (1984). OGDEN NASH: Curtis Brown Ltd for 'The Adventures of Isabel' from *Bad Parent's Garden of Verse* (Simon and Schuster, 1936). ALFRED NOYES: Hugh Noyes for 'The Highwayman'. IONA AND PETER OPIE: Oxford University Press for 'The Blue Beard' from *The Classic Fairy Tales*, © Iona and Peter Opie (1974). JENNY OVERTON: Faber and Faber Ltd for the extract from *Creed Country*. BRIAN PATTEN: Viking (1985) for 'The Trouble With My Sister' from *Gargling With Jelly*, ©Brian Patten, 1985. PRUNELLA POWER: the author for 'First Day at Boarding School' from *Messages*, edited by Naomi Lewis (Faber and Faber Ltd). SUSAN PRICE: Faber and Faber Ltd for the extract from *Ghost Dance*. JAMES REEVES: James Reeves Estate for 'Little Fan' from *Complete Poems for Children* (Heinemann), © James Reeves. JUDITH RODRIGUEZ: University of Queensland Press (1988) for 'Eskimo Occasion' from *New and Selected Poems*. ANNE SEXTON: Sterling Lord Literistic, Inc., for 'Young' from *All My Pretty Ones*, copyright © 1962 Anne Sexton. SHEL SILVERSTEIN: Edite Kroll Literary Agency for 'Sick' from *Where the Sidewalk Ends*, copyright © 1974 by Evil Eye Music, Inc. STEVIE SMITH: James MacGibbon for 'Girls!' from *The Collected Poems* (Penguin 20th Century Classics). CATHERINE STORR: Faber and Faber Ltd for the extract from *Marianne Dreams*. ROSEMARY SUTCLIFFE: David Higham Associates Ltd for the extract from *Song for a Dark Queen* (Pelham Books). ARTHUR WALEY: HarperCollins Publishers for 'The Ballad of Mulan' from *Chinese Poems*. JUDITH WRIGHT: Carcanet Press Ltd for 'Eve to Her Daughters' from *Collected Poems* (1994), and ETT Imprint, Watsons Bay (1996) from *A Human Pattern: Selected Poems*.

Faber and Faber Limited apologize for any errors or omissions in the above list and would be grateful to be notified of any corrections that should be incorporated in the next edition or reprint of this volume.

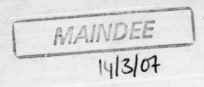